# REST IN PEACE
# BOOK ONE:
# THE BEGINNING

Evelyn Sciarratta

First edition May 2012
First edition - revised – December 2012

Front cover illustration by Michael  J. Pohrer.

Printed in the United States of America

Dedicated to my forever best friend,

and one-of-a-kind husband.

My darling Joe, you gave to me a fairytale life.

I will live forever in that memory.

# CHAPTER ONE
## HAMPTON BAY, NEW YORK 1953

The limousine followed the eight-foot-tall cobblestone wall seemingly for miles before it pulled into the driveway. A teenage girl watched as the window on the driver's side descended. Anchored into a stone pillar several feet from the gate entrance was a black box. The chauffeur pressed a button, said a few words, and in seconds, a high black steel gate swung open, allowing the driver and his passengers to enter. The young girl could not begin to comprehend the wealth that lay beyond the gate.

They continued on the cypress-tree-lined road for at least a mile before their destination reached its end. A nun in charge of the girl's care was seated at her side. She was the first to accept the chauffeur's extended hand.

Subsequently, the same courtesy was given the young girl.

The teen, with the appearance of a small child, scanned the grand house. There were no words to describe either the stately Chadsworth mansion or the grounds surrounding. The mighty castle appeared to be from a distant time. Of course, she would have welcomed anything compared to the drab and dreary place she was forced to call home; a ghastly orphanage. She was moved beyond words. Could she, too, have a life like the rich and famous? She would dream the impossible.

The nun, with the credentials of Mother Superior, took charge as soon as her booted feet touched the snow-covered ground. She raised her long black cloak as she struggled to mount the eight platform steps, many times stopping to gasp for breath. She tried to stand rigid in form, lungs fighting for air. She finally managed to climb the last step, trembling from exhaustion. She had barely enough strength to press the doorbell.

The small girl, five feet tall, with pale blond hair to her waist, brown eyes, and full lips complemented by one dimple, stood fidgeting from the weight of the lone suitcase she clutched to her chest with gloved hands. Fear stood with her.

The highly detailed teak door opened, displaying the beauty beyond. The Chadsworths' butler, Franklin, a tall, distinguished gentleman who appeared to be in his fifties, with thinning brown hair, slightly grayish temples, and sideburns, greeted the guests.

"Good afternoon, Mother Superior. Please come in. Mrs. Chadsworth is expecting you."

She'd been received into the home many times before, and Franklin was well-acquainted with her presence. As Mother Superior was about to step forward, she noticed her charge, moving away; anger set in. Franklin, now standing off to the side of the entrance, did not notice the Mother as she slammed her fist into the young girl's back, forcing her forward.

Franklin took the young girl's suitcase from her clutched hands. He noticed her apprehension. He gave her what she desperately needed, a smile. She gave hers in return. His was stamped with assurance, hers with gratitude. After he relieved them of their outerwear, he escorted them into the parlor. His time with them was at its end.

"Mrs. Chadsworth will be with you momentarily. Please make yourselves comfortable. "

The Mother chose an armless, hand-carved oak chair that suited her character, straight and formal. She also took in account her enormous size. She stood at the lofty height of six feet, coupled with a scale weight of 380 pounds. Her eyes, with no visible lashes, were brown and close-set. The nose was of normal proportion, but she lacked lip formation. Comparing the size of her head to that of her body would be like comparing a baseball to a basketball.

Entering the convent had really been her only choice; how else to hide gross deformity? The young girl seated herself in a matching chair next to the Mother.

The sixteen-year-old, if chosen today, would serve as a governess/nanny. She was heartsick she could not wear something more pleasing to the eye, but it was not to be. No, she would be seen by the mistress of the house wearing her customary brown jumper with its long-sleeved white blouse and the hideous brown loafers with knee-high white socks. This was the customary uniform designed and sewn by one of the nuns. Every deserted child wore the drab garments, ugly at its finest.

She copied the Mother's posture. From the moment she was forced into a life of loneliness, she'd been taught the stringent rules regarding etiquette; she learned to always obey, the tree switch the early lesson.

But she never gave up on wishes. She wished daily to escape the Mother's parade of being shown off to prospective parents as the very best the orphanage had to offer.

She continued with the daunting task of keeping her back straight, hands folded on lap, legs neatly joined together, a perfect lady. She had been well-trained in her ten years at the orphanage.

The hardwood floor bore various rugs shipped from different ports around the world.

The draperies, made of the finest tapestry, flowed magnificently from the ceiling to the floor, where they billowed out in perfect folds. The combined textures of wood and marble formed the fireplace, making it the focal point. The temperatures were such that a fire was indeed called for. The giant opening bearing the fiery logs was large enough to consume a small divan. Tables, lamps, chairs, sofas, and paintings could never overcrowd the room.

The young girl extended her neck as far back as possible so she could see the high ceiling; she counted the chandeliers, six in total. The scrollwork on the ceiling was indeed a master's work of art. The girl, known as Jennifer Carr, was beginning to feel engulfed not only from the heat of the flames but the castle itself.

She began to feel sick at her stomach; she was losing the confidence given by the butler.

The Mother never missed a thing. "Jennifer, what in the world is wrong with you?" she demanded. All Jennifer had to do was move and it irritated the Mother.

"I'm really sorry to upset you, Mother Superior, but I worry about the 'if.' If she doesn't take me in, I'll have no other resources; I will have to return to the orphanage. Oh, my…I don't feel well…I…I need to use the restroom…I'm going to throw up."

The Mother quickly grabbed onto her arm, and with spittle spraying about, she let Jennifer have it.

"If you dare to upchuck in this fine house, you will return. Then there will be hell to pay, beginning with the trip back." Hell hath no fury like when the Mother speaks.

The Mother leaned as close as possible as her anger exploded. Jennifer closed her eyes to avoid direct eye contact. By doing so, though, she entered into a trance.

She saw before her the Mother, lying face down with a twelve-inch butcher knife shoved deeply into her back. The knife met resistance when the brown wooden handle could penetrate no further. Blood would remain unseen upon her black habit until it pooled onto the hardwood floor of her study. Sixty days flashed as if on a screen.

But just as quickly as Jennifer fell into the trace, she came out of it. She was horrified at what she'd seen, but if she told the Mother, she would be labeled as crazy. The Mother would like nothing better than to watch with a smirk as Jennifer, hogtied and chained, was led off to an asylum.

It did not take long for Jennifer to reach a decision. She would tell no one. On the sixtieth day, when Lydia is informed of the Mother's death, committed by another teen in the Mother's care, she, too, will make a decision.

Never will Jennifer hear the details from Lydia's lips, and because she will never be informed, Jennifer will come to believe the vision was a figment of her imagination.

Jennifer could not describe the odor that the Mother's mouth brought forth as the Mother continued with her say.

"You have been a noose around my neck from day one. I am sick of your impudence. The sting of the tree branch is the only thing you seem to understand, and trust me, that is what you will feel if you do not get your act together. If I have to parade you around one more time, I pray God will forgive me, for I just might kill myself."

There, the Mother said it. Jennifer was her display model. But she need not worry about taking her own life. That was in the making.

But still, the Mother was not finished.

"You must make the lady of the house believe you are like no other. Beg, if you have to. I want you out." She gave Jennifer's arm a twisted pinch for emphasis.

"If I were you, I would start praying to God for His help, because if you do not make this happen, I will make the remainder of your stay unbearable. Do you understand me?"

Jennifer understood the switch better, but she was a hard nut to crack. She insisted upon being heard.

"Yes, Mother, I do understand, but…"

The Mother was about to slap her across the mouth, but caught herself when Mrs. Chadsworth stepped into the room. But the Mother managed to get the last say.

"Your lip time has just expired, Jennifer. It's Showtime."

Jennifer felt the start of tears. She quickly brushed them aside, collecting herself accordingly. She prayed she would be accepted. She feared she wouldn't see sixty more sunsets should she return to the orphanage.

The Mother and Jennifer stood when they came face to face with the "Lady."

Jennifer was accustomed to looking up when engaged in conversation, but this time she would see eye to eye with the mistress of the house. Never did she envision someone so beautiful she was to be envied. Hair the color of ivory was pulled back and fashioned into a double knot. Eyes that shared the color of blue in the sky were complemented with thick brown lashes. A perfect nose and full lips with a hint of rose color were additional bonuses.

She wore a tailored dress of mauve and blue silk. Tapered sleeves ended just below the elbow; above the square-cut bodice, a single strand of pearls graced her throat. She wore plain low-heeled blue shoes. She was regal in her movements.

The fear Jennifer was experiencing was no longer evident. All she could think of was how this grand lady chose her resume' among so many applicants.

She felt privileged and would remain forever grateful.

"Mother Superior, I'm pleased you could make it."

Mrs. Chadsworth extended her hand, followed with another comment.

"My prayers were answered, that this sudden snowfall would not keep you housebound."

"Mrs. Chadsworth, I wish you had been at the orphanage when Jennifer awakened. The poor child was in hysterics. It took some doing to convince her the trip was still on. Please allow me to make the introductions."

But Jennifer took the initiative. Never before had she spoken out of turn. This was a turning point in her life.

"I'm pleased to meet you, Mrs. Chadsworth. My name is Jennifer Carr. I've been looking forward to this day for quite some time." She followed with a curtsy, wondering why the Mother fabricated the story about waking her and crying about the snow.

"Is that a rehearsed speech, Jennifer?"

"No, Madame. I..." A flushed Jennifer began again. "I..."

"Jennifer, relax. I'm just playing with you." Mrs. Chadsworth's smile was genuine.

Jennifer had finally found her place in the sun.

Mrs. Chadsworth extended her hand, palm up, toward the chairs. " Please make yourselves comfortable; this could very well be a long visit." Mrs. Chadsworth sat across from them on a settee that matched the now occupied two chairs.

A black-uniformed maid, quite thin and tall with short black hair and wearing a white cap, delivered a silver tray laced with warm cakes and hot tea. She placed the tray on the table before them.

"That will be all, Caroline. We'll serve ourselves. Thank you." Mrs. Chadsworth did the honors.

"Now, tell me. Is that what everyone calls you? Jennifer?" asked Mrs. Chadsworth, as she began pouring the tea.

"No, Madame. My friends call me Jena."

"Then Jena it will be, for I would also like to be your friend. I do believe friends call each other by their first names. My name is Lydia."

"Yes, Madame... ah... Lydia."

"Now that the names are taken care of, let's talk about you.  Okay?"

Jena complied with a radiant smile.

"All I really remember are fragments of my life. Most of what I know was told to me by Sister Magdalena when I was found and placed in the orphanage's care. Shall I tell you of that conversation?"

"If that is where you wish to start, that's fine. But if there is anything that makes you uncomfortable, you need not tell me. All right?"

"Yes…Lydia."

"I was told the history of how my parents came to be placed in an orphanage, but it is much too tragic to talk of. Maybe I can speak of it at another time."

Lydia nodded with understanding. Jennifer wished she could shove that grisly information back into the throat of the giver, Sister Magdalena, but never would this be repeated in her lifetime.

She looked onto the face of the woman whom she prayed would be her savior.

"I will tell the story exactly as it was told to me by Sister Magdalena and finish with the parts I remember."

Lydia nodded.

Jena began her sad story.

"My parents were involved in a tragic accident that took their lives. An investigation was conducted because little was known about them. The results proved to be vital in regards to my placement.

"My parents met in an orphanage long before they entered into their teen years and quickly became friends, and as the years played out, they fell in love. When they became of age, they were forced out. They married, and nine months later, I arrived.

"They worked hard, but things were never easy. They never had what others take for granted, a family to fall back on when jobs were lost, and evictions stared them in the face. Shelter was hard to come by and food stamps were never enough. Many times they slept in what others would describe as a poor excuse for a car, but it got them where they needed to go.

"But they never took the easy way out. To leave me on someone's doorstep was never an option. But of their many losses, their faith sustained them, and through that faith came a steady job, providing food and permanent shelter. They called a single seventy-foot trailer their 'home 'til Heaven opens its gates.'

"There were many that considered them gutter trash; this was noted in the investigator's report. But when all was said and done, no one could discredit their love for me. Six years of age did not wash away the memories of hugs and kisses, the nights of lullabies and stories to lull me to sleep.

"And never will I forget our long drives. When they had free time, they took to the road. They called it our vacation time. It gave them an excuse to pack a basket of food, though never did we cross the state line. Gas was the culprit.

"It was on my sixth birthday that my life had no further meaning. To have one's parents taken at such a young age is something no child should bear alone.

"The day started out being the best day of our lives. We were going to see the mountains. We were leaving our home state for the first time. That trip would be our last. To this day, I remember the songs we sang and the many storybooks my mother read as my father sped along the rocky road, higher and higher."

Unaware, Jena stepped out of her body and entered that of a six-year-old. She was in a world unknown to those in attendance. She began to tell a nightmarish story to anyone that would listen, starting with one tear, then followed by many.

"My daddy was driving really, really fast. I told him to slow down, because he was scaring me. But I guess he didn't hear me, because the car went faster and faster.

"He hit a really big tree and I fell onto the floorboard. I screamed for my mommy. I wanted her to take me in her arms and tell me everything will be okay, but she didn't hear me either.

"I began to really, really cry. I was really afraid. I wiggled my way over the front seat so my mommy and daddy could see me, but their eyes were covered in blood. Blood was everywhere. My daddy had a first aid kit in the glove box, but it was crushed. Band-Aids were everywhere. I needed a lot of Band-Aids, they had big boo-boos, but the Band-Aids wouldn't stick. Mommy and Daddy just kept bleeding. They needed really big Band-Aids.

"I screamed and cried for someone to help fix my mommy and daddy, but no one was listening. No one came. I guess no one cared." The weeping sounds of a six-year-old filled the room.

Mrs. Chadsworth was at a loss at what had just taken place. Jena had been speaking in the voice of a child. Had she actually returned to the accident, reliving that tragic moment? Mrs. Chadsworth had her doubts, but what she did know was that this child desperately needed a family that would love her and care for her.

Jena's out-of-body travel would not be remembered as she returned to the present. She could feel the wetness upon her face and was bewildered by its presence.

Her story continued as if she had never had an out-of-body experience.

"My parents' car swerved off a road high in the mountains, hitting a tree with such force that a branch entered through the windshield, nearly decapitating them.

"I was suspended in a treetop over a deep valley for three days and nights before I was rescued. After viewing the pictures of the accident, the doctors were in disbelief that I survived such a crash. But the x-rays did not lie; I had neither a scrape, cut, nor bruise.

"I defied the odds. I was given a clean bill of health. But I did lose the use of my vocal cords. The doctors speculated it was caused from my ongoing screams for help. But as the saying goes, time does heal, and within three months I began to speak.

"In the final analysis, the doctors summarized their findings: I was a 'Miracle Child,' a child of God put on this earth with a special purpose.

"When the records were searched, they revealed there were no living relatives to care for me. I was then placed in St. Mary's Orphanage. I've been there ever since."

Jena never realized how her words shocked Lydia, nor did she notice how she seemed visibly shaken by what she had been told.

Mrs. Chadsworth stood abruptly, tipping her cup of tea into the saucer. She did not hold back her fury.

"Sister Mary Francine, why wasn't I told of this?" She used the Mother's chosen name when she had taken her final vows.

Jena was shocked by Lydia's sudden display of anger. She, too, could no longer stay seated. She took to the floor, and the words she uttered were of a child desperate to belong to someone, anyone, just not the orphanage.

"Does that mean you don't want me?" Jena was now an out-of- control weeper, unable to wipe the tears fast enough.

"Oh, my dear, poor child, no. Heavens, no. I'm... I'm just at a loss for words. Would you please excuse us, Jena? I need to talk to the Mother."

The small child, still thinking no one wanted her, continued to wail.

Lydia went to her. She cupped her face into her hands.

"My dear, sweet Jena, there is no need for tears. You are going nowhere. You are here to stay. Our home is now your home." Lydia's smile and warm embrace would stay with her when she closed her eyes that night.

The Mother followed Mrs. Chadsworth into an adjacent room that looked to be a library. She closed the doors behind them and lit into the Mother Superior.

"Sister Francine, who in the world could have told Jena such an appalling story?"

"Mrs. Chadsworth, it is not a story. It is the truth." The Mother stood more rigidified than ever, if that were possible. She was determined to defend herself.

"The truth? My God in Heaven, why would you tell her such a thing?"

"You're directing the blame at the wrong person. Sister Magdalena will attest to that."

"What utter nonsense. You're their Superior. Is it not your responsibility to advise them of the proper thing to say and not to say?"

"I leave it to their discretion, Mrs. Chadsworth."

"You should be ashamed. I know I would be. But that is not all that is troubling me. Why was I not told of the circumstances surrounding this child's life?"

"I didn't feel you could handle it, Mrs. Chadsworth. Jennifer should never have told you that part of her life."

"I couldn't handle it, but a child of six could? You are unbelievable. You could have destroyed her life with that kind of knowledge. Apparently she has strength of character you could never achieve.

"You had better start re-thinking what to say to those under your charge. If not, the funds made available to the Archdiocese to care for the Children's Orphanage could very well come to an end.

"I believe it is time for you to take your leave, but first you need to think what you will say to Jena in the form of an apology about her unfortunate life."

The lady of the house walked swiftly from the study; the Mother, with head held down, followed.

The Mother's walk to Jennifer was slow. Was she trying to think of the words she would use to apologize to someone that, in her opinion, deserved none? This was the first time someone in her standing was given a mouth thrashing.

She was downright humiliated. She did have one consolation; no one outside that room heard the put-down.

If she had to get on her knees (although impossible) to beg forgiveness, she would do so. The Archdiocese would hold her accountable if the orphanage were to lose those much- needed funds.

Jena's face glistened from the aftermath of tears, and she was still standing when Lydia and the Mother re-entered the room. Lydia put her arm around Jena's shoulder with a comment.

"The Mother has something to say to you." Jena looked from Lydia to the Mother.

"Jennifer, I pray you will find it in your heart to accept my apology for the grave injustice that was done to you. I have no excuse for releasing information that should have been kept in strict confidence. Never again will this happen to another. This is my sincere promise."

Jena was stunned to hear the Mother apologize to anyone, least of all her.

Jena's reply was simple. "Apology accepted, Mother Superior."

The Mother no longer gave the impression of someone totally in charge. She finally found humility.

Jennifer's excitement over her new life would be short-lived.

# CHAPTER TWO

## YEAR 1985

Sloan J. Parker's hometown, Mason's Mill, the place of her birth and for eighteen years the place she reluctantly called home, was a small community in Illinois. With only a few exceptions, the majority of the residents were farmers.

Three generations of Parkers thought themselves farmers, with little apparent success. Saul Parker was, in reality, a dreamer. To say they were in debt over their heads is an understatement. They were sinking into a slow, painful non-existence, and no one within shouting distance was capable of saving them.

Their homestead, by county records, was well over two hundred years old, evident by its deplorable condition brought on by years of abuse and neglect, a two-and-a-half- story farmhouse that would be condemned if they lived anywhere but here.

A hen house provided eggs and flesh, the barn housed two cows for milk and butter, and there was a large garden for canning their vegetables. What they didn't have was workable machinery and implements on which to depend to bring in their main source of income, one hundred acres of corn.

Saul spent endless hours tinkering with repairs on his deceased pa's two-generation tractor to no avail. Beth, his wife, knew, without a tractor, there would be no crop. She confided in her closest friend, Harriet Anderson, her dilemma. Harriet came to the rescue, soliciting help from surrounding neighbors, families that Saul didn't take the time to know or welcome, yet the farmers stopped what they were doing to help a neighbor in need. More and more came, offering him assistance; some offered parts they knew would get the old tractor running. Saul turned his back on them.

"Thanks, but no thanks. I was raised to take care of my own."

He was determined, more than ever, to make things easier. For the benefit of the parishioners, the church hung a corkboard for posting items for sale or wanted. He trudged up the road. He felt what he needed would be listed. His fingers scanned the slips of papers scattered haphazardly.

The people who operated the hardware store in town seemed to have the perfect deal on a later- model tractor. The fantastic deal, though, came with no guarantee. Saul hesitated.

"Take it or leave it," was the owner's tart comment.

The bank's loan officer was equally sharp with his tongue.

"It's a good thing you have no other debts. Your income is barely within our guidelines."

His comment did not sit well with Saul. Saul made a promise to himself; he'd make damn sure that loan was paid off as soon as possible. After one month of operation, that tractor also ceased to function. He threw up his hands in disgust. "That's it. No more."

He requested a second loan, this time on a new tractor, plus all the farming equipment he would need for his corn crop. He sweated the outcome.

When the call came three weeks later, he was told his loan would only be approved using his land, farmhouse, and their meager household contents as collateral. But it was the addendum that would have caused Saul to laugh if the situation wasn't so serious. They would also take his chickens and cows.

He would never know the outcome of that disastrous decision to sign over everything he owned.

Beth also had her own problems. The kids were growing at a fast pace. She sewed long hours into the night, making clothes for those in need. Whenever her friend Harriet came to visit, she never came empty-handed. Bags of clothes and material were tucked in her arms. Neighbors were many, friends few.

Saul had acquaintances, not to be mistaken for buddies. It's not that he disliked people. To socialize meant to wine and dine, for which he had neither the time nor the money. The only social activity he felt like pursuing was bedding down his wife. It was a pity. He didn't realize all work and no play makes for a dull and lonely wife.

You had to pity Beth; she would have open house if not for him. She thanked God for Harriet, for without her strength and determination to make and keep her as a friend, she would have had no outside communication.

Saul in time realized that no matter what he did or didn't do, Harriet would never disappear. She was here to stay. Defeated, he started being kind of friendly -- not overly, but at least civil. That made Beth a far happier person.

The clothes Sloan had were few. She wore only what her mama had sewn, but things went from bad to worse when her mama's headaches continued to worsen, forcing her to her bed. Sloan's wardrobe was becoming almost nonexistent.

Saul's call to the Doc had been put off far too long. Sloan's concern was also evident; she would sacrifice her own life to save her mama's. She could never imagine life without her folks. God had to have felt the pain she was going through, for when the Doc announced his diagnosis, "severe eye strain," she hugged the Doc, thanking him over and over.

"Don't thank me yet, Sloan. You may not like what I'm about to say. Your mama's headaches will never let up if she continues sewing for you and your siblings. You're the oldest; it's time you learn to sew for yourself and the others. If not, you'd better think about taking clothing from charitable organizations."

Mama sighed and was forced to agree. The Doc had some nerve, but for Mama to agree angered Sloan. She'd rather die, but sew she did.

Sometimes good things do happen when you are born on the wrong side of the tracks. Sloan's good fortune came from someone she least expected. She was offered, from her best friend, Sunni, a dress she coveted. Her pride, for the first time, was shoved to the side. The sleeveless dress with a zippered back was pale yellow with a white rolled collar that scooped low, both in the front and back. A white tie belt gathered at the waist. The straight skirt was just short enough to be acceptable. The woman wearing this dress would bring sweat to a man's brow.

Sunni showed courage to offer such a gift. Even though Sloan was poor, you had to tread carefully when it came to her pride, her papa a living example. Sunni knew how horrid Sloan could act over petty things, and offering a dress was the extreme. She was always there for her, suffering many times in silence at the hurling of her insults, but she took this in stride, for when all was said and done, she knew Sloan loved her.

Sloan was working the vegetable garden when her papa called her into the house. She was led into the sanctuary, her mama and papa's "off limits" bedroom.

"Baby girl, I brought you in here so we could have total privacy. I've put aside a few dollars just for you. It's been far too long since your mama and I bought you anything nice. We got to talking, your mama and I, and we agreed it's time for you to get out and have some fun.

"We thought maybe you'd like to spend a day in town. You could take your time, mingle with the people, browse through the shops, and maybe even grab a bite to eat. What do you think?"

Sloan threw her arms around him, smothering him with kisses. "Oh, yes, Papa, I would love that. When? When can I go?"

From his pocket he extracted a folded twenty-dollar bill, placing it into the palm of her hand. To give her such an amount when the electric was in jeopardy of being discontinued was quite a gift. His ulterior motive had nothing to do with it; he would do anything for his kids.

"Would tomorrow be soon enough?" She was already thinking ahead. She'd wear the dress Sunni gave her, and finally the opportunity to wear her still-hidden pantyhose.

"You are not to tell your sisters about the money. This is our little secret, baby girl.

There is one other thing: I expect you home on time to join the family for dinner."

He need not have worried. She always obeyed her papa.

"One other thing, baby girl. I have some business that needs to be taken care of tomorrow. I won't have the time to take you or pick you up. I hope you don't mind walking." Her papa was being overly generous, for to be taken out of the fields or away from her inside chores was quite a treat. The size of her family demanded everyone's help.

Tomorrow finally arrived, and on this rare occasion she wore Sunni's dress and was proud to do so.

Town was seven miles or better. It could have been fifty; nothing would have held her back. Her hair, usually worn in a braid, flowed freely to her waist. One thing her mama insisted upon was that her kids had decent shoes to be worn for church. She thanked God for Mama's insistence to Papa that they all attend church. Those shoes now would serve a dual purpose.

God got an extra thank-you for the package that was delivered last spring. A parcel addressed to "Occupant" contained a pair of pantyhose, noting one size fits most, an introductory offer to a world of beauty and comfort.

Sloan remembered well what transpired on that day last spring.

Her Mama laughed when she opened the package.

"Pantyhose. This is just what I need for doing housework and tending to the kids, like I could get them over this." Mama rubbed her hands over her well-rounded stomach, another baby due that week. Without further thought, she discarded them into the wastebasket.

Sloan's mama showed no favoritism, at least not outwardly. To offer them to her would have been unfair. Today was Sloan's day to do laundry, her sisters' to work the fields. It was nap time for Steven and Tony.

When the phone rang, getting her mama's attention, Sloan snatched the package out of the trash. She stuffed them in the waistband of her jean shorts, pulling her short-sleeved knit shirt out as to cover the ever-so-slight bulge. She raced up the stairs to her room, jumping onto her bed. She carefully removed the nylons. She marveled in their feel until her mama called to her.

"Sloan, honey, where are you?" She knew her mama never stayed on the phone for very long. She should have waited.

"I'm upstairs, Mama." She quickly replaced the nylons in the pouch, surveying the room. What had originally been partitioned to make four small rooms her papa removed. The layout now resembled a dormitory. Bed after bed lined the walls, with more than enough space to walk between.

She and her seven sisters occupied the top floor; her two brothers shared a room next to her folks on the main floor. She and her sisters also shared four small chests of drawers. Some of them used milk crates as nightstands, the opening facing outward, holding their more personal items. Their main source of light hung suspended from the ceiling by a long electrical cord. It was a dreary and depressing room.

Sloan's mama had sewn pink curtains for the two large windows that faced each other on the opposite ends of the room. Bedspreads were given as gifts from Harriet, Mama's friend; the bedspreads were a mismatch of colors and designs. There was no semblance of style in their house.

Sloan really tried to liven up the dreary room. She would tear colorful pictures out of magazines (Harriet's personal gift to her) and tape them to the drab walls, frequently changing them when Harriet arrived with more. Sloan would then stand back and admire her display; she was making a huge effect to make her world a pretty place in which to live. There was nothing she could do to disguise the rough, ugly wood floor beneath her shoed feet. She was still deep in thought when her mama again called out.

"Sloan, your chores will never get finished if you keep diddling your time away."

"Yes, Mama, I know. I'll be down in a minute."

She had to find a place to hide the pantyhose, somewhere where no one would think to snoop. The attic came to mind. A ladder with a rope attached was used to gain access. Standing fully erect was nearly impossible. Nothing but cobwebs, spiders and dust resided there. She quickly doused that idea.

"Sloan, what is taking you so long?"

"I'm coming, Mama, I'm coming." She had to think fast. She continued to survey the room. More minutes passed. Her mama was now standing at the foot of the stairs.

"Sloan, I'm not going to call you again. I need your help sorting the laundry. If we don't get it out of the way soon, we'll be eating our dinner on top of the baskets."

"Okay, okay, I'm coming." She kept her tone light. She could not mistake the slight edge to her mama's voice. Before long, she would be stomping up the stairs. She needed to find a place quickly.

She knew her time expired when the steps squealed, their age apparent; this was now to her advantage. Why she pulled her bed out from against the wall will never be known. Maybe fate was looking out for her while forcing her to look downward at a warped floorboard.

She could hear her mama on the landing. She was past anxious; the sweat beads began to appear. She couldn't hurry any faster. She managed to get a good grip, shaking the board back and forth; amazed that it was now in her hand. The pouch sailed into the opening, and the floorboard shoved back into its place. All she could do was pray the opening wasn't so deep that she couldn't retrieve them if ever necessary. She was proud of herself; she now had a small place that was hers alone.

"What in the world! Sloan, what are you doing with your bed?" Sloan jumped up, startled. She quickly shoved the head of the bed back against the wall. With a tug, unseen by her mama, she pulled a locket off the chain she wore around her neck, a graduation gift from Sunni. The locket contained a picture of her and Sunni, taken two years ago at a church picnic, arms wrapped around each other, eyes crossed, tongues sticking out. She loved that picture. She loved Sunni.

"Mama, you scared me to death!"

"What in the world is going on, Sloan?"

"The locket Sunni gave me was missing from my chain. I was trying to find it."

"Sloan, you were just downstairs. I noticed you had your locket on then. You should be looking downstairs, not up here."

"No, Mama, I came up here to change my heavy knit top; it was way too hot. When I pulled the shirt over my head, the locket must have gotten caught on some threads and broke off." She could tell from her mama's expression that she didn't believe a word she said.

"Sloan, I'll ask again, what is going on?"

"Nothing is going on, honest, Mama. Here's the locket." She extended her arm, exposing the locket in the palm of her hand. Beth took the locket and sat down upon her daughter's bed. The steps did her in, and the baby must have felt the same way. He or she was kicking fiercely.

Sloan's lips began to quiver, and the tears started.

"Oh, Mama, my locket is broken. How will I ever explain to Sunni?" She knew her mama would believe anything she told her if she saw her face wet with tears.

Beth looked up into her beautiful daughter's green eyes.

"Honey, there is no need for tears. Why I persisted in questioning you is beyond me. I'm just so tired. I hope this baby decides to come on time, not two weeks late like Tony."

She then looked at the locket. The link holding the locket to the chain had broken off.

"I'm sure your papa can find something to repair it. Come now, wipe your tears. I really need your help downstairs." Sloan's papa would keep putting off the repair; she would never again wear that necklace.

"And Sloan, honey… can you forgive me?" Tears began to form in Beth's eyes.

"Oh, Mama, there's nothing to forgive."

Beth extended her arms and Sloan walked into them. It was just a little lie. Sloan forced herself not to feel guilty.

The pantyhose were kept in their original wrap. They could collect all the dust they wanted under the floorboard; they were well-protected in their plastic pouch. She got them out only when she felt she needed reassurance that there was a better life ahead. Those nylons gave her that confidence. She seldom tried them on, for when that special day came, they would be like new.

Today was that day.

# CHAPTER THREE

Sloan was to begin her trip to town.

Saul left the fields reluctantly. He knew what he was about to do would break his daughter's heart. He had called ahead the night before; it was to be a personal call at the Doc's home. His time would not interfere with the Doc's scheduled appointments in town, which started at 9:00 a.m. It was also made in accordance with the departure time Sloan was to leave for town, somewhere around 8:00 a.m.

Saul's entrance into the farmhouse did not go unheard. The hinges on the door's frame had pulled loose many years back, causing the door to squeak and rub on the worn chipped tile floor. He made a mental note that he had to replace the rotted wood soon, very soon, before the door's frame would totally give way.

Beth quickly wiped the tears from her eyes when she heard the rattle of the broken chain as Saul entered the kitchen. He could see she had been crying. He cradled her in his arms, kissing the top of her head.

"I just saw Sloan leave for town. That yellow dress sure captures her beauty. I also noticed she didn't have her hair in her customary braid. I can't remember the last time she wore her hair down.

"You know, honey, this could have been where we went wrong. We haven't given her any space. From now on, she goes to town once a week.

"But enough chatter. I, too, better get going. I don't want the Doc waiting on me."

Beth did not hear a word he said. All she could think about was how the man she adored was going to put a huge hurt on their daughter.

Beth couldn't help herself; she exposed her feelings for what seemed the hundredth time. Maybe this time he would listen.

"Oh, Saul, do we have to do this? We're taking away the only friend Sloan has ever had. She works so hard for us and we give so little. To take Sunni away could be her breaking point. She could turn against us, if she ever finds out."

"Honey, we've been over this many, many times. Now is the best time. Sunni is away at school most of the time. The transition will be easier now than when she graduates."

"Why can't we just wait and deal with that when it happens? She seems to be doing fine the way things are, but if she knows she won't ever see Sunni again, I don't think she'll be able to handle it."

"Then you know what will happen when Sunni graduates? She'll return home just long enough to collect Sloan, and they'll both be gone. It's foreseeable, unless we end their friendship now.

"In a couple of years, she'll accept the fact that Mason's Mill is where her future lies. And before we know it, she'll find a nice young man to settle down with. And as a wedding gift, we'll give them some of our land. They can take their time and build themselves a nice home while living with us; they will then be our neighbors. You yourself said you couldn't stand it if she were to move from Mason's Mill.

"Honey, you'll see, everything will work out fine. You just need to trust me. You know I would never do anything that would bring harm to our daughter."

Beth, though, was not finished with her say.

"She just seems so unhappy lately. I can see and feel her pain, and it breaks my heart. I want to do everything we can for her. We just don't have the means.

"I'm not criticizing; you know I'd never do that. It's just that she's completely different from the rest of our children. She seems to need more, more than we're capable of giving. The sad fact is I don't think she will ever be truly happy, and that frightens me.

"You know, we still could make a phone call and maybe her expenses would be taken care of. She could then take that offered scholarship. Maybe, if given this one chance, her life could turn completely around.

"I've never told you this, but lately I've been having some terrifying dreams, and it's always the same. It's late, very late in the evening. I'm getting ready for bed. But first, I must check on the children. They all appear to be sleeping. Sounds of the night disturb me. I'm restless. I try waking you; you roll away, ignoring my touch. I'm pacing the floor, back and forth, back and forth. The sounds of the night are getting stronger, crackling in my ears.

"I stop pacing, straining to hear… suddenly a scream blasts my eardrum… 'Make amends; make amends, before it is too late.' I awaken to find myself on the floor, sobbing hysterically."

"Honey, you're putting yourself on a guilt trip. You have done nothing in your life to be sorry for. Think about what you're asking. Have you forgotten what it was like, living with them? You didn't have a choice. How could you even think about turning our daughter over to them?

"But say, for the sake of arguing, we decide Sloan could spend a couple of weeks with them, maybe a few months. Now, picture this… she gets caught up in their grander way of living. She no longer has household chores, no more working the fields. She's pampered and powdered and made new. She won't be our little girl anymore. She'll change, all bought with the power of money.

"If you were given a choice and had known no other kind of life but what Sloan has now, wouldn't you, in all honesty, grab hold of that brass ring?

"There will be no turning back the hands of time if we decide to do this. It's up to you, honey. If you decide you want to take that chance, then I'll go along with your decision." He could feel the anguish she was going through, the weight of that choice. If she could have read his mind and knew that he himself was unsure of his decision, she wouldn't have walked to the telephone, she would have run.

"You're right. The risk is too great." She would never know if she had made the right decision.

Saul held her close; he needed her strength as much as she needed his. He could not get to his truck fast enough before the tears spilled from his green eyes. His handsome rugged face was etched in pain. Once in the truck, he clasped his hands over the steering wheel and began to pray.

"Dear Heavenly Father, I love my kids, maybe too much, and just the thought of parting with them, especially my first born, is more than I can bear. I know Sunni would take our daughter from us in time; I can't sit by and let that happen. If what I'm about to do is wrong, please give me a sign. Please, God. Help me before it's too late."

He continued to weep and pray, trying to make it as easy as possible for God to grant his prayer.

"Maybe if You could disable my truck, that would take care of my problem." His truck barely started with a charge. This could be an easy prayer to answer.

In his heart, he knew it was wrong to separate friends. He knew this could cost him his daughter.

The key was already in the ignition. His foot, usually on the gas pedal, ready to pump, sat relaxed on the floor nowhere near the pedal. He would not give it the added boost it always needed if it were to start at all. His thumb and index finger gently turned the key. He kept praying.

"Please, God, please." He cried harder than he thought possible.

The beat-up, run-down truck fired up on the first try. He would not have tried again if it had not started. He would have gone along with Beth's way of thinking. He could have walked to the Doc's house, he really didn't need the use of the truck, but that would not have given him the excuse he needed to forego his plan.

God's sign was made clear. Saul's knock brought his part-time nurse, Alice, to the door.

He was early. Scheduled appointments were still hours away. Alice was dressed in a form-fitting uniform; nothing could hide a well-defined body. Thick auburn hair with a mass of curls extending down her back were held back with jeweled barrettes, and long lashes and eyes with a hint of violet joined an array of freckles that not only covered her face, but her arms as well. She was a beautiful woman in her mid-thirties.

A story circulated about how her husband left for work one day, never to return, deserting Alice, leaving her with four young children to feed, clothe, and for whom to provide a roof. She was forced to return to the only profession she knew, nursing. Four years had since passed, and still she had no news of her husband's whereabouts.

The Doc had a small office and an examination room set up to assist those who felt more comfortable in the privacy of his home. His hours were from 4:00 p.m. to 8:00 p.m., Wednesdays and Thursdays. Alice took appointments in the mornings. She left at noon to return again at 3:30 p.m. She bid Saul a good morning and proceeded to show him to the Doc's office.

Doc was busy sorting out papers, dealing with various case studies, when Saul appeared in his doorway.

"Good morning, Saul, come on in. Please take a seat. Your call last night seemed urgent. I'm just having a hard time trying to figure out what that could be; since you said it's not related to medicine."

Saul took a seat in front of the Doc's desk facing him. He didn't hesitate with what he had to say.

"Doc, you've been good to us. I don't want any hard feelings between you and me or my family. I'm here to ask of you a favor."

"Saul, I'm not only your doctor, but your friend as well. I'm here to help in any way I can."

A knock from the waiting room brought their attention to Alice as she poked her head into the door.

"I was wondering if you all would like a cup of coffee. I just made a fresh pot." Both men in unison said, "No, thank you," and then proceeded to laugh. A serene atmosphere followed for their discussion.

Doc had three doors for access to his office. The main door to the reception area stayed the same, but the Doc felt he needed easier accommodations to the bathroom and a place to rest between visits. Getting up and going into the waiting room, then down a long hall, he considered a hassle.

He hired a contractor to tear out two openings in his office wall and install two doors in an already established bathroom and guest bedroom. He now had access to both facilities.

The door leading into the bathroom was not completely closed, giving an unobserved person the opportunity to hear the conversation in progress.

Saul, now seated, began his tale of woe.

"This is the hardest thing I've ever had to do, but here goes. Doc, I'm here to ask you not to send Sunni plane fare each time she gets a whim to escape the responsibilities that come with college life. When you and Miriam feel the need to see her, maybe you could take time away from your practice to fly up to New York.

"I know I'm asking a lot, but if you hear me out, then maybe you'll understand my bizarre request."

The Doc nodded his head as if he already understood.

"I... that is, Beth and I feel it's time for Sloan and Sunni to go their separate ways. Sunni has always had a great influence over Sloan. When they were small, it didn't matter, but Sloan's got it in her head that when Sunni finishes college, Sunni will settle here to find employment. You and I know that will never happen. Sloan's just not being rational.

"If we can put a stop to Sunni's periodic weekend visits home, Beth and I feel that Sloan will eventually come to live in the real world. This can only happen with your cooperation."

Saul was working hard to keep his emotions in check as he continued.

"From day one of Sunni's departure for college, Sloan's been unhappy. This constant turmoil of 'will Sunni or won't Sunni come home this weekend' is draining the life out of her. She no longer makes an effort to play with her sisters or brothers. There was a time you'd never see her without one of her brothers attached to her hip.

"And read, God, she was always reading to the kids. Harriet is still dropping books off at our house, books she buys when there's a book fair in town, books that now collect dust instead of fingerprints.

"Beth has given up trying to coax a smile out of her. It's pointless. The only time we have our happy, cheerful girl is when Sunni shows her face."

Saul's face was beginning to crumble with despair.

"Don't you see, Doc? We're losing her. All we can do is pray we haven't lost her already. Please, Doc, I'm begging you. I'll get on my knees, if that's what it will take for you to agree to this arrangement."

Saul didn't bother to brush the tears from his eyes. His dignity was forsaken. His love and concern for his baby girl was all that mattered.

"Oh, Saul, I'm deeply sorry for the grief you and Beth are going through. I never realized their friendship went that far, and from what you told me, it's bordering on obsession. For you to be burdened with this situation is unnecessary.

"I'll explain everything you've told me with Sunni. She's a good girl. I know she'll understand and cooperate. She'd never want to hurt Sloan. She knows the day will come when she will have to leave to pursue her career, leaving Sloan behind. I'm just glad this talk took place now that Sunni is home on summer break.

"I think this will work out to their advantage. This will give both of them more than enough time to accept what has to be done. I'll talk to Sunni the first chance I get.

"At present she is visiting with one of the neighbors. She's off again on one of her 'I've got to have' purchases. She heard that Larry Goodman has a puppy for sale, a Yorkshire terrier. She can't sleep, thinking about owning one, since her roommate found one hiding in the bushes outside their dormitory.

"Of course, the roommate couldn't keep it in the dorm, so she took it home to her parents. I guess Miriam and I will be back to potty training and babysitting. Maybe, if we're lucky, the pup has already found a home.

"Here I am, going on and on about a dog, when I'm sure you want to get home and tell Beth the good news."

The Doc stood with his hand out, a final comment on his lips.

"Saul, my friend, I hope I've put your troubles to rest."

Saul, with the force of Samson, gripped the Doc's hand so tightly the Doc let out a yelp. Saul offered an apology as he rubbed the Doc's hand, thanking him over and over.

The night caller had come in and left the same way, unseen. The caller was furious. "Why is it some people think they have the right to decide another's future?"

The caller had to find a way to prevent what was about to take place. The night caller was about to make another call on unsuspecting victims.

As Saul was preparing to leave, Sunni ran up the steps. The force of the screen door as it swung out slammed hard against her head. Saul's apology was swift. He couldn't stay around; he was eager to share the good news with Beth. Doc made him a promise, a promise he knew the Doc was determined to uphold. He and Beth no longer had to worry about their beloved daughter. He all but ran to his truck.

Sunni was still holding her head and totally teed off with his abrupt apology. She felt he could have at least taken the time to see if she was all right. She could feel a tender spot and knew it would leave a mark.

She decided to dismiss what she was feeling for Mr. Parker.

Her mind was on something more important.

# CHAPTER FOUR

Harriet was preparing for her own visit at the exact moment Saul was taking his leave from the Doc's home office, only hers would be at the Doc's office in town. Her scheduled appointment was for 9:00 a.m. She had twenty minutes to finishing dressing to arrive on time.

As she left her home, she noticed Marc's truck parked in the driveway next to her red Chevy Malibu. He'd mentioned his plan to hunt this morning; he could be gone a long time. She wished she had told him of her appointment. He worried about her living alone when away at college; although he spent nearly every night in the home he was raised in. But when he did not, he was close enough, if needed.

Marc has but two loves in his life: Harriet, his beloved mother, and Sloan, a young woman he considered his personal property. Sloan would beg to differ.

Harriet knew she had to leave a note explaining her absence. Marc could find the game-hunting unproductive and return home sooner than she. The memo would serve as a safety measure. Lately she was feeling lousy, always tired and uptight. She wasn't up to Marc scolding her for not telling him where she would be.

She arrived ten minutes early. The reception area was small and crowded. The office space was shared between the doctor and dentist, though divided. The waiting room for the patients was combined. The enclosed area was limited to eight chairs; she was fortunate to find seating. Standing for any length of time caused her undue stress.

The Doc's other part-time nurse, Ethel, a tall, very thin woman around sixty years of age with close-cropped white hair and half-glasses, escorted Harriet to one of the examination rooms. She was given a smock and told to remove her bra and panties. It was noted in her records she had not been to see the doctor in over a year.

When Nurse Ethel finished with the routine testing, she sweetly stated, "The Doc will be with you shortly, Harriet."

Harriet was self-conscious. She hated being exposed. She knew she'd never get over these awkward situations even if the doctor were a female.

The Doc knocked before entering.

"Well, well, it's been a while since I've seen you, Harriet."

She gave no response. She was pale and drawn. He knew this was not going to be an ordinary visit.

He spoke gently, taking her hands into his.

"Now....what's the problem? You look stressed. Have you not been getting enough sleep?"

"Sleep, it seems, is all I do lately," she softly replied, saying nothing more. She continued to sit. It bothered her more to lie down. She needed to be face to face with the person she was to talk to. She stared at him. She was speechless; the subject matter was about to prove to be embarrassing.

Doc noticed her delay. He could tell the subject in question was something she dreaded.

"You know, Harriet, anything you say is confidential. Nothing ever leaves my office. You need not be afraid." He continued to hold her hands.

She first looked at the floor, and then her eyes focused on the ceiling. She proceeded to twist her hands and sway her legs. She finally began to speak. Her eyes were unable to connect with his.

"I haven't had a period in over three months. I'm worried. I surely can't be going through menopause, and I know I'm way too old to get pregnant. I am…aren't I?"

"Do you think there's a chance you could be? I, for one, would never judge you. Please believe that."

She felt ashamed. She still could not look him in the eye.

"Yes, there's a possibility. I just thought I no longer needed that protection. I guess that's stupid on my part."

"Harriet, that's one thing you're not. Many women think the same as you. I think the responsibility lies with us doctors. We need to inform our older patients about the do's and don'ts on relationships.

"But we're leaping ahead. We don't know if you are pregnant. So, why don't I just examine you, and we'll go from there. Okay with you?"

"I guess I have no other choice." She scooted back on the table, positioning herself so that the heels of her feet rested in the stirrups. God, how she hated them. Talk about being exposed. She held the sheet tightly to her neck.

The Doc was gentle as he removed her hands, placing the sheet below her breasts. She made a slight move, her breasts very tender to the touch. When finished, he returned the sheet to its prior position, making idle conversation as he then prepared to exam her internally.

"Did I tell you that Sunni will be returning to school hopefully this weekend? Summer break or not, she can't stand to be away from school for any length of time. I'm going to see if there's a flight available Sunday evening."

And no… the Doc had not yet spoken to Sunni. It was a harmless lie to engage in a conversation that would put Harriet at ease.

Harriet was calm and relaxed as he finished up. It helped to keep her mind off the exam, with the Doc's chatter. His back was to her as he removed his rubber gloves. She righted herself to a sitting position, making sure the smock was back to its original placement, concealing her most intimate parts. She was indeed a very modest person.

"Well, I think I know what you would like to hear, but then that wouldn't change the fact. Harriet, I would estimate you to be about fifteen weeks pregnant, give or take a few days."

She had a choice to smile or cry, but she was too tired and worn out to do either. She thought a few days ago that she was probably pregnant. She started feeling flutters many times in the last few days. Denial was easy until the Doc proved otherwise.

Twenty-two years had passed since she had a baby. Could she cope with the gossip that was sure to take place? What would Marc do? Would he lose his respect for her?

How would she tell Ben he was to be a father? He'd never been married, let alone fathered a child. Would he think he was way too old to be a daddy? Would he now accept a "yes" to his proposal of marriage after always hearing things were fine as they were?

The Doc interrupted her thoughts.

"Harriet, if there's anything I can do to help, please don't hesitate in asking. Could you at least tell me if you're happy?"

"How could any woman not be happy, knowing she's to have a baby? There are just so many changes that are going to have to be made. I'm staring at the fifty-year mark. What if, because of my age, my baby's not right? Don't get me wrong, I would accept it no matter the circumstances. I just wouldn't want my baby to be put in an institution if I were not around to care for him or her."

"Harriet, you're getting way ahead of yourself. You'd be surprised at how many healthy babies are born to older woman today.

"Of course, with all doctors, there is concern because of the age factor. There's a slim, very slim possibility the baby could be born with Down's syndrome, but we have a test that we can do, called amniocentesis. That's where we inject a needle into the sac surrounding the baby. We then withdraw what's called amniotic fluid.

"This will tell us if the baby has a problem, though I must tell you, this, too, has its risks. Sometimes, though rare, this procedure could cause a miscarriage."

"Then it's out of the question. There's no way I'll jeopardize the life of my baby. I'll just have to take my chances."

"Why did I already know that? You're an exceptional woman, Harriet. I'm proud to know a woman of your strength and character."

He then handed her a prescription for vitamins, a must in her condition. She was to see him again in one month, unless she experienced any problems. He also told her she was to consider this a high-risk pregnancy and to avoid any strenuous exercise. No heavy lifting, and get as much rest as possible.

If she thought she was somewhat surprised with the news of her pregnancy, she had no idea how shocked she was going to be with the unexpected news that would be awaiting her when she returned home.

Clay had just finished with his shower. He never thought this day would come. It took him months to find her. His excitement could hardly be contained, but would be no match compared to Harriet's.

Harriet arrived home at 9:40 a.m. No sooner had she unlocked the front door, throwing her purse and keys onto the entry foyer table, than the telephone began to ring. Instead of answering, she collapsed onto a chair that was closest to the front door. Her feet were beginning to swell from the confinement of her shoes; they met the marble floor with a thud.

The phone was on its seventh ring. Her thought was not to answer. She had far too much on her mind. She needed time to absorb all that was to change in her life.

The phone continued to ring; the caller refusing to hang up. It was useless to ignore persistence. She forced herself to leave the comfort of the chair. She did not recognize the voice, nor should she. It was a call she thought she would never live to receive.

He thought he dialed the wrong number when the voice at the other end spoke. She sounded old, too old for whom he thought she should be.

"I'm sorry; I think I made a mistake in my dialing. I was trying to locate a woman by the name of Harriet Anderson."

"This is she, but I would prefer you to call back another time. I am not up to doing any readings today."

Hardly a day went by that someone didn't call to see what lie in their future.

When she took residence, her friend Beth suggested posting flyers in all the storefronts to generate business. She was met with a profound "No" each time, until she made a proposal of X amount of dollars that would be paid on a monthly basis with or without a guarantee of clients. Now, instead of turned-up noses, she was met with palms up. It is really pathetic how the almighty dollar can cause a person to do something he or she would not normally do. Chalk it up to greed.

The gentleman caller had a ready response.

"I'm not calling for a reading… whatever that is…" But before he could respond further, she had her own reply.

"Then what is it that you are calling about, sir? If you are selling something, today is really not a good day to listen to a sales pitch. I'm sorry."

He skipped over her words and got to the point.

"I thought I would never find you, Mrs. Anderson. I think you know me very well; in fact, better than anyone. I'm in town, and I think the time has come for us to meet again face to face."

She felt as if she was going to faint. She quickly grabbed hold of a chair that was within her reach. It couldn't be, could it? Her physic ability pounded within her. She knew her past has made itself present. All these years, it finally happened. He was here. She could not contain the tears. The trembling in her voice also could not be controlled. Minutes passed. Harriet finally spoke.

"Do you know where I live?"

"Yes, your friend Marnie was free with that information. I've rented a cabin in town and would like to see you as soon as possible. Now, if that's convenient."

Marnie, her dearest friend, gave to Harriet what no one else could accomplish: her son.

"I'll be waiting," was Harriet's brief reply.

Soon, everything about her cover-up would be unveiled.

# CHAPTER FIVE

Sloan wanted that day to last, that trip to town, a trip taken so seldom, lest forgotten.

The unpaved road she walked was dusty and rocky, the sounds of wildlife sharp and clear. Birds were singing and chirping, busy in their intent as they gathered twigs and leaves to ready nests for their young. If she were granted one wish at that moment, she would have chosen to be one of God's feathered creatures. She would spread wings wide to fly high, traveling to sights she'd only read of in school. State law enforced that privilege.

Sloan's thoughts took her back to the most miserable time in her young life.

The church basement, divided into sections according to grade level, served as an elementary school. The wall dividers were made in such a way they could easily be moved together for special functions. To attend high school, located in Pine County, they were bussed.

Sloan's graduation from Valley High in Pine County took place a little over a year ago.

Graduation day is the happiest day in a person's life. Her life ended that day. School taught her everything. Her thirst for knowledge made her feel alive, and she could feel another world was beyond the one she was living. Graduation took her hopes, shattered her dreams. College was not for the impoverished.

Sloan was offered a two-year scholarship in art. She was forced to turn it down. Saul, her papa, always had the last word.

"I'm proud of you, baby girl, but tell me, where is the money you'll need to pay for food and clothes, and what about the cost for books? How do you plan to get there, walk?"

Her tears did not go unnoticed.

"Baby girl, it breaks my heart to see you cry." Saul gathered her in his arms.

"Even if I had the money, how would I endure life if you were not at my side?"

Everyone is given choices. Papa made hers. She wondered why Sunni had to have it all. She also wondered why the poor are given the capabilities of bearing so many children, while the well-to-do bear one or two, or none at all. Beth, Sloan's mama, has already given birth to twelve babies. Sloan, the oldest, is eighteen years of age. She wondered if her folks would have more.

Saul, when alone with Beth, or so he thought, would brag about how all he had to do was drop his pants and Beth was knocked up again, while the old Doc shot blanks.

Sloan had just come out of the recently installed bathroom replacing the outhouse. The bathroom was located just off the kitchen. She could hear her papa's vociferous words. She pressed her body against the wall near the opening that leads into the huge kitchen. She was not about to miss out on her folks' conversation.

"See, honey, all the money in the world can't give Doc what he's always wanted: kids, lots of kids, like we've got." Saul was a proud man when it came to his children. He chuckled as he made a grab for Beth. It was evident how much he loved her.

She giggled along with him, telling him to hush, for their kids might hear.

"Now, honey, you know those kids are nowhere in sight. They know if they stay around, you'll put them to work."

Sloan couldn't stand it; she had to see what was going on. She boldly peeked around the opening. She wondered what her papa would do if he caught her.

Saul's 220-pound body was carried well on his six-foot-four-inch frame. His looks were such that he could have been a stand-in for Tom Selleck. Sloan could not believe the passion he displayed as his massive hands wandered over her mama's body and up under her long skirt. Beth held a belief: all married ladies wear skirts, no excuses.

Mama moaned as papa moved his lips around her face and neck, nibbling at her ear.

"Saul, please, we have to stop messing around during the day. What explanation would you give if we got caught in the act?"

He paid her no mind. He knew the second he laid his hands on her; she would be climbing all over him. She was like a stick of dynamite with a short fuse; she couldn't get enough of him. She was now telling him how much he turned her on as she continued to rub up and down against his body.

Mama's moans were really turning him on. His arms lifted her high, while her legs circled his back. His attempt at walking backwards in the direction of the kitchen table paid off. He steadied himself, almost knocking some of the stacked laundry onto the floor as he struggled with the fly on his bib overalls.

Moans began to ring out; he pleaded with her to hold on. He somehow managed to expose himself without releasing her. Her body was on fire, her arms pulling him closer and closer...

A yell sounded outdoors for Papa to come quick. Steven was beating up on Tony again and his nose was bleeding. Mama and Papa pulled apart, panting heavily.

But Sloan was more than shocked when her mama took control.

"Apparently Chrissie has her mind on something other than watching her brothers. Fetch Sloan. She's working the garden; they can exchange chores. I just put DanDan down for his nap. He'll sleep for hours.

"And please hurry. You got me so excited, I can hardly stand it. I'll be waiting for you in the bedroom."

Her legs worked themselves down from around his back. She stood in front of him, her hands stroking his lap.

It was hard for Sloan to see exactly what her mama was doing, but whatever it was, her papa appeared to more than like it, for he crushed her body to his, his lips searching for hers.

In short order, Papa pushed her away. He could barely contain himself. His words said it all.

"You little tease, you just wait; I'm going to make you beg for it."

Sloan couldn't believe what had just taken place. She was unable to see all that was going on, with multiple baskets of laundry stacked not only on the table but the floor as well. The chairs also blocked some of her view, but her hearing wasn't impaired. They were not finished.

She couldn't believe the rapid pounding in her heart, why she had difficulty breathing.

Whatever was happening to her, she didn't want it to end. For the first time in her life, she felt excited. Her body was going through a change. She wanted to feel what her mama was feeling. Something good was happening to her, and it was not to be, all because of her brothers.

She knew if Sunni had been a witness to this, there wouldn't have been any interruptions. She would have gotten to see the finish.

Sunni's father was the town's doctor, Dr. Malcolm Harrison. Dr. Do-gooder always felt the need to help the less fortunate. He was fifty years of age, his height five-foot-five inches. His dark hair was very thin and he wore those stupid half-glasses, always straining his head upward when talking to someone.

If he had to depend on his looks to make a living, he would be living in a box under a bridge. Maybe that was the reason he chose to be a doctor. All doctors get noticed by those seeking to upgrade their life. It's called wanna-be wealthy.

Sloan wondered what Miriam, a woman who came to the table with her own money, had seen in him, for she was a strikingly beautiful redhead with body freckles that would take a lifetime to count. But it was her emerald green eyes and her never-seen-without smile that everyone talked of. Miriam proved to Sloan that love is truly blind.

Fifteen years ago, the Doc packed up his family and moved from a thriving Florida practice to Sloan's farming community, replacing Dr. Merlin Forrest, a doctor who, at the age of eighty, regretfully was forced to retire. He was on his way to an emergency when he lost his way. Twelve hours later, the old doctor was found wandering in the woods, his car abandoned miles from where they found him.

Doc Harrison was on staff at two hospitals: County Valley in Pine County, a ten-minute drive from Mason's Mill; and St. Mary's in Franklin County, a thirty-minute drive. The Doc chose to have two offices. He alternated between his main office in Mason's Mill and the one in Pine County that offered Saturday hours.

The hospitals were known to have 400-bed units, serving not only the residents of Pine and Franklin Counties, but Macon as well. Doc gathered up the majority of his money from the surrounding communities.

Sloan knew many of the farmers held a running tab, including her parents. Tabs the Doc knew could never be paid; he more or less rendered his services free. He knew his farm friends well, very well, for if a bill was not received, they would think of themselves as charity cases. They could owe month after month, year after year, feeling good each time his bill arrived.

Sunni's property was adjacent to Sloan's. What used to be farmland no longer existed. The old farmhouse, barn, chicken coop, and fencing for the pigs' quarters was cleared away to make room for a large brick house and a new barn that housed Sunni's first pony.

Dr. Malcolm Harrison was Sunni's savior. He made sure Sunni and her mother, Miriam, had their every wish granted. "Need a vacation? Take one. You say two? Go right ahead." More or less those were his words, according to Sunni.

"It's a good thing that crops fail, or even better if there's a drought. My people are sure to get sick over that. I'm sure that pads your pa's wallet for all your fabulous trips." Sloan knew it showed her envy. Sunni's face would look stricken with horror, eyes downcast. Sloan's attacks were always followed through with kindness.

"Sunni, I'm sorry. I didn't mean that."

Sunni traveled places Sloan only read of, spoke languages she would never speak. On each return, she took Sloan back through time, filled her in on all the fascinating places and exciting people. She wasn't being vindictive, for she knew of Sloan's pleasure in listening to all those stories. Through Sunni, she lived a part of her dreams.

Sunni was four to Sloan's three when they became neighbors. Sloan's May 22nd birthday made the September deadline for entering school, while Sunni's November 6th failed. Consequently, when the time was right, they entered into kindergarten together.

From day one, Sunni was like another daughter for Sloan's mama and another sister for Sloan. They were inseparable, except when Sunni was off on one of her travels.

Sloan's school was Sunni's school from elementary through high school. Their separation came when Sunni took her leave for college, receiving her acceptance from the New York School of Interior Design.

Their properties benefited them with a creek separating the two properties. This favorite meeting place offered just the right amount of trees for privacy and enough sun for tanning. Old logs formed platforms for either lying or sitting.

On the day of Sunni's departure they were neither lying nor sitting. They stood clutched together like conjoined twins. Sloan crying like a baby.

"Please don't cry. I swear I'll be home every weekend." Sunni's eyes clouded with tears. Sloan cried that much harder.

Sunni left that day, working towards her future. Sloan walked to hers, the cornfield and home.

Sunni kept her promise; she was indeed home every weekend in her first year of college. But with her upcoming second year, she knew it would be impossible to keep that promise. Sunni's weekly letter arrived on its expected day of Thursday, telling Sloan she would be arriving on the 20th of June, summer vacation.

Every week the content of the letter was the same, except for the date. This weekend she will tell Sloan that after her summer break is over, she will no longer be coming home on weekends. Sunni knew it would be a hard sell.

Sloan and her mama were on their hands and knees, trying in earnest to plant seeds to grow flowers. Each year they tried; each year they failed. All Beth needed to put sunshine in her life was a few flowers. It was a shame. How did she expect anything to grow in this dried-up section of the world?

Beth was dried up, showing age way before her time. She no longer turned heads in church, her five-foot frame hampered by a figure long gone. Blond hair no longer had the shimmer of being well cared for, dark circles covered her large brown eyes, and her lips were void of color.

Sloan looked down at her hands. No amount of lard will keep them soft. In time, she, too, will be like her mama. She knew there was no way in

God's name that she would ever escape this hell called home.

Sloan and Beth turned towards the sound of the Doc's car as he pulled into their rutted, graveled drive. He leaned out the window with a repeated request.

"Hi, you all. We were hoping Sloan changed her mind about going to the airport with us."

Sloan shook her head.

Miriam threw in a few of her own words. "You know, honey, Sunni will expect you to be there. Your papa said it was okay with him, so how about it?" Miriam's persistence did not pay off.

"I'd rather wait here. Besides, you all need to spend time with her before I butt in. Sunni knows where to find me. Thanks anyway."

A two-hour drive to the airport and then back would make Sunni's return seem like a very long day. When Sloan thought the time right, she headed for their spot. An hour passed, then another.

She was not prepared for what happened next.

"Oh, great, just what I needed. Rain to put a damper on Sunni's welcome home." Droplets were just beginning to fall. She looked up, thanking God anyway. Their cornfields desperately need rain. She decided to head home, heartsick that Sunni probably wanted to spend more time with her folks than with her, when a splash of water hit her back.

"What in the ...?" She turned, crying with delight at the sight of her best friend's beautiful face. She propelled herself into her arms. A pail Sunni had found nearby, sparsely filled with water from the nearly dry creek, now empty, fell from                                her                                hand.

"Sunni, Sunni, I missed you so much!" Sloan desperately clung to her.

"I swear, Sloan, I could have drowned you, had I had enough water."

"Oh, Sunni, what took you so long? It's been more than six hours. I could barely stand the waiting."

"You really missed me, huh?"

"Sunni, quit teasing me. You know I have."

Within seconds, they began laughing, hugging, and crying all at the same time. Sloan's Sunni was finally home.

Sunni's arrival home played out well, for within that week Sloan was gifted the trip to town. She was excited with the prospect of having Sunni along. That would have been like adding icing to the cake. But her thoughts took her back to their conversation on the telephone after Sloan offered the invite.

"Sloan, I really wish I could, but relatives I haven't seen for over three years are supposed to be here tomorrow. Mother wants me to stay around. Their visit is only for the day."

Sloan pleaded and pleaded, to no avail. She slammed down the receiver. She did not say good-bye.

She also remembered last night at the dinner table how she felt as if she were seeing her family for the first time. Papa was seated at the head of the table. Mama's place would have been at his side, had it not been for the two high chairs placed between them.

Sloan's youngest brothers – Tony, age two, and DanDan, age one - occupied those chairs. The oldest of her brothers – Steven, age three - used a booster chair. Sloan's sisters took up the remainder of the space, bodies packed together around a large table, shoveling food into their mouths like inmates in a prison.

Sloan looked at each one.

Christina, seventeen years of age, was the carbon copy of her mama, with blond hair, brown eyes, and a height of only five feet.

Jessica, sixteen years of age, was the tallest of all the girls. She stood five-feet-eleven inches. She favored Sloan, but lacked Sloan's bust line.

Katie, fifteen years of age, was fair of skin, had light hair, and was considered cute, and was only five-feet-three inches.

Kaily, fourteen years of age, in all honesty, was the most beautiful, surpassing Sloan, though in all honesty, they could be mistaken for twins. She stood five-feet-ten inches. Every night you could find her on her knees, praying to God to make her shorter. Oh, well, if you must pray, you may as well pray for something you really want.

Lecky, thirteen years of age, had a look all her own. Hair the color of wheat with heavy blond highlights, grey eyes, a darling pug nose, and a deep, dimpled smile made her height just under five feet much more adorable.

Courtney, twelve years of age and still growing, was a combination of her mama and papa, standing five-feet-eight inches. Her prayers matched Kaily's. She had blond hair, a dark complexion with alluring greenish- brown eyes, and one dimple. When she smiled, she walked into your heart.

Payton, ten years of age, was the smallest, and possibly the prettiest little girl in town. Everyone adored her. She stood only four-feet-five inches. She also prayed nightly, only her prayers were for God to make her taller. She had a mass of tiny black curls with eyes that copied her hair color, a barely noticeable nose, and lips that appeared puckered, ready for a kiss. Her features certainly matched her size.

Steven, three years of age, was dark-skinned with light blond curls, blue eyes, and was the only one born with three dimples, one in each check and one in his chin. He was all boy, always ready with the fists.

Tony, who just turned two, was a little sweetie and was Steven's punching bag. He was the opposite of Steven, light-skinned with dark brown hair, large round brown eyes, and no dimples. If you had to pick someone perfect, Tony would win hands down. All anyone had to do was look at him and he would give a humongous smile. He knew no strangers.

And finally, the baby, DanDan, who, at the age of one, owned the family. He had no hair, no teeth, no dimples, and hardly ever smiled. Yeah, just maybe he knew more than the rest of us. Life is no bowl of cherries.

Sloan knew there had to be something wrong with all of them. They seemed not to care how they lived or what lay ahead. Did they just live for that moment and to hell with tomorrow?

She felt isolated. She did nothing wrong; her only crime was being born into the wrong family. And because of that, she was to serve a life sentence.

If she had known the hideous nightmare that awaited her, would she have taken that unnecessary trip to town, even if it meant never meeting the man that was destined to be in her future?

There are no options when it comes to destiny.

# CHAPTER SIX

Sloan refused to allow her disappointment in Sunni to cloud her day. She had forgotten how long it took, that walk to town. Still, she stopped to capture squirrels scurrying up trees or running for cover under brushwood and rotted pieces of timber. There were many rabbits; she couldn't begin to count them. When they noticed her approach, they began to scatter in all directions. She watched as two collided. The ring of her laughter sang out, all other sounds extinguished.

Suddenly, without warning, a shiver ran down her spine. She froze. Neither sounds nor a whisper of life could be seen or heard. It was there, a movement somewhere behind her. Something was desperately wrong.

She began to shake. Perspiration formed on her face. Her legs were glued together from the sweat of fear. She was not a coward, yet what she was experiencing never crossed her path until that day. She lowered her head as if in prayer.

"Please, someone help me...I know I'm being followed...Oh, God, I'm going to be sick." Bent over, everything in her stomach from breakfast hurled forth, spraying the trees, weeds, and her. Still slightly bent, she wiped the vomit off her face with the back of her hand.

She glanced to each side, refusing to look behind her. She strained her ears for sounds... nothing. She compelled her eyes to see something…anything. Again, nothing.

Slowly it dawned on her; she was off the frequently used path, wandering around in an unfamiliar area, a part of the woods dense and dark.

"How in the world did I get off the main road?" She stood silent for what seemed an eternity, when she felt something brush against her back. The scream of terror that echoed forced her to pee her undergarments. No longer did it matter how she looked. Thoughts of survival were uppermost in her mind.

She broke out in a run, hiking up her skirt, allowing her more leg room. The stench of urine filtered through the air. She did not stop until she was free of the woods. Her breathing, put on hold through the ordeal, slowly returned.

She collapsed onto the road frequented by the townspeople. Her senses returned. Her heart no longer pounded, her lungs were able to breathe, and her body sweats were gone. All functions returned to normal, except for the way she looked. She began to weep at the appearance of her scuffed shoes, torn nylons, and the vomit that covered her beautiful dress. She refused to think about her hair and all the time spent on it.

She was a mess. She knew she should go home. If she couldn't stand to look at herself, who else could? But thoughts of town were uppermost in her mind. Her escape from reality was the only thing of importance. She voiced her decision. "To hell with my appearance."

A lake, or so-called swimming hole, lay ahead. Tons of white sand years ago was hauled in and paid for by one of the wealthier farmers, giving the appearance of a sandy beach.

The "hole" was enormous and well-hidden. You had to be a local to know the place existed. Privacy was provided by numerous large trees that enclosed the area. Brush, weeds, wildflowers, and tangled ivy added to that security. Large rocks, many resembling boulders, also worked as a shield.

It was sad, for the "hole" wasn't used anymore. The sheriff of Mason's Mill, Ben Davidson, posted a "No Swimming" sign forced on him by the town's council.

Sloan remembered well how that came to be, as she again traveled back into the past.

Sloan was ten years old when Timmy Fossold, also age ten, a playmate of hers and Sunni's, met with a tragic accident. Timmy had light brown hair with humongous brown eyes. He was really quite cute, although that really shouldn't apply to a boy.

He was called Peanuts by his mama. He loved that name, for he was born a dwarf and the name suited him. Others thought of it as an insult, but not everyone thinks the same.

He was quite the jokester. That could have been why everybody did love him in spite of his physical condition. And no, not everyone thought of this as a handicap. Only the small-minded people with nothing to do would make fun of what they perceived to be a horrible misfortune that the Fossolds would have to endure.

But Timmy, like everyone, had his moments where he showed his serious side, making those around him quite mad. This was one of those times.

The day of the accident, or "murder," as the sheriff seemed to think, Sloan and Sunni had been playing at Timmy's house. They loved playing there. He had a massive sandbox that his papa built, securing a hose that supplied water needed for building sand castles. Added to that were swing sets, a jungle gym, battery-operated cars, bicycles, and all the toys any kid would envy. This was the neighborhood playground. Not a day went by that two, three, or more kids weren't there playing. But Sloan and Sunni were Timmy's best friends.

There was no way Sloan could have forgotten that day. Anger like nothing she had ever experienced took over when Timmy fired off a remark about how her papa loved her baby brother more then she, how she no longer was her papa's favorite since Zac came along. He even went so far as to laugh about Zachary's stupid nickname, ReRe.

Sloan threw sand at him, telling him it wasn't true, her papa loved her the same as he had before, and that she loved her baby brother's nickname. But Timmy kept riding her till he had her crying.

She told him he was cruel and she would never play with him again, as did Sunni. Sloan took off running towards her home, leaving Sunni behind. Sunni told Timmy he should never have said the things he did, for his words could come back and haunt him.

Sloan and Sunni could not believe that, within hours, Timmy would no longer be making fun of anyone.

Theory has it that Timmy attempted to dive off a boulder the older kids used as a diving board and lost his balance, plunging head- first onto a formation of rocks below. The brutal blow, in all probability, caused him to lose consciousness.

His cause of death was listed as "death by drowning." No one was present at the time, and the circumstances surrounding Timmy's death caused the sheriff to be more than a little suspicious. He knew there was much more to Timmy's death then what was being revealed.

Sunni and Sloan were questioned, but they were little kids. What could they know that would help? They told Sheriff Ben about their fight, but that really was insignificant. Kids argue all the time.

No one is aware that a night caller who is a demented killer is living among them and has made a move on its first victim.

The intense investigation that followed took months. The outcome provided no clues. Something felt wrong. Ben felt it in his gut, and when that hurt, his instincts were always right.

Sunni overheard the grotesque story as it was being told by the sheriff to her father, the Doc, and then retold it to Sloan.

Three boys were involved in the discovery. Two of the boys, Buddy Fox and Ronnie Hubbard, the youngest of the trio, were both seventeen years of age, while the third, Junior Thornton, was nineteen. They had planned a day of swimming until a posted sign stated the hole was closed. A cleaning crew was hired to rid the sand of all the debris that uncaring folks left behind. They had yet to show-up. The boys eye-balled one another. Grinning, they began discarding their clothes the instant their feet hit the sandy beach.

It was the highlight of their young lives to swim in the buff. Two of the three raced to see who would make it to the "hole" first. The third ran up a boulder to dive in, until he saw what appeared to be a body on the surface of the water.

A blood-curdling scream erupted, causing the boys on the ground to abruptly end their leg race. Their necks jerked towards the sound that caused their hair to stand on end.

Their friend looked like he was doing a war dance as he jumped from one foot to another in rapid succession. He began spurting vomit, which fell like a torrent of rain on the water below.

Ronnie and Junior thought their friend was having some kind of fit. They started to laugh, but then realized the seriousness of the situation. If he should fall from the estimated height of ten to twelve feet, he could really get hurt, maybe even die.

Junior yelled up at Buddy to hang in there, they were going to bring him down. Junior told Ronnie to get up on the boulder and help him; he'd get below in the water in case Buddy should fall. Ronnie just stood there, looking stupid like he normally did, until Junior yelled at him. "Hurry the fuck up there."

"But Junior, what if he's gone crazy and tries to kill me with a knife or something?"

"You dumb shit, he's naked. You think a knife's up his ass?"

Ronnie reluctantly made his way up to Buddy as Junior swam over to the huge boulder. Junior slowed his strokes as he began to tread water, his eyes continuing to focus upward. Ronnie's head finally appeared, but before he could utter a word, he too started screaming, mouthing words inaudible, shaking his finger in Junior's direction.

"Ronnie, what the fuck is your problem? You're supposed to be helping Buddy. If I have to come up there, you'll see what my fist looks like."

A stammering Ronnie finally mouthed the word "body."

"You stupid fuck, what body?"

Ronnie managed to get more control.

"For cripes sake, Junior, there's a body in the water with you!"

Junior turned to his left. After seeing nothing, he then turned to his right. A scream of hysterical proportions sounded. The body in the water was poor little Timmy's. He was jammed between two large rocks.

It was a sickening sight to witness. Junior began wildly flapping his arms about in an effort to escape, each time slapping poor Timmy. Junior was going nowhere in his panic to get away. Timmy kept drawing closer and closer. At last, Timmy's little body broke free from his captor, the rocks.

Now Junior was caught in his own chamber of horror. Timmy, from the neck up, no longer resembled anything remotely human. The top portion of his head had been cracked wide open. Brain matter had spilled over what was left of his mangled face.

One of his eyes appeared to be missing, while the one that remained bulged outward toward the center of his forehead. He resembled the Cyclops.

No matter what Junior did, it was not in his favor. Timmy also appeared to be on a quest of his own. His lips brushed Junior's face, like a kiss thanking him for his release from hell. Junior's fierce swim to escape the horror he came face to face with did not end until he felt the safety of the sand beneath his feet.

With their clothes forgotten, Junior and Ronnie somehow managed to carry Buddy, running when possible, to the sheriff's station. Gasps could be heard by those they passed on the way. Some turned away, embarrassed.

The sheriff had a lot to worry about when he saw the condition the naked boys were in. Whatever happened to them might hinder an investigation, if one were called for. He was not about to be accused of mistreatment when questioning the boys.

A rookie cop named Billy was told to round up the boys' parents, while the sheriff grabbed up blankets to cover the boys.

That rookie was assigned another district after that episode. Why, who knows? The fact of the matter, before the sheriff would acquire Deputy Robert Davis three years down the road, he would have had his share of rookies. He stopped counting after ten.

He was given different reasons why they needed to be reassigned. He questioned their loyalty to the profession, or maybe it was just boredom from working in a small town. It really didn't matter much to the sheriff; his thoughts on the matter were that if you were unhappy, move on, and do not wear him down with a bunch of whining.

The sheriff tried fruitlessly to question Buddy, the first to see the body. He was a gangly kid, standing six-feet-four inches with severe acne, oversized ears, large hands, and big feet.

The sheriff had a hard time keeping his mind focused on the job before him. Buddy would have to fall to his knees and pray really hard if he ever wanted to have a girlfriend. His parents were told to take him home.

Ronnie was the next in line to be questioned. He had already acquired his full growth of five-feet-six inches. He was a fairly good-looking kid. His only setback was that he was born into a family who were not given a full deck of cards.

He was the Hubbards' only child. There would never be a genius born into that family.

Ronnie offered way too much information. The sheriff knew half of it was fabrication. When he told him he could go, he made no move. His parents also remained seated. The sheriff shook his head, having one thought: "God, they are a strange bunch." He had to physically escort them out of the door and onto the road.

The best witness was Junior. He was tall, with a dark complexion, dark brown hair, and the most incredible blue eyes. He had the qualities all girls dream of. He was from a wealthy family, extremely handsome, a super personality, and a high I.Q. He was also voted valedictorian in his senior year in high school.

And yes, he did have a dirty mouth, but never in the presence of young women. Maybe what he portrayed to his male friends was not how he perceived himself. Maybe the skeleton he kept hidden was his own self-esteem.

Junior by no means was calm, but managed to tell word for word what transpired. Afterwards, if anyone spoke a word about that day, Junior's look alone ended all future conversation.

Ronnie did not care about Junior's look. It was Ronnie's turn to act the big shot, for he was always treated as the underdog. Did he lap it up? You bet he did. Each time he told the story it got more grotesque. The horror he wrecked upon the kids forced them to stay within the confines of their homes. Many of these children would be found by their parents, hiding under their beds. Not a child could be found playing outside.

The sheriff knew it was time to put an end to Ronnie's reign of terror. He drove to Ronnie's house. Mrs. Hubbard, short, fat, and ugly, with misery written on her face, answered the door on the first knock. The sheriff told her he was following up on some leads, would she mind if he questioned her son again?

When Ronnie appeared, Mrs. Hubbard took her leave, leaving behind a strong body odor. Mrs. Hubbard began praying that Ronnie was going to be locked up, hopefully for life.

She never could understand why the sheriff insisted that she and her beer-guzzling, non-working bum of a husband be present when they questioned Ronnie the first time. She couldn't care less if the sheriff took her only child away in handcuffs; she was tired of raising him.

Ronnie was an annoying brat beginning with the day of his birth. He was forever in her face, reminding her of all the things she could have been, had it not been for his arrival. Now all she wants is to be left alone with her soap operas, beer, and cigarettes. There was definitely something wrong with this family.

The sheriff got to the point with Ronnie. He put it rather bluntly.

"If you don't shut your God-damned mouth, I'm going to tell everyone about the knife your friend had up his ass."

Ronnie's pedestal fell down around him. His rise to fame had taken a nosedive.

Buddy was never the same. Nightmares climbed into bed with him, his screams heard deep into the night. He took to sleepwalking. That walk took him into his parents' barn, then up a ladder. He threw a knotted, looped rope over the rafters, secured the rope tightly around his neck, and jumped. He finally laid his body and nightmares down to rest.

Timmy's death was a blow in itself, but Buddy's death left fear behind, fear of the unknown.

Mr. and Mrs. Fossold, both in their fifties, were the nicest couple you'd ever want to meet. John Fossold was tall and thin, with grey hair that was fast becoming a receding hairline. His brown eyes had yet to show crow's feet, and he was a fanatic when it came to his mustache and goatee, always trimmed to perfection.

His wife, Joan, was short to his tall. She had long, dark brown hair that was worn in a double braid, and with that, huge brown eyes that appeared to show a mischievous side. She was very pretty and made friends easily.

The Fossolds had just left town the day before, due to the death of Timmy's grandpa, his mother's father. They had packed enough clothing for five days. Timmy's grandpa had been in a nursing home for well over three years and had been in extremely bad health for the last two months of his life. His death was expected. Timmy's was not.

Mrs. Fossold dreaded having to take Timmy. He was her only living child. She had lost twin daughters eight years prior. Their gestation time lasted a mere six months, each weighing not quite two pounds. Their struggle for three weeks ended when they succumbed to pneumonia.

After that, Mrs. Fossold never allowed Timmy out of her sight. She was so afraid for his life; she purchased a whistle to be worn around his neck, should he encounter trouble.

From the time he took his first step, when not in her presence, he was never without his whistle. It made no difference; he had not yet mastered the skill for its use.

He would remain her only child. She would be unable to have another child due to the complications following the birth of her twins.

When Mrs. Fossold's father died, she decided to leave her Timmy behind. She thought him much too young to be exposed to death. Fate sure had a way of playing a dirty trick when their backs were turned.

Word had gotten back to the Fossolds that Cindy Bingington was in town for a visit with her folks before she set up permanent residence in Chicago, her place of employment. She had just finished taking her bar exam and finally graduated from Northwestern University.

She had signed on as an assistant with a prestigious law firm, Hartford, Crawley & Mansfield. She was a true redhead, freckles and all. She was of average height and weight and was never without her black-rimmed eyeglasses. She dressed conservatively, taking on the role of what a lawyer should look like, passing that grade with flying colors.

Cindy did not hesitate for a second when asked by Mrs. Fossold if she would care for Timmy in their absence. Cindy babysat for him while home on weekends and summer breaks from school since Timmy was a baby. She felt as if he were her own.

Malicious allegations ran rampant, accusing Cindy of having a hand in his death. She was given no trial. The townspeople found her guilty beyond a reasonable doubt.

Shortly after Timmy's burial, those accusations stopped when she was committed to a nursing home. She was twenty-eight years old, and when told of Timmy's death, she never again spoke a word or uttered a sound.

She left behind the original model of herself and became a shell of what she used to be: bright, cheerful, and outgoing.

Ken and Sarah Bingington, Cindy's parents, owned a thriving antique business in town, which was quickly sold at a great loss, along with their personal property and household contents. They took up residence within walking distance of Alshore Nursing Home, located in Chicago.

A city in which Cindy was to begin her future sadly became the place of no tomorrows.

Many so-called friends of Cindy's parents wrote to keep in touch, but received no replies. They were the same people who judged their daughter. Those were the ones who gave birth to the name "hypocrite."

The townspeople gradually learned about the day that Sheriff Ben was crying when he had the unpleasant task of getting in touch with Timmy's parents. He informed them they were to return home immediately, that their son had met with an accident. He would tell them nothing more until their arrival.

He earlier in the day removed the yellow crime scene tape, all the available evidence collected, if that's what you would call it.

Mrs. Fossold, when told of the tragedy that had befallen her young son, became stark-raving mad. Mr. Fossold's grief was to be put on hold. Screaming and tearing at her hair, she attacked and clawed everyone near. The Doc had to be called. An injection was administered. Doc, in his desire to try and lessen the blow, stressed the fact that if Timmy had not gone to live with the Lord, he would have been a vegetable; the damage to his brain was that severe.

Mrs. Fossold's savage attack was vented on the Doc before the shot had time to take effect, her teeth tearing a huge hunk of flesh and tissue out of his arm. Extensive bleeding incurred, a tourniquet applied. Doc was rushed to his own hospital. A plastic surgeon would have to perform reconstructive surgery.

The Doc minded his own business from then on, putting to practice only what he was trained for, general medicine.

Timmy was not buried in Mason's Mill. Mr. Fossold sadly and quietly made arrangements with the undertaker who was in charge of his father-in-law's burial to also take charge of his son's.

On burial day, as the oversized casket made its descent, Timmy's journey ended. He was placed in his grandpa's protective arms in a small cemetery plot in Wisconsin. He and his grandpa would spend eternity surrounded by weeping willows.

Mrs. Fossold took a journey herself, entering a void of darkness; her madness forced her into seclusion. She was unable to attend her father's and her son's burial. Mr. Fossold said his good-byes the day his son left Mason's Mill, never to return.

Mrs. Fossold became crazed and was kept guarded under her husband's watchful eyes. As bad luck continued, she escaped, running from farmhouse to farmhouse, telling her used-to-be friends that if they didn't put her Timmy back together, she would put a curse on all their children.

Mr. Fossold took it upon himself to replace the original door locks with hardware that was sure to keep her indoors. He finally realized there was nothing more he could do when the bits and pieces that should have restrained her were lying about the floor.

Mr. Fossold found his naked and distraught wife running through the fields with a scythe, screaming obscenities, blaming everyone.

"I'll remove all your heads for what you did to my poor baby Timmy."

Sometime during that night, the Fossolds left. They took nothing of their personal belongings other than their old brown station wagon.

Today the house still sits in wait for the family to return and pick up where they left off. A bulb on the porch is left to burn to light their way should they return like they left, in the night.

The church offered to pick up any expenses occurring from the upkeep of their property. The fields were left unattended. The yard surrounding their house was kept mowed and watered. Flowers planted in the flower boxes sat on the front porch. Maybe the townspeople believed in curses.

Sloan again turned back the hands of time, remembering when Sunni initiated the subject of Timmy.

They were then fourteen years of age. Sloan had put Timmy out of her mind. She wanted to forget it ever happened. Not so with Sunni. She refused to forget. Her main topic of conversation revolved around him. She was a bore. As educated and traveled as she was, you would think she could have found other things to talk of.

They happened to be at their favorite spot, lying on the platforms, splashing their feet, sunning their bodies, when his name was mentioned.

"God, Sunni, is that all you can think of to talk about? Timmy's been gone for years. We were ten years old when that happened. If I hear you say his name one more time, I'm going home."

"But Sloan, this is really important. Just last night I heard Sheriff Ben talking to my father, asking if Timmy was found face up, and his lungs were absent of water, how the pathologist could rule 'death by drowning.' Father told him he suspected someone turned him over and, fearing the reprisal, did not report it.

"As to the absence of water, he was stupefied, but they needed a cause of death and that seemed the logical choice.

"But it didn't end there. Sheriff Ben said they could have considered murder. That blew my mind. But father jumped right in, telling him he had to consider the consequences of such a finding, how we live in a small town and the impact that would have on the townspeople: how they'd take to keeping their kids inside, never letting them out of their sight; how our peace-loving community would turn into a town full of anger and hate, each accusing the other; and how Sheriff Ben's phone would never stop ringing. Was that what he wanted?

"Father pleaded with him to let it go, but Sheriff Ben shook his head. He told my father he must be losing his mind if he didn't remember being called in to examine Cindy, because in the sheriff's opinion, she appeared drugged. And because of that suspicion, Sheriff Ben wanted a blood test.

"Father appeared a little teed off with that comment, but gave Sheriff Ben a slight dose of his own medicine. He told Sheriff Ben his memory had never been tampered with and that Sheriff Ben was the one lacking in the recollection department.

"You should have seen the look on Sheriff Ben's face. For once in his life, he was at a loss for words.

"Father didn't take a breath. He told Sheriff Ben he had more important things to deal with, and the past was not one of them. And besides, it was too late to do anything about it.

"Sheriff Ben stood his ground, stating nothing is ever too late, and he would continue to call the sanitarium, and until Cindy talked, the files would remain open. Father shook his head, ending any further discussion. After all this time, you'd think Sheriff Ben would hang it up. I'll say one thing for him -- he sure has determination."

"God, Sunni, you're worse than the worst when it comes to gossip. Why do you insist on talking about Timmy? You're as bad as the sheriff. You just won't let it alone."

"Come on, aren't you the least bit curious? You know you really would like to know what happened. After all, we do live here. For all you know, we could have a psycho running around. What if your mama turns her back one day and one of your sisters slips away and gets killed?"

"That will never happen. They're never out of my mama's sight. And besides, it's been four years and nothing else has happened, has it? No. So what I'm saying is, I don't care. It's done. It's over. I want to forget it ever happened."

"I bet you'd feel differently if it were your brother Zac. You'd want to know then, wouldn't you?"

Glaring, Sloan jumped up. "I'm sick of the talk of death. I can't take it anymore. And you're cruel to bring up Zac's name."

Sloan's heart felt as if it were about to explode. The painful mention of her baby brother Zac was unbearable. The memory of his death could never be erased, but Sunni had no right to dig up his tiny remains and rub her face into his coffin. Tears blinded her with agony in her race for home.

Sunni regretted those words the second they rolled off the tip of her tongue.

"Oh, God, Sloan, I'm so sorry. I wasn't thinking. Forgive me, please forgive me." Sunni's tears were no match for Sloan's.

Sunni forced Sloan's memories of the birth of her precious ReRe to resurface.

Another Parker baby was on its way. That particular day Sloan was trying to remember the comments of the townspeople, but it was hard since Mama just never stopped having babies, although one did come to mind when the news circulated.

"I wonder what the Parkers do in their spare time." The town's gossipers speaking out, giggling like the fools they'd become. Lip movement revealed what they did in their spare time.

Sloan wished she could remember how old she was when her mama, heavy with yet another child, sat her down and tried to explain the importance of having a son to carry on the family name, how her papa prayed nightly and

Sloan should do the same. But prayers were not heard when the Doc, for the seventh time, broke the news.

"It's another girl, Saul. It's God's will."

Afterward, Mama again drew her to her side, telling her how she found Papa hiding in the barn, weeping and questioning God.

Mama repeated the words of her papa. They took root in her memory.

"Dear God, why are you punishing me? I promised to follow you all the days of my life, but where are the boys? Am I not praying hard enough? Do I not have enough girls?"

Mama finished the tale by telling her how she went to him to show comfort, promising she would give him a son.

Sloan was counting the months when she would celebrate her ninth birthday when her mama got that way again. That pregnancy was etched for eternity. Nowhere could she run or hide to erase what was set in motion.

Beth wasn't her usual self. She was sick all the time. Smiles and gentle hugs were past tense.

Saul was also showing a side of himself no one recognized. He was frantic, worrying he might lose his precious Beth, refusing to leave her bedside. The kids were on their own. Her condition seemed to worsen with each passing day. Her bedside friend was a bucket, emptying stomach contents frequently. Saul was putting undue stress on everyone he came in contact with, and Doc was the worst recipient. Papa had the Doc out so often, the Doc felt as if he should pay room and board.

"Saul, you need to stop worrying about Beth and focus on the care of your kids. Sloan is shouldering your responsibilities and she's just a little girl. You need to take a look at how your behavior is affecting them. If I had a penny for every tear they cry, I could retire a wealthy man. You need to get your priorities in order and let God take care of Beth."

Doc's words got Saul's attention, putting him more at ease while adding a bit of humor.

"Just between you and me, I think after this one, you might ought a think of separate rooms."

Time passed. Beth had her good days, but most were bad. She tried to assume her responsibilities, but with each effort, she could feel the breath being sucked out of her. Determination no longer came into play. She ended up bedridden.

Sloan's memory replayed the words her mama spoke on that fateful night while sitting by her bedside.

Beth tried to sit up, but failed miserably. Sloan offered to help.

"Mama, you really need to rest. I'm a big girl. I can take care of everything." She threw in the age of nine, proving she was capable.

Beth was moved beyond words. Tears came to the surface, while bringing forth a smile not seen for some time.

"My beautiful baby girl, you are the sunshine that starts my day and the stars that light my nights. Never have you been a problem, always mama's helper. And I want you to remember, if anything were to happen, I couldn't have asked for more."

"Mama, you're scaring me. Are you going somewhere? Are you going to leave me? Are you going to die?" When that last word registered, she grabbed onto her mama, pleading with her, through a mass of tears, not to leave her.

"Oh, honey, I'll never leave you. Don't you know we carry each other in our hearts?

"Now, wipe those tears and give me a hug. It won't be but a couple more weeks and I'll be giving you a little brother or sister. Then I'll be my old self, just you wait and see."

But it wasn't a couple of weeks. That night, her pains started. Screams ricocheted in and out of Mama's room. Saul didn't hesitate to call the Doc. He, too, never heard such piercing screams. The seconds it took for Doc to show himself, you would have thought he had been standing at the door, bag in hand. He rushed through the door announcing his presence, his orders quickly shouted out.

"Saul, have you the hot water ready? Have you timed her pains? When did they start?"

Question after question were asked and answered promptly. He settled Saul down in the main part of the house and then rushed down the hallway to their bedroom.

Minutes ticked away into an hour, then two. Saul refused to stay put, but the second Doc departed, he began pacing back and forth in front of the bedroom, wringing his hands, and then wiping his forehead.

He would stop and listen, and then he would be back to pacing. Three hours, then four. The hands of time were creeping at what seemed like a snail's walk.

Sloan's sisters' hours ago had fallen asleep. Sloan would not allow her eyes to sleep. Her mama might need her.

When Doc appeared, Saul showed a measure of relief, thinking the baby finally arrived. This was not the case.

"Saul, the baby is in the breech position and the outcome may not be good for Beth or your baby. I can't hide my concern. Her labor is intense, and it's taken a toll on her. I wish I had transferred her to the hospital hours ago, but at this point I think there would be dire consequences to pay if I were to move her now. I need your permission to sedate her.

"Now, I know her feelings on this, but she is in desperate need of rest. What do you think?" Saul didn't hesitate to respond with a yes.

Doc patted him on the back, with an additional comment.

"When she's comfortable enough, I'll attempt to turn the baby. If I'm successful, the baby should come quickly."

Doc felt time was of the essence, the reason behind the emergency call to his nurses. Alice and Ethel were due to arrive within minutes.

The Doc put his arm around Saul's shoulder, trying to sooth his anxiety.

"I'm going to get a cup of coffee. I suggest you do the same. Come on, Saul. Coffee's on me."

They wearily made their way to the kitchen, where a huge pot of very black coffee was made hours ago.

No matter how hard Sloan tried, her eyes wanted sleep. She wanted her mama. Curled in her papa's chair, where she had been all evening, she did not know the sandman arrived.

Suddenly a scream bellowed out into the hallway. Sloan's eyelids shot open. She was back from the world of slumber. Running as fast as nine-year-old legs could go, she and her papa collided in front of the bedroom door.

The screams continued for what seemed like hours, but were a matter of minutes… then dead silence.

They stood looking at one another, neither saying a word. Was silence better, she wanted to ask? But her mind said this was not the time to ask questions, she didn't.

Time stood still.

The sun was rising to envelop their home with warmth for the beginnings of a new day. Silence continued in Beth's room. Saul's silence ended with a sign, commenting to no one in particular about a fresh pot of coffee. He padded toward the kitchen.

The patter of feet was heard above. His daughters were rising like the sun to begin their new day.

Alexis, the sixth born, was four years of age, and the instant the lids of her eyes opened, she started her daily ritual, whining for the baby bottle she refused to sacrifice.

Lecky, as everyone called her, asked nothing of anyone; she demanded, everyone complied. She was built like a tank and moved as one. She was the spark that lit Sloan's fire. She was her favorite.

Then it happened. The door to her folks' bedroom opened.

Doc held a wrapped bundle close to his chest. Saul approached cautiously. He feared the worse. He had heard a piercing wail, then quiet. His baby did not make it. There will be a burial.

"Congratulations, Saul, you have a beautiful baby girl; a wee bit small, but feisty. I would put her weight at four pounds."

Saul fell to his knees in gratitude. There would not be a funeral.

"Is Beth okay?" Doc's wide smile convinced him all was okay. He had more to say, but Saul would not let him finish. Saul rose and gathered his baby girl gently into his arms, his lips longing to place kisses upon her tiny face. It was love at first sight.

"Saul, congratulations are again in order." The Doc repeated himself for the second time.

Saul was so into his baby girl, he had no time to respond until Nurse Ethel appeared with an additional bundle. Saul was confused. Sloan was to be a witness to a miracle.

Doc's words rocked Saul's world.

"You may be a big man, but I'm wondering if your arms are capable of holding the most beautiful babies I have ever delivered." If you had to gauge the Doc's excitement level, it would be over the top.

"Yes, you finally did it, Saul. You have a son, and is he a whopper. I could be wrong, but he's eight pounds or better. He was the one giving his mama all the problems. But if you were to ask Beth, she would reply, 'Don't be foolish. He was no trouble at all.'

"And I have to give credit where credit is due. Without my nurses' expertise, I don't think I could have turned that big boy. And let me tell you this: when he showed himself, he let out such a high-pitched wail, it was if he was telling the world to make room, a new voice has been heard.

"That big boy and his mama went through quite an ordeal, but his wee sister showed her patience by calmly waiting her turn. I brought her to you first because I wanted to see your reaction when I told you that you have a son. I just couldn't help myself. I hope you can forgive me."

Saul sank to his knees, his daughter safely cradled in his arms. He looked upward; thanking God over and over, for his prayer was surely heard. His son's name would be Zachary, the Hebrew meaning 'remembrance of the Lord.'

Sloan stood beside her papa's fallen body and watched his actions as everything unfolded.

Papa turned, giving his firstborn Sloan her baby sister. He then removed himself from the floor, taking his son from the arms of Nurse Ethel; never would anyone be more important.

The morning was perfect to welcome new arrivals. The glorious sun bore down brightly upon Saul's son, a sure sign from God that there will never be another to equal. He walked the grounds, showing his son what would one day be his, talking to Zac as if he were a child years older.

The arrival of Sloan's baby brother would forever change everyone's life, especially for Sloan, for she had always been her papa's favorite.

Beth was resting peacefully; well aware she had given birth to twins. She gave to her beloved husband the one thing she thought would never be accomplished, a beautiful son.

Sloan took it upon herself to feed breakfast to the younger of her sisters: Lecky, four, and Courtney, three. The four remaining managed to create food a chef would find to be deplorable, but eat it, they did. Mama allowed them this luxury, for they thought it to be a treat. Of course, the masterpieces they created left quite a mess, but the honor of the cleanup was given mama.

Their baby sister's name was left up to the siblings. Each took their time writing the name they thought best on a piece of paper. The ones unable to write legibly whispered their choice to one of their sisters.

When finished, they ran to the bowl their mama held in her lap. She had the privilege, with eyes closed, to draw out the chosen name. Anticipation was great. Finally, the slip of paper revealed their sister's name would be Payton, the name chosen by Sloan.

She would take first place in Sloan's heart, moving Lecky to second. The tragic circumstances surrounding that placement could well have been the reason.

In a matter of days – six, to be exact -- Papa announced there was to be a celebration. He would send invitations to all his friends. Sloan was confused. Friends? What friends? He never made friends. He kept to himself.

She remembered his age-old comment, "If we allow neighbors to become friends, they would take up valuable time. Plus, food and drink would have to be served, a substance that would benefit my children. No way is that going to happen.' And now he has friends? His acknowledgement to a greeting was always met with a nod, never a word.

This celebration was to show off the twins' arrival. Truth be told, it was in honor of his son, Zac. It wasn't as if he ignored Payton, for when he would pass her cradle, he'd give her a kiss, telling her she was daddy's girl. But when it came to his son, she would never be shown that kind of love.

Beth couldn't help herself. Her opinion should matter.

"Saul, this so-called party will be disastrous. Do you honestly believe our neighbors will come, when we never attend any of their functions?"

He was lacking a sense of reason.

"Absolutely how many of our neighbors have twins? Oh, ye of little faith, do you not believe? This will be an affair to be remembered."

She was a believer in the realistic, not in his kind of nonsense. But instead of telling him a flat "No way," she asked, "When would you like to have this party?"

"Today is Sunday, so the following Sunday would do just fine."

She looked at him as if his senses took flight. One week notice and the invitations had yet to be written. The way his mind was working, he must also believe money does grow on trees. But she would do as told, although she did throw in a comment.

"Saul, do you expect the not-yet- purchased invitations to spread wings and fly? The little money we have should not be used on postage. This just isn't feasible."

His comeback was quick.

"Handwrite the invites on sheets of paper. I'll deliver them myself. In the meantime, call Harriet and tell her to get the word out. She knows far more people than we."

As the words continued to spill out of his mouth, she was convinced he had approached the edge.

She kept a daily accounting of their funds stored in an old coffee can. At last count, a measly $240.00 was left, money desperately needed for past-due accounts, staples, and feed for the livestock. Very little money was used for food. They canned what they sowed, virtually living off the land. She felt sick, her stomach tied in knots. She knew this was wrong. When invited to a party, are you not to bring a gift? Was this not a form of begging? Did her husband wave as his pride left?

Beth knew Harriet would come, but she wasn't about to ask her best friend to run around town. She made the right decision due to the circumstances. She will not prepare food for a celebration that would end before there was a beginning. She refused to be a participant to such an obscene act, throwing money away on food that would never be eaten.

The day of celebration arrived. The party was to start at 1:30 p.m. Saul escaped into his own world. His morning was spent walking the floor with Zac. When the day ended and he was still walking and talking to Zac, Beth would tell him the party was over. If it turned out he didn't believe her, that was his problem.

Sloan felt as if her mama was losing it. Did she really believe he wouldn't notice there was no party? Something was happening to her family and she didn't know what to do to help them. After all, she was only almost nine years old.

Before the commotion started, Sloan gathered her sisters to get them away from the crazed madman, the title she bestowed on her papa.

Trucks, cars, flatbeds and the like began rolling into their driveway, but it wasn't long that space was filled; making weeds that should have been grass their only other source on which to park. The children were more than ready to have fun. A teenager gave to each a helium balloon tied with a weight.

Name a child that wouldn't be thrilled to have a balloon. Neither a hand nor an arm was free of a gift. People that pray together, stay together. The same principle applies to a close-knit community.

Men and women began taking banquet tables and chairs off the flatbeds, placing them around the yard. The older children entering into their teen years shook the folded tablecloths, readying the tabletops for God's bountiful blessings.

Dozens of women came laden down with baskets, platters, and bowls of food. The designs on the tablecloths quickly disappeared.

And leave it to the men to haul in the necessary beer by the barrels, while the old galvanized washtubs filled with ice held the soft drinks. Several BBQ pits were set up, charcoal getting fired up to accept hot dogs, pork steaks, and hamburgers. And what would a party be without the all-time favorite chicken? All would be consumed by day's end.

Legs of all sizes, shapes, and heights were on the move constantly, rushing about, making sure the newcomers' party would be the talk of the decade. A never- ending parade of new-found friends and neighbors came from far and wide. They were a part of the community, but the Parkers knew few of them.

The congratulations continued throughout the day. Saul's pride grew and grew with each handshake. Beth was surrounded by many women she did not know. She was told to sit, relax, and enjoy herself. It was her turn to be waited on. She obliged. Payton was passed from arm to arm. Never once did she cry. She was and always would be a good baby.

Saul refused requests for his son to be passed around. Beth noticed his apprehension when people would gather around to take a look; she wondered what excuse he gave to those who wanted to hold their son.

The day finally came to a close. Everyone was exhausted. Sleep came quickly to Sloan's sisters.

Wherever their body took them, that is where the fairy sprinkled her dust, closing their eyes in sleep. Two were found lying on benches in the yard. Three were scattered in the house: one on the sofa, another on the rug under the dining table, another curled in Papa's chair. The last of the bunch, Lecky, with baby bottle stuck in her mouth, was the lone child claiming her own bed.

The twins could not share a crib; Zac was double Payton's weight. Sloan's folks felt more comfortable with their separation.

When the night beckoned for everyone to return to their homes, there was no evidence a party had ever taken place.

The entire group of neighbors that supplied the food and drinks were the same crew for cleanup.

Saul and Beth felt the comfort of each other's arms as they escorted a tired, but happy, Sloan to bed. She no longer dreaded the crazed madman, for he left when the party started.

Sloan awakened much earlier than usual, and in what was turning into a habit, she peeked in on her new babies. They were fast asleep. She slipped quietly into the kitchen, enjoying the peace and quiet. She was met with mounds of baby items covering the length and width of the kitchen table. The larger items, double of everything, took up space against the walls.

Highchairs, baby beds with mattresses already assembled, pumpkin seats, cradles, playpens, wind-up swings, play mats with an attached jungle gym, changing tables, humidifier, hampers, diaper pails, stairwell gates, bathtubs, walkers, and a twin stroller completed the assortment.

When she thought she'd seen all there was to see, she noticed her papa and mama hidden behind a barricade of gifts sitting at the far end of the table, deep in conversation. They took no notice of her approach until she let out a gasp.

Stacks and stacks of money lined the table. She was young enough to let her imagination take over. She would have a pony (Sunni would have nothing over her) and new clothes for everyone. No more hand-me-downs, all new appliances and furniture, and Papa would have the finest truck ever. Mama broke the spell, forcing her back to reality. Dreams last for only so long.

"We've been up for hours, counting our blessings with every gift we opened, but it was the last of the gifts that left us speechless, a huge bag tied with blue and pink ribbons, stuffed to the brim with nothing but money.

"We both agreed the money would be returned, until we came across a sealed envelope with a brief note: 'Please accept this donation in God's name.'

"The money will be put aside for Zac and Payton's benefit, for it was given in their names."

They were not in a discussion on what to do with the money. They were praising their Heavenly Father. Sloan's dream came crashing down; she would not ride her pony.

Weeks and then months quickly passed. The twins were now 15 months old, walking to the point of running. Words were being tried out, most just baby jabber. Payton was still a petite little person, but her size did not diminish her capacity to keep up with her twin. Zachary got a quick name change almost from birth.

Lecky and Courtney, who Mama still considered toddlers, had a problem saying Zachary. Somewhere in the pronunciation of his name, ReRe came into play and soon gained popularity with everyone except Papa. To him, Zachary was powerful, ReRe was wimpy, but soon he caved in when Zac responded to only his nickname. This little guy, just fifteen months old, was already taking a stance in life, proving he was in charge.

During the early morning hours, Sloan was aroused from her sleep. She heard what sounded like the screen door opening or closing. Its scraping sound could not be mistaken, but that could not be. It was much too early for Papa to tend to outside chores. She continued to listen, but there was nothing more. She was about to claim her lost sleep when the sound was repeated. She looked around her shared bedroom. Apparently no one else had heard what she heard.

She convinced herself she must have been dreaming. She settled down to dream about things only ten-year-olds dream of, and that did not include boys. Those dreadful words 'if only' would not come into play in her young mind.

The night caller was paying an unwelcomed visit. Appearing out of the darkness and entering their home, the caller was there to commit the most heinous of crimes. When finished, a tiny pair of blue socks would be within the caller's grip.

Beth was finishing up with breakfast for Sloan and her sisters. Saul had eaten much earlier. The slam of the screen door with the broken hinge that dangled like a noose signaled his departure.

Beth was beginning to clear the tables when the now familiar cry sounded in the twins' room. She told Christina and Jessica to finish clearing the table. It was Sloan's turn to wash the dishes. Katie and Kaily were to take Lecky and Courtney out to play, with a stern reminder to keep them away from the hen house. She didn't need any more eggs broken like the last time Lecky and Courtney were left to fend for themselves.

She made her way to the twins' room. Oats were fixed and waiting, along with glasses of juice, buttered pieces of toast cut up into bite size. Bibs lay across the back of each high chair. Everything was ready and waiting, food stored on gifted heating trays. Beth was extremely efficient; she didn't waver off her schedule.

She entered the twins' room, prepared for Zac's demand to be picked up first. He was so like Lecky.

Payton was jumping up and down in her crib, smiling and talking her baby talk. Beth wondered why Zac was not doing the same. She went straight to his crib.

He was face down, his hands tucked under his baby pillow, his legs drawn up under his chest. He was sockless. His diapered butt stuck high in the air. Beth giggled at his antics.

"What are you doing, my little man? Are you playing hide and seek with Mommy? Where is ReRe hiding? I think I see you."

She reached down to tickle him. A piercing scream erupted, followed by a howling.

Sloan's head jerked up when she heard the scream, for she was doing what was expected, washing the breakfast dishes. Christina and Jessica, carrying the remainder of the dishes to the sink, dropped them when the scream erupted. If there was a clutter of breakage, it could not be heard. They reached for each other.

The water running for washing the dishes was totally forgotten as Sloan rushed towards the room that contained the howling. She stopped suddenly, a hand pressed against each side of the door frame. Her mama's back was facing her. Cries of anguish were echoing in the small room.

Sloan steeled herself from joining her mama's cries, but she was definitely not calm.

"Mama, what's wrong?" Slowly her mama turned towards her. Clutched to her breast was her ReRe. Mama was a pasty white. Eyes void, her mama looked dead.

Sloan ran screaming from the room, mouthing words her mama surely did not hear.

"Don't tell me, I don't want to know." Her tears were plentiful. She needed her papa; her papa would make everything okay. She ran screaming out the back screen door, practically pulling the framework away with the door.

She could barely speak; calling for her papa was barely above a whisper. Her efforts finally paid off when she found her voice.

"Papa, Papa, something bad has happened. Mama needs you."

Saul was hoeing a part of their vegetable garden when he heard his daughter's pitiful cries. For just a second, he hesitated. He felt evil lurking, waiting to plunge a dagger into his heart, draining the blood from within.

But no sooner had that thought entered, he brushed it aside. He didn't believe in such nonsense.

He would come to believe in the power of being forewarned.

He dropped the hoe as he raced towards his baby girl, wiping her tears as he folded his knees to rest on the ground. Gently he placed his hands on her trembling shoulders, trying to calm away what appeared to be a panic attack.

"Baby girl, it's okay. Papa's here. Nothing can be so bad that your old papa can't fix. Come on, dry those tears and tell me what has you so upset."

His attempt to calm her was not working; he had to show a harsh side of himself.

"Sloan, you need to put a stop to your crying. If you don't, I'm going to walk away."

She had no choice. She always obeyed her papa. She dug at the tears coating her young face.

"Something is wrong with Mama and ReRe."

Saul's hands now felt like vises. She trained her eyes on his as he looked up behind her towards their home. He rose to a standing position, giving no thought to the excessive pressure upon his daughter's shoulder, causing her to fall backward.

She quickly righted herself as she watched in wonder at the swift movement of his body. He gave the appearance of a well- trained athlete racing to the finish line. This is one race that would have no winners.

She willed herself to stay put. Lightning struck, the sound of thunder bore down, lights went out, for that is what it truly felt like. Mama's screams continued to explode throughout their home. Papa's spark in life ended that day. Mama barely existed.

Sloan had to take control. It was up to her to try and hold together what was left of their family, no matter what happened inside the walls of their home.

Saul's approach into the twins' room was without caution. He ran to his Beth. She was cowered into a corner, sobbing one minute, screaming the next, as she rocked her baby.

He pulled her to her feet, telling her everything would be okay. He took his son from the arms of his mama, holding him close. He did not look into his eyes; he did not want to see the face of death.

He grabbed a blanket nearby and laid his beloved baby boy gently upon it, the wood floor much too hard for his precious son.

He pried open the mouth of his only son and began mouth-to-mouth resuscitation, breathing for him, then applying compressions to his chest.

He would not stop. He would continue to breathe for his son. He refused to give up. Tears mingled with the saliva gathering on his son's face.

Beth was hysterical, looking upward, praying like she'd never prayed before.

"Oh, dear God in Heaven, where are You? We need Your help. Please, God, help us. Our baby needs You.

"Are You listening? Are You there? Don't leave us in our time of need, please, please."

Her rocking and weeping continued as she huddled in the corner.

Sloan was a witness to the unspeakable tragedy that would destroy her papa and mama's unwavering faith in God. She ran to the telephone. Little fingers traced the numbers written on a small notepad placed beside the phone, Doc's emergency exchange number. She grasped the phone tightly. The operator asked what doctor she was calling for, her name and phone number, and the reason for the call.

Sloan was now weeping as she told the operator everything that was asked of her.

"I think my baby brother is dead."

The operator's intake of breath was clearly heard. She could not mistake the voice as belonging to that of a child.

"Sweetie, I am going to have the doctor call you back right away. But what I need for you to do is to hang up the receiver. But you must stay by the telephone. Okay?"

Sloan's tearful response of "Okay" could barely be heard, her sobbing nearly drowning out her reply.

She answered on the first ring. Doc's familiar voice brought forth a fury of tears, tearing at his heart. When she was able to take a breath, Doc had the opportunity to relay a message: "Tell your papa I'm on my way."

The Doc's arrival seemed like an eternity when he rushed into the house, a useless medical bag in hand.

Sloan's sisters were huddled together, some crying. Others, too young to understand, were sitting on their older sisters' laps. Chrissie, nine years old, had already taken Payton out of her crib. A baby bottle was given to quiet her sobbing. She was now content.

Doc was shocked to see the scene being played out in front of him. A home, once full of life, now dissolved into one of emptiness and despair. Saul was oblivious to everyone around him. He was still performing CPR on his son. Doc needed access to the baby, but Saul refused to release his son's body to him.

He did not need the Doc to tell him his baby boy would no longer take him by the finger and guide him to the great outdoors or ride his shoulders into the cornfields or hear the magic word when his baby boy cried for his dada. His firstborn son, his only son, was gone. He couldn't give him up; he wouldn't give him up.

Doc began rubbing Saul's shoulder. He prayed his words would get his attention.

"Saul, I need to examine your son. I promise I will not hurt him, okay?" Saul's tear-drenched face looked onto the face of not only his doctor but his friend as well. He stood, taking Beth away from the security of the wall, drawing her close to his side.

Doc played his role well, baby Zac was handled gently, but all the medicine in the world was not about to bring their baby back. Saul and Beth's long-awaited son was gone. Rigor mortis had set in. There would be no miracles today.

The Doc wrapped his arms around Saul and Beth's baby boy, cradling him close to his chest while he looked up onto their faces. They were still holding on to their faith.

The Doc was grief-stricken when he spoke three words: "I'm so sorry."

Sloan watched as her mama slid out of her papa's arms onto the floor. Papa could not hold onto her; his arms fell to his side as the flood of tears washed over his body.

He turned, pounding the walls with his fists, and then he slowly sank to the floor, taking his fury out on the old floorboards. Wailing sounds could be heard over several roads.

As a young teenager, he stood by and watched his mama and his only baby brother die during childbirth. Six months later, his papa by his side died in the fields, and now his only son will join them.

Doc removed Beth from the floor, guiding her into the living room to be close to her other children, while Sloan took her papa's hand, leading him into the same room.

Saul and Beth reached out for each other, their love stronger then death. Their children gathered around them. Sloan sat on her papa's lap; with his hands, he pulled her head to his chest. She was still her papa's baby girl.

Doc made no attempt at finding the words to give comfort, for there were none. God will face quite a challenge.

"Saul, Beth, I wish I could tell you with certainty the cause of your son's death, but I cannot. It could have been crib death, though rare at fifteen months of age. To be absolutely sure, I would recommend an autopsy."

Beth jumped up screaming.

"How dare you suggest such a thing? No one will take a scalpel to our baby. He will not be butchered. Do you hear me? I will never allow anyone to hurt our baby, never, never, never."

Saul was quick to comfort his wife. There would be no autopsy.

Sheriff Ben's gut started to hurt when the Doc called him about the Parkers' son.

He told the Doc over the telephone he should conduct an investigation, but the Doc said ever so quietly that the Parkers were extremely distraught, and that could send them over the edge.

Ben decided not to heap on more misery by invading their home with inquires. If the Doc felt SIDS was the culprit, he would accept his diagnosis. He had a huge heart. He would let it be.

The hearse from the mortuary was called in to pick up Zac's tiny body to ready him for burial. His sisters were lined up, huddled together in the front yard waiting for Henry White, the coroner, to finish with their baby brother.

Henry dreaded having to walk pass Zac's sisters with the tiny body. He would hide his tears well. Believe it or not, he had never had to deal with such a terrible, terrible tragedy. That in itself was a blessing. He knew the history of the Parkers extremely well. Losing a baby is something no one should have to go through, but these wonderful people had waited years for a son. Now all the expectations and dreams for this little guy's future had come to an unthinkable end.

Henry would think about early retirement. This was something he did not think he could cope with. No one would understand his feelings unless they, too, lived in a small town.

Saul and Beth were seated upon their well-worn sofa, tightly holding on to each other, their faces awash in tears. They watched as Henry gently wrapped their beloved baby boy in his favorite blanket.

Beth rushed over to give Henry Zac's favorite daytime friend and bed buddy: a miniature white polar bear, threadbare, but loved just the same.

"Please, Henry, ReRe never goes anywhere without his little friend."

The blanket would be Zac's cover-up when Henry exited their home with his small body. There would be no black body bag to store their beloved son.

Ashes to ashes, dust to dust. The memory of those last words spoken as his tiny coffin was being lowered into the small opening would never leave the minds of all those in attendance.

Saul tried to hold Beth back, but she broke free, throwing herself onto her baby's coffin, screaming for God to have mercy, but that was not part of His plan.

Saul, choking on his own tears, stood back and watched as his beloved tore at the white rosebuds that blanketed his son's coffin. Her piercing cries of anguish caused the strongest of men to drop their heads and weep. Saul could do nothing to help himself. How was he expected to help his wife? Nobody could help them.

Sloan stood by and watched, bringing to mind the story of Moses when he commanded Pharaoh to let his people go, and when he refused, he called down a darkness for three days, whereby killing the firstborn in Egypt. And the people of Israel escaped by putting the blood of a lamb on the doorpost so the Lord would pass over them.

Moses was gone, as was Pharaoh, and her baby brother was not the firstborn in Egypt, but the firstborn son of her papa and mama born in Mason's Mill. If she had the blood of a lamb smeared on their door, would the Lord have passed over them? Only the workings of a young mind could think such a thought.

Sloan cried no more, for their home was already buried in a fountain of tears.

The same neighbors and new-found friends that organized and executed the celebration of the twins' birth now gathered to weep and say their final good-byes to a baby boy who had yet to experience the wonders of life.

Sloan was haunted by the memory of the outrageous comments of the so-called grievers.

"Boys were just not meant to be a part of your family, Sloan. Imagine raising a boy amongst all you girls. He most certainly would not have taken on a manly role, but of course, you are much too young to understand the significance of that."

That snobbish old broad managed to find an unoccupied chair that would withstand her weight when Sloan got right in her face.

With her hands on her hips, Sloan spat her response to that despicable remark.

"You mean he would have turned out to be a queer, a fruit, a gay guy, a fag, or a homo like everyone knows your son to be?"

This woman, with rolls upon rolls of fat that waddled like a duck when she walked, and whose name was Bertha, was struck dumb with that sarcastic comeback.

A friend of Bertha named Dorie, who was in competition with Bertha's size, jumped on her companion's remark.

"You should have never gone there, Bertha. You never know when to keep your big mouth shut. The kids today know more about the facts of life than you or I will ever know.

"I think it's time for your son to come out of the closet. It's apparent his sexual preference hasn't been hidden very well, if it has reached the ears of the young ones."

If a 10-year-old could cause Bertha to wobble away, hiding her face in shame, imagine what an adult could do.

Another offensive remark stored in the deep recesses of Sloan's mind came rushing forth.

"Wounds heal. It just takes time."

Sloan's ReRe was considered a wound! Now, just how dim-witted did that sound? Sloan never forgot her brazen comeback.

"Yeah, he was like a boil on my ass. Never thought I'd get rid of it."

Mouths dropped, shocked at the language pouring out of the mouth of a child. Sometimes adults needed to be put in their place. This was one of those times.

Sloan was again waiting for her age to change. Eleven was a good number and she was quickly learning how to be her own person. Speak when spoken to no longer applied. She was taking notice of the stupidity of adults.

She made a vow from that day forward to never allow anyone to speak ill of her family. She would protect them, no matter the means or the method.

It would be years before another baby was conceived in that house.

Papa turned his back on the church, and it would take years for Mama to forgive God. But for Beth to punish her children by refusing them the teaching of Christ was something even she could not do. They would never miss Sunday services.

The tongues started wagging when the years started rolling and no further birth announcements were forthcoming. The mention of divorce spread like a virus. Then one Sunday, when none of the Parkers' children attended church services, the wagging tongues began again, and continued as the Sundays added up with no-shows.

No one had seen Beth for several months, although the children were always visible. Many wondered if she had packed her bags and left in the night like others before her, although for different reasons.

Then the unexpected happened.

Pastor Riley turned the pulpit over to the Doc before church services began.

"Many of you have wondered, or I should say some of you have spread rumors about the Parkers getting a divorce. Well, I'm here to inform you nothing is further from the truth.

"They have been grieving for a very long time over the loss of their baby boy, Zac, and in the process, lost their devotion to God. Beth forced herself to come to Sunday's services only because of her children. She and Saul needed time to accept God's will.

"We cannot judge them, only our Redeemer has that right, and God in his goodness understands what drove them away.

"Well, I'm here to tell you that Beth and Saul received a blessing from God today.

Very early this morning, I delivered to them a beautiful baby boy. The name they chose for him is Steven.

"They renewed their faith in God several months ago when Beth and Saul paid a visit to Pastor Riley, asking for his blessings and to be reborn into Christ. They gave me their permission this morning to speak to all of you in this revelation."

The congregation stood, applauded, and in unison, spoke.

"Praise be to God in the Highest."

There would never again be another welcome party. That honor was bestowed upon Zac and would remain so.

Sunni's cries of regret for bringing up Zac's name also forced Sloan to remember how the love she felt for her best friend reversed into hate.

She had left Sunni behind, tears blinding her path in her race for home. Once through the door, she stumbled up the stairs into her bed, telling everyone in hearing distance to never again mention Sunni's name in her presence.

Forgiveness had never been easy for her. Life, as she struggled through it, taught her many things. Adults as well as children could be very cruel. She cried through the finish of the day and long into the night.

Sunni pleaded with her day and night, banging on the door, begging for forgiveness. The telephone also did not produce results.

Sloan refused to give Sunni absolution. Sunni fell into a deep depression, refusing to eat, and took to walking the floors when sleep should have prevailed. It got so bad that Miriam, Sunni's mother, made tracks to see Sloan's mama. Beth told a distressed Miriam she had already tried to reason with Sloan, but to no avail.

Beth tried to give some consolation.

"Whatever has caused this much anger, only time is going to heal the pain."

They decided to play the waiting game. Days turned into weeks. Finally Sunni's persistence paid off.

Six weeks to the day, Sloan drug Sunni to their spot. She had to swear on her life never to bring up Timmy's name again, but most of all, never, ever mention her baby brother ReRe. Sunni swore.

Four years have passed since Sunni's swearing day. Sloan is now eighteen years of age, and the only time Timmy's name is mentioned is in church. The pastor, on the eve of his death, says a few words in his memory.

The Parkers' tragic loss will remain their private memory.

# CHAPTER SEVEN

Sloan's tragic memories faded, bringing her back to the present day.

Everything was as Sloan remembered. When the "No Swimming" sign was staked, all the townspeople showed respect, including Beth. She cried as her kids cried. Their one day a week for two or three hours of swimming ended as abruptly as Timmy's and Buddy's. Their death affected many lives. Sloan felt as if a huge billboard was hanging over their house, an arrow pointing downwards, written with the words, "Destroy Contents."

She had to tug and push at the weeds and vines blocking the swimming hole's entrance. Birds bathing, interrupted by her appearance, took to the treetops. Cautiously, she looked over the entire surrounding area. Everything appeared normal.

She dropped to the ground, exhausted, mouthing a few words to no one.

"Now what do I do? First things first. Pitch the nylons. Don't even think." Kicking off her shoes, tears flowing, she pulled and tugged viciously until shreds of nylon were bunched tightly in her hands.

Kneeling in the sand, she began a digging process, deep, deeper, sand flying through the air, the opening now the depth of her arms. The nylons, no longer able to fulfill their intended use, were placed into the gap.

Tears flowed heavily; they were as plentiful as the handfuls of sand she slowly sprinkled into the opening, handful after handful, until at last the opening closed.

Her reassurance was buried, like her baby brother, both gone for good.

She then stood and shouted to the unseen entity that earlier had the gall to touch her.

"You want to touch something? Then touch this." She removed her dress. She wanted to make sure that whoever was out there would get an eyeful.

The tie belt that secured her twenty-dollar bill revealed no telltale signs of vomit, but the money's safety would best be stored in her shoe.

It was time to take inventory of her wearing apparel: a very skimpy bra, pee-soaked panties, and the vomit-free belt that she flung around her neck. If her mama could see her now, she would have thought she lost her senses.

Modesty then came into play. She tried to cover what the dress was used for, hands a poor substitute.

She could not have been any poorer had they taken her shoes away, but this young girl/woman was like no other. She was an attention-grabber. It made no difference whether it be man, woman, or child, they would stop what they were doing in awe of such perfection. She was her papa through and through.

She again took inventory of her life.

She did not know her grandparents on either side. She always wondered how her family could afford the luxury of a telephone when they barely the means to cover necessities.

Papa's explanation saddened her.

He and his pa had been in the fields since sun-up. It was time to head home. The daylight was ending. It was nearing time to show its black side.

He told his pa he'd race him to see who could make it home first. He did not have a chance to respond.

His pa gasped, clutched at his chest, and then plunged facedown onto the ground that had sustained him and the generations before him. And because his pa did not believe in the expense of a telephone, Papa had to run for miles to get the doctor, crying all the way. It did not cross his mind to call on his closest neighbor, the same neighbor that would care for him until he was able to care for himself.

He did not feel or take notice of the condition of his torn and bloody foot when he lost one of his shoes, racing against time. But God's will was already in place, and by the time the doctor got to his pa, too much time had lapsed; his pa was with his "Maker."

He was buried alongside of his wife, Papa's mother, who six months prior hemorrhaged in childbirth, taking with her pa's only sibling, a baby brother. The umbilical cord supplying the nutrients to sustain him did a reverse and strangled the life it was meant to care for.

The only service the doctor was able to perform was the treatment of a badly cut foot.

Papa swore before God, beating his fist onto the ground where his pa had lain and died, that he would never, ever, be without a telephone, even if it meant no food on the table. Papa was true to his word.

Mama's folks died when Beth was just a youngster. Her pa died of cancer shortly after her mama died of a stroke. The care of Beth was left to her great-grandma, who was barely able to care for herself. But she took Beth into her home and heart.

As Beth entered into her teens, her granny's strength began to deteriorate and her bed became her closest companion. Beth spent her free time hearing and sharing stories with her granny. Granny would end the evening with a prayer that Beth would meet and marry someone that would love her as much as she.

Granny was making preparations to meet her "King." She was getting her house in order. Within three months, Granny's prayer was granted, her great-grandbaby married, and two months later, Granny did meet her King. Sloan and her sisters and brothers grew up with no one to share their time with other than their mama and papa.

Sloan ignored the attention she generated. She was much taller than her female classmates, standing five-feet-nine inches. Younger classmates who were in awe of her and who stuffed their bras with toilet tissue or their papa's handkerchiefs believed that they, too, could have Sloan's measurements of 38-24-34; they just needed to grow a little taller.

She would make Venus weep if she were alive. It is nearly impossible to describe perfection. She has hair the color of approaching night that shades her back from the rays of sun. Her thick-lashed, almond-shaped, emerald green eyes hold you spellbound, while her lips, full and sensual, beckon men to taste of them.

She could never escape from one class to another without a hound of boys performing as sexually aroused animals. One such animal would hold himself and moan as if in a great deal of pain.

"Hey, Sloan, baby, I really have an ache. Do you think you can rub it away?"

Add to that another…

"Hey, Sloan, if you're looking to see if the shoe fits, you need look no further."

And yet another…

"Hey, Sloan, baby, what I have doesn't require batteries."

The disgusting remarks were endless, and the least offensive of these did nothing to jeopardize her self-esteem.

"You need help with your boobs, Sloan, oops, I mean your books," each guy slapping the other's hand, bellying over with laughter.

If she allowed herself to waste time on those that roamed the hallways, she would be no better then they. She turned a deaf ear, but not Sunni. She had more balls than all of them. She wouldn't think twice about kneeing them in the only place they thought made them a man.

"Look and say all you want, assholes, but never will you touch nor have what's in your small minds."

Sunni considered herself Sloan's protector and problem-solver. Sloan's mama did not consider a bra a necessary item. They could hang and sway. Who would notice? The same principle could apply to a man's genitals hanging loose minus his underwear. Sunni thought differently. She had the funds, and

Sloan now had the bra. A very large problem solved.

Sloan shook herself free from the past, returning to the present.

Bath time was further delayed for the birds as they fluttered from tree to tree; waiting for Sloan to finish what she came here for.

She stopped at the tip of the water, hesitated a second, then shouted.

"To hell with all of you!" She removed her meager cover-ups, the tie belt, bra, and urine-soaked panties. She admired the naked form that mirrored her image on the water's surface. How blessed she was to be given such a body, but wondered if anyone of importance would get the pleasure of touching the splendor of such a body.

Sloan and Sunni were noticeably different in their looks. You could categorize them as Beauty and the Beast. What they had in common was their height, weight, hair color, and length.

Sunni was a sad piece of work. No amount of talent on an artist's part could make her canvas come alive, with her small, close-set brown eyes, long, slender nose, and lips that lacked contour. Broad shoulders with a small bust and virtually no waist was a guarantee she would never turn a head.

But they both had crosses to bear, Sunni carried the cash, but lacked the looks; Sloan had the beauty, but lacked the bucks. Sloan surmised that was God's way of evening the score.

Sloan knelt at the water's edge, plunging her dress and panties, praying the water would remove all evidence of her mishap.

When she had gotten dressed this morning, she wrestled with the thought on whether to wear underwear. The pantyhose, ultra sheer, left nothing to the imagination. Modesty won, she thanked God. She would never have gone to town, putting it bluntly, bare-assed. Or would she?

After soaking the garments for several minutes, she stared at them intently, giving herself a thumbs-up. Now all she needed was a place for them to dry. A large, flat rock would have to do. The sun was near its boiling point; July never wavered in its intense heat. The dress should dry quickly. The panties were another story. They were the heavy-duty kind, meant to last a lifetime, her lifetime.

She stood back with her hands on her bare hips, cursing the unfairness of having to wear such ugly underwear.

"Damn those panties to hell. They will take forever to dry."

She lowered her body to sit, but instead found herself stretching to lie in the sand, the warm, warm sand. When she thought about it, what purpose would it serve going to town? Seeing all the strangers happy with their lives would only add to her misery. They got to leave; she had to stay.

The town's shopping center faced the highway with a bridge built over a creek, the same creek water that flowed between Sloan and Sunni's properties. Once over the two-lane bridge, it transformed into a tourist paradise.

Parking was no problem. Wide cobblestone walks lined the storefronts. The tourist trade was heavy during early spring on through the Labor Day weekend. That trade gave the store owners the necessary resources that provided affluent lifestyles.

Once over the bridge, if you were to look to the left, a newsstand was anchored into a wide stone walkway located forty feet from the front of the gas station and car repair. Following is a hardware store, a grooming station for pets, a laundromat, a hair salon for men, women and children, and a dry cleaner.

But a must to stop and shop was the fabulous two-story antique brick clothing and accessories store. It was known for its rare and hard-to- find items. And what's a town without the yummy taste of homemade ice cream? A parlor with the comfort of booths inside as well as outdoor tables and chairs is considered a nice gesture for the tourists to enjoy the weather.

And then there is the most talked-about restaurant, called Shelby's, serving the finest of country-style cooking. And yes, they had a license for selling booze for those who felt the need to quench their thirst.

On the opposite side of the street is an antique shop, and because the owner thought of himself as a reporter, he added a printing press.

The owner's idea was not to deliver per se the town's news, but to gather gossip meant to insult and embarrass. A drug store, a shoe repair, a post office and bank, a grocer & meat market, a furniture store, a five and dime variety, a bait and tackle shop, and finally, the doctor and the dentist sharing the same, but divided, office building.

The police station could not be ignored; it faced the shopping district. Protection was available at all times. If you stroll this far, maybe just to say hello to the sheriff, the smooth paved streets will transfer into a rocky road.

On this heavy graveled road sat sixteen cabins, with the rental office first. It faced the same woods that backed to the sheriff's office. The sixteen cabins were air-conditioned and furnished with a full-sized bed and, upon request, rollaway beds.

On the nightstand sat a current newspaper, Bible, lamp, telephone, and clock. A dresser and chair sat side by side. A small area rug to add a bit of color laid upon the wood floor. A closet and full-sized bathroom did not lessen the space of the cabin.

It would be hard to imagine the cabins would be used that often in a small town, but most were rented to people wanting to fish from the town's well-stocked lake. Set back off the road relatively close to Cabin 16, pits for barbequing and picnic tables with benches were scattered over a large plot of land. A small field with playground equipment was set up for the kids; a beautiful, fun place to visit, not only for adults but children as well.

So, who was Sloan going to impress with a town that was geared towards family-oriented people? Surely not the drivers that exited the highway, seeking to fill their gut after noticing the miles of billboards advertising country cooking or fishing the ever-popular lakes. It was designed for families who enjoyed the great outdoors.

Did Sloan really expect to meet someone? Not in this quaint old town.

An example was Martin Sizemore, the grocer who told all the women that entered his store that he was looking to end his bachelor life, if they knew of someone who might be interested. They would quickly gather their purchases and race for the door. He was round, short, and bald. If not for hair-curling eyebrows and hair sprouting out of his ears and nose, he would be hairless, and not to forget toothless. Following that description, did age matter?

Or there's the bank's president, William Hewlett, or "Willie Boy," as his never-ending bedding companions called him. He was a good one, that one, a real charmer, married five times and in debt up to his you-know-what, while paying child support for his twelve children. Supposedly he swore off women. Yeah, well, no one sees pigs fly either.

Just recently a rumor ran rampant throughout the town about how a former girlfriend chased one of Willie's girlfriends out of a cabin, swearing she'd kill her if she continued seeing her Willie.

On one specific occasion, as the black swept over the sky, Sheriff Ben, doing the night shift, grabbed  hold of "Willie Boy" as he was attempting to escape yet another cabin with only his shoes in hand. Why his shoes and nothing else remains a mystery. But as all rumors go, some of his cronies at the bank said his shoes cost more than his child support payments, so he wasn't about to leave them behind.

Another story, while inebriated, he told his drinking buddies his bare feet couldn't walk the rocks, let alone run. His shoes were his means for a quick getaway.

The sheriff, on that particular night, stated loud and clear: "If I ever catch you again in any of the cabins, I'm going to jail your hide. These nightly rituals end as of this night. I refuse to bury someone over your shenanigans."

So far, it seems as if "Willie Boy" is keeping a tight rein on his zipper.

When Sloan really thought about the eligibility of the store owners, they were either married or divorced, making them liable for many hang-ups, and if single, way too old to be of any benefit to Sloan.

The only one left, God forbid, is Marc Anderson, nicknamed Pimp, short for large boils that covered his entire face. He owned the name "ugly." He was twenty-two years of age, a single man, and sure to remain that way. Even though he stood six-foot-three, with a fantastic muscular body. He needed a face replacement.

He worked part time at the gas station while attending Brown College, seeking a degree in architectural design, a college located in Lincoln County, forty miles from town.

Marc was his mama's boy; her home was his home. Transportation presented no problem. When his high school diploma was placed into his right hand, his mother placed truck keys into the other, figuratively speaking.

Sloan again journeyed back into her past.

Beth told Sloan years before how the arrival of Harriet and her son Marc began.

Someone placed an emergency call to the sheriff, telling him to hurry over to Mac's land (the prior owner). It looked to be a burglary.

"Of all things, a burglary. Who'd believe that?" A shake of his head is a part of the sheriff's makeup, a habit he will always carry.

Sure enough, as he pulled up and climbed out of the patrol car, someone or something was pushing and shoving its way through weeds and mountains of trash. The small house, hidden from view, lost its appeal a half-century past. It now resembled a well-worn shack.

Sheriff Ben shouted at the intruder, "You in there, show yourself!" Ben's hand held steady on his holster. "Stupid, stupid," were his thoughts.

The so-called burglar tumbled out, looking somewhat like the place he escaped from. He was a rather small man with hardly any meat on his bones, but he wasn't lacking in the looks department.

He rudely voiced his opinion of his surroundings.

"This place appears to be the town's dumping grounds."

Ben didn't appreciate the man's tactless comment, but said nothing in that regard. He remained stern, but calm.

"And sir, just who might you be?"

"I think I'm a real estate agent, but to look at me, who knows? My card, Sheriff. The name is Thomas Langsby. I'm here representing Harriet Anderson. She bought this property, sight unseen, for reasons I hope to never understand.

"At her request, I'm here to check it out to see if it's livable. Now, tell me, Sheriff, should I call her and tell her to rush right over because it's ready for occupancy?"

Ben decided to also let that remark slide. He also decided to put this agent in his place.

"You say this Anderson woman bought this here place, sight unseen? Well, then, it looks like it's her baby.

"Now, before you say another word, I'd advise you to inform your client what a choice piece of property she got herself. And if you want to keep clients like her, I'd also advise you to hire in a cleanup crew, pronto."

With a wave of his hand, he was gone, leaving the small but manly real estate agent with his foot in his mouth.

Ben took it upon himself, as he looked at the agent's card, to call him and get some background information on this Anderson woman. The agent this time was cordial and polite.

"Sheriff, I really don't know what information you are seeking. All I can tell you is what she told me. She at present lives in a big city and wishes to settle down in a small town and live a quiet life with no hassles.

"When she hired me to be her agent, I was grateful. The economy sucks. The only thing she asked of me was to find a house, any house, which she could make into a home for her and her three-or four-year-old son. There was no mention of a husband. Of course, that doesn't mean she's not married. Trust me; she wasn't forthcoming with any information other than the mention of the little boy. I wish I could have been of more help."

Ben appreciated everything the agent told him and bid him good-bye.

Ben did not waste any time preparing the townspeople about their intended tenant. He figured if given enough time before Harriet moved in, they would not be so condemning. The sad part was that most of the families had roots dating back several generations; they did not take kindly to outsiders, especially Silva Felders.

Silva headed the town's council and thought she ran Mason's Mill. In part, that was true. Four generations had left her extremely well-to-do, very old, and cynical, and without doubt she would remain single until death did her in.

Thankfully, she was the last of her generation. She was at her best destroying the lives of people she felt would not fit in, which meant no outsiders would ever be permitted to live in her community.

She gathered her closest conspirators to formulate a plan to rid her town of this so-called 'city gal.'

But Harriet Anderson had a plan of her own. She was here to stay. She had found her place to set down roots.

Cruel gossip, not excluding harassment, ran rampant, continuing for months, stopping to take a breather, and then picking up again.

Eventually, if given enough time, things can turn around. The townspeople were taking a liking to Harriet and her small son, Marc.

Silva refused to let go of the badgering. She hounded her co-conspirators.

"What is it that you low-life scrums do all day, sit on your asses? We have a stranger living among us, weaving her way into our homes, with evil as her weapon. And yet you sit here like stumps on a log."

Silva did not receive the response she demanded. They stared into space. She began punching those closest to her, while she continued to blast their eardrums, damning the woman that brought so much pain into her life. She continued with irrational insults until she lost her voice. The townspeople could only pray it would be a permanent thing.

Finally, a few co-conspirators found the guts to speak up. They were about to turn the table on Silva.

"No more, Silva. We're through hurting people. If anyone should be run out of our town, it should be you. You're vicious and contemptible. May God help you, for one day you just might suffer a terrible demise."

"Yeah, and one day you all are going to regret this day."

Contractors were hired to tear down what was left of the old farmhouse, and in its place was to be a beautiful three-bedroom, two-bath brick home with 2,100 square feet of living space. An office and a storage unit would be added years later.

Never at any time did Harriet Anderson apply for credit. Everything was paid with a cashier's check. She was courteous, kind, and extremely thoughtful, always going out of her way to help those in need, whether it be money, food, or help with caring for a sick neighbor. The townspeople in time would come to think highly of her and label her as one of a kind.

She did have a fault, if you would call it that. She would hesitate before she answered direct questions, if she answered them at all.

Questions such as:

"Your little boy is a darling. I bet his pa's as proud of him as you are?"

Harriet would just smile.

"Will your husband be joining you and your son when the work is finished on your land?"

Again, her answers contained only a smile.

In a way, it was surprising they didn't directly come out and ask:

"Do you have a husband?"

"Does your son have a father?"

"Are you in hiding?"

"What is your source of income?"

Stupidity had become the trademark of Mason's Mill. And then one day, it just stopped. The townspeople began to make appointments, anxious to see what their future held in store for them. Each time they got more than expected, always leaving with a smile.

Never question believers; no one can sway them away from their beliefs. This psychic ability provided Harriet a steady income, and soon her clients became friends, barring Silva Felders.

As the calendar years changed, so did Sloan. She was a seeker of knowledge, always wanting to know more, whether it be places, objects, or people. This time her curiosity centered on the Andersons. She gathered a few known facts, but craved more.

Harriet and her son Marc moved here ages ago, and whatever title Harriet chose for herself, whether it be a psychic, clairvoyant, or medium, it required a lot of hand-holding. Once moved in, no man took up residence; she was alone with her son. She was single, married, widowed, or divorced. She had an endless supply of money. Marc's father was either dead, gone away, or never was. That was the extent of knowing the Andersons.

Sloan finished hanging the seventh load of line-drying the family's clothing. She collected the now-empty baskets, heading indoors for refills. She decided to quiz her mama. It was common knowledge her mama knew Harriet far better than anyone.

Beth stopped what she was doing, taking Sloan's face into her hands.

"Honey, you have such an inquisitive mind, always seeking answers, but to this question, I have not the right to answer. If you feel you must know, then you must go directly to the source, for only there will you find the truth, though I prefer you didn't.

"If Harriet wanted the townspeople to know her business, she would have taken it upon herself to tell them. There is no escaping evil, for it lurks everywhere. Silva is living proof.

"On the opposite spectrum, if anyone were to be given a halo for being all that God wants us to be, the honor would be bestowed on Harriet. And if everyone acted as such, Jesus would be walking among us."

Beth bowed her head when she spoke of Jesus, then continued.

"Harriet has been a victim far too long, and I, for one, am sick of it. Gossip is hurtful and can destroy people's lives. It starts with folks that have nothing to do. They feast off the kindness of others. Then, the minute you turn your back, they turn into leeches, sucking the life out of the innocents.

"We have not the right to interfere with God's work; He will take care of the wrong-doers when the time is right. So for now, let us take care of the work set before us. Time waits for no one."

Sloan thought her mama was through with her say when she turned away, furiously cutting away at vegetables that would soon be a part of the family dinner. Sloan was about to head out the door, clothing baskets refilled, when her mama, apparently lost in thought, began to speak.

"Dear God, hear my prayer. Please take Silva's tongue and silence it once and for all. Harriet has had enough hurt in her life."

The tone of her mama's voice indicated a great sadness; she knew more than she was willing to tell.

Sloan turned back. The baskets of wet clothing would have to wait.

"Mama, you seem sad. I'm a good listener, if you need to talk."

Beth turned to face her daughter, gently stroking her cheek with her fingertips.

"How could I be sad, when God blessed me with so much? You'd better get going; I've never known clothes to hang themselves."

When Sloan turned to do what was asked of her, her mama had one more thing to add.

"I love you, honey."

Sloan turned back to hug and kiss her, adding a bit more.

"Not nearly as much as I love you."

Sloan tearfully confided in Sunni, telling her how sad her mama was with Silva's lips always moving, never having a kind word for anyone. Sunni knew how close Beth and Harriet were. She was sympathetic.

"Sloan, your mama's not the only one who's tired of Silva's tongue-lashings."

Sunni wrapped her arms around her best friend.

"Don't cry, honey. Everyone is beginning to turn their backs on Silva. It won't be long until she'll only have herself for company."

Maybe Silva hated those that could see into the future, reveal the past. Maybe she has a skeleton in her closet. Maybe Harriet will see and know about that skeleton and reveal those findings to the townspeople.

Silva wasn't stupid; she was aware that most of Harriet's predictions did come true. And the townspeople were not stupid, either; they noticed that every time Harriet's name was mentioned, Silva would fiddle with her hearing aid, no doubt turning up its volume.

Silva refused to let Harriet roam around her town. She had to know at all times what Harriet was up to. She'd be damned if she allowed anything to get pass her.

Sloan also felt vulnerable. She never knew of anyone who could predict things before they happened. She wondered if Harriet possessed the power to know things about her without asking.

She posed that question to Sunni.

"What if Harriet knows my future and sees something bad?"

"Sloan, for God's sake, get real. I sure hope you're not losing sleep over that stupid thought.

"You need to really think about this. If she knew something bad was going to happen to you or even your family, she would warn you to be on the lookout. She loves you and your family; she wouldn't allow any harm to come to any of you."

Sunni was one of these nonbelievers, but she would say and do anything to pacify her best friend.

Sloan kept it to herself, but she wondered if her mama ever asked Harriet to look into her future. Now, that would be something even Sloan would like to know.

Sloan began questioning other avenues. She asked Sunni for her opinion.

"There are two things that have me puzzled. Why didn't Harriet foresee the death of Timmy and Buddy?"

"Those are two examples why she's a fake. God, I can't believe you swallow all her garbage."

No matter what her best friend said, she believed the dead walked among the living, spirits watching over those they love. It did not matter that Harriet could not see all, nor did it matter that some of the things she predicted never came to be. Harriet was truthful with her clients; she told them only what she could see and nothing more. If they were not satisfied with her findings, she would return their money. Never at any time was there a request for a refund.

Ben was going nowhere in his quest for answers into Timmy's death. He himself was no believer in psychics, but what the hell, it wouldn't hurt to talk to this Anderson woman; it wasn't as if he were going to ask for advice or guidance into the supernatural. He just wanted to see if she had heard or seen anything.

She told him she had not. He was no believer in the world beyond, but he did believe that when lightning strikes, it always strikes twice. Months passed, and Ben continued to see Harriet.

Silva's tongue started rattling again. This time she received no help; she was on her own. Silva's feet pulverized the rocky roads. She ran from farmhouse to farmhouse almost as well as she ran her mouth. She pounded on the farmers' doors. Doors left unlocked and unanswered, she stomped on in.

"I told you nothing good would come out of that bitch living here. But no, not one of you imbeciles would listen to me. I didn't acquire all this money from being stupid."

Silva's screams could be heard by the surrounding neighbors, and that is not something to be proud of.

If only the townspeople had enough courage to say what they felt: "No, all the money you inherited made you a smart-ass." But they kept their lips and tongues intact.

Silva continued her show of disapproval.

"The sheriff and that slut are having illicit sex, and them not being married, the shame of it all. The sheriff's shoes should be on his floor beside his bed, not beside hers."

The townspeople knew beyond a doubt that she had finally crossed over the line. She should be certified as insane. They wouldn't think about calling in the Doc. He would never cross that line again.

That evening, the monthly meeting of the town's council held in the church was called to order. Silva was, if at all possible, at her worst.

The townspeople's hushed tones were about Silva falling over the edge.

She banged the gavel unmercifully. They refused to keep quiet.

"Shut your God-damned mouths. (God, are You not listening to Your name being taken in vain?) I'm not here to pass the time of day to a bunch of assholes."

Silence always followed when filth came charging out of her mouth. Her sinister smile did not go unnoticed.

"I have an announcement."

The silence was beginning to make everyone sick. Something was going to happen.

Silva continued. "The money I contribute to my church, added to all that I have done for you and my town, apparently has no gratitude. I just spent hard-earned money on the cost and installation of a new roof for our parish, not to mention the potholes in the roads that needed repairs that the state would not pay for.

"I have a packed folder showing each and every good deed I've done. I bet you didn't think I'd keep a record, huh? Maybe I'll take this red folder and read each item one by one."

She shook the thick, blood-red folder above her head for emphasis. The townspeople's mouths dropped open. They would not be home for breakfast. Silva fed on the reactions of the townspeople; she was satisfied with their dropped jaws.

She continued where she dropped off.

"No, I don't think so. I refuse to lose my beauty sleep over this."

Heads shook and eyeballs rolled on that comment.

Silva was on a roll. She would not let up.

"As of this day, my contributions stop. I'm withdrawing all future funds."

The townspeople gasped, stunned that their main source of money was at an end, money desperately needed to make their town function. The quiet was anything but natural. Everyone was in shock.

Silva, with the same stupid smirk on her mouth, gathered up her useless set of papers. She then stood to finish her announcement.

"Now, I want all of you to see just how you'll manage without my money. And then, when you all come to your senses and decide I and only I know what's best for my town, then maybe, just maybe, I might again reconsider funding everything."

On a further note, she added, "I also advise you all not to wait too long, for it could end up being the sorriest mistake you will ever make."

Her smirk was still lodged on her mouth as she left her place of self-centered honor.

After her departure, the townspeople could think of nothing more to say to each other. Most of them stood shaking their heads in disbelief.

For the first time, the townspeople were ashamed at how they allowed Silva to buy their friendship, how she controlled them by the use of her purse strings. They formed a line to take their leave, heads bowed as if at Sunday mass, though this was not in reverence, for that night many wished Silva dead, even if it meant taking her money with her.

Heavy rains beat upon the grounds that night, adding to the gloom of the townspeople.

The night caller was at it again. The darkness would soon turn to light. The caller had to hurry.

The rock thrown into Silva's bedroom window was right on target. Glass blew inward and some fragments dropped on the ground below. The caller was positioned against the framework of the farmhouse, sight unseen.

Silva screamed out, for the rock struck her in the head. She rubbed her forehead; a trickle of blood smeared her hand. She was beside herself. She was utterly pissed. She felt the urge to kill.

She rose from her bed, taking notice of the rock lying at her feet. She reached down. Hate was raging as she clutched the rock tightly into her hand; she would do to them what they did to her, only much, much worse.

She was careful as she leaned out the broken window.

"I'll get you bastards for this. You all need a strap taken to your asses so you won't be able to wipe for weeks. Nobody breaks my window and gets away with it. Your folks will pay dearly for this."

Silva came tearing out the back door, her robe beltless, nightclothes already showing signs of the downpour of rain. Boots readily available for wet weather were totally forgotten.

The caller slung a baseball bat onto her back. The output of breath sounded forced as she plunged forward, her face striking the mud with a thud.

The rock toppled from her hand, joining the rock bed from which it came. She was temporarily knocked out as the caller grabbed onto her arms, pulling her forward.

The caller had difficulty dragging her body, the mud adding extra weight to the already heavy load. She was a big-boned woman and grotesque, standing a minimum of five-feet-ten. Her weight was tipping the scales at 300 pounds.

The caller swung the gate open to the pigs' quarters, their hooves buried in the rain-drenched mud. She started to respond, when the caller's booted foot slammed onto the back of her head. She started choking on the mud and slop in the pigs' den.

The activity caused the pigs to stir. More and more gathered around the two figures. The caller knew it was time to finish up.

The caller rolled Silva over, wiping the mud and feces from her face with a gloved hand. The caller wanted her alert. She wasted no time coming around. Her eyes blinked once and then twice, as she recognized her attacker.

"You... I can't believe this... how dare you! Let me up!" She was now fully responsive.

The caller's fist pounded into her face. Blood gushed from her nose, while part of her lip was ripped away, hanging at an odd angle. She could feel several teeth trying to make their way down her throat. Eyes locked onto her assailant; she never felt such pain. She began to cry, choking on blood and teeth, but still she managed to run her mouth.

"You are going to pay dearly for this. Everyone in this town will see and know what you've done to me."

She couldn't hold back from the horror of the pain. The crying turned into hysteria.

The caller had no sympathy.

"You really are a bitch. All these years you've slung shit at people, rubbed their faces in it, and laughed. Now how does it feel? What, no comment? Too bad. Now it's your turn to eat shit and die."

The caller laughed hysterically. A heightened pleasure would define the caller's state of mind. The caller then grabbed up glops of the pigs' shit and began stuffing it into Silva's mouth and nose.

She was suffocating. She fought hard to free herself from the brutality of her attacker. The mud and the pigs forced her to remain immobile.

"Gee, Silva, the pigs don't even like you." The caller laughed. Silva's last moments of life would not have been something she would have held onto. The caller closed the gate, watching as the hogs closed in for what was to be their kill.

Silva took her last breath when the gate closed behind her. She would not hear the caller's last words.

"Gosh, I'm really rather tired. I think I'll go home. But before I go, I will claim ownership of that red folder, for it will no longer be of service to you."

The caller's high-pitched laughter echoed through the downpour.

When early morning came, an urgent call was placed to the sheriff's office. The rain had finally stopped, leaving soggy fields and mounds of mud behind.

Deputy Robert Davies took the message. He shoved his shoed feet into his oversized boots. He felt as if the message should be delivered immediately. His boots made tracks to the sheriff's place; a mobile home parked no more than a hundred feet behind the sheriff's office and jail.

Ben was on his way out when the storm door slammed into his deputy, knocking him off the steps onto a now mud-covered yard.

Robert's sprawled body landed backwards. The mud splashed onto his face and into his mouth, causing him to gag. Ben did not laugh; Robert was not the kind who took to anyone laughing at him. Ben wrestled with him, trying to return him to a standing position.

They were both big men, each well over 200 pounds, their height nearly the same. Their difference was in their ages. The sheriff was in his fifties, whereas his deputy was only thirty-one.

Ben may have been older, but if looks counted, he would win hands down. He was six-feet-three, with hair the color of a Hershey bar and eyes to match. His smile would send shivers down a woman's back, his teeth perfect and white as snow. He has a slight stomach bulge, but with everything else in his favor, who would care?

Robert… well, he wasn't what you would call ugly; it was just hard to describe him. But Ben was the best when it came to description. After all, he was a cop.

Robert had light brown hair that was rapidly receding, small brown eyes that looked over a very crooked nose held up by his rather large lips. He wasn't married, but desperately wanted to be. He would accept a "yes" from any woman as long as she had a head, two arms, and two legs.

He was on the prowl, constantly looking. The women couldn't run fast enough when it appeared as if he were going to approach them.

Ben had a hard time trying to juggle his own weight in the rain-drenched mud, let alone Robert's. After a number of attempts, Robert slapped Ben's hands away.

"Damn, you're getting more mud on me than I had to begin with. Just move away. I'll get up by myself."

He couldn't have been more pissed. Ben turned away, grinning. Whatever brought him here, Ben would lay odds that Robert wished he had stayed at the office.

Robert righted himself. He knew he had to return to his house for fresh clothes, but not before he told Ben about the call.

Ben knew Silva would start something again. She didn't do enough damage last night. What she did this time, he had no idea. She'd do anything to get attention.

Ben was not in the mood for Silva's antics, and he told Robert so.

"She'll just have to wait."

"I don't know, Ben. It sounded pretty serious. That Mexican, you know, the one I can barely understand, he said, 'Hurry, be quick, somethin' bad happen.' Those were his exact words."

"Everything is an emergency when it comes to Silva. Is there ever a time that her problems are not serious? What is the purpose of having the Mexican place the call? Oh, what the hell, come on. I'll drive you home so you can change. We'll leave from your place and see what she's up to."

Ben stuck his head in his office, telling his soon-to-be-retired dispatcher (economy will prevent a replacement) he was on his way to Silva's, should she call.

No more than fifteen minutes had passed since Robert informed Ben about the call from the Mexican. The patrol car approached Silva's farmhouse slowly. There appeared to be another council meeting, only this one was held outside.

Ben looked at Robert.

"Now, what in the hell do you suppose is going on?"

Robert took to shaking his head, ready with a reply.

"Do you think something bad did happen, like the Mexican said?"

"I don't know, but whatever it is, I have a feeling this is going to be a long day."

The patrol car inched its way into the crowd. The townspeople took to the graveled drive, avoiding the mud-soaked ground. Pulling the patrol car as near as possible to the farmhouse, the sheriff and his Deputy attempted to climb out, when a flurry of the farmers and their better halves started talking at the same time, although making no sense.

Ben was in no mood for their nonsense.

"Quiet, all of you. If any of you have any information as to what is going on, I'll listen; if not, please return to your homes."

The townspeople reluctantly took their leave. Never did they dare cross beyond the front of the farmhouse, fearing the wrath of its homeowner. They had enough of Silva last night to last their lifetimes.

Ben still did not know where Silva was. She, of all people, should have been the first to run to his patrol car. He really wished he had taken up a different line of work.

Milling around were the hired hands, totaling forty. Ben wormed his way through the huddled men. It didn't take long for him to find the Mexican; he had positioned himself on a tree stump far from the others. His head was buried in his hands, sobbing uncontrollably.

The Mexican called Johnny was no more than five feet tall. He was dark-skinned with dirty, shoulder-length black hair. He was a nice enough looking young man, only very short. Ben put his age between twenty-six and thirty.

Ben gently touched his shoulder, causing him to leap into his arms.

"It bad, it be bad, Sheriff." Ben appreciated that he could speak English. This would make whatever the problem less difficult.

"Now, calm down. It can't be as bad as all that. Your call said it was urgent. Do you feel up to telling me what it is that has you so upset?"

"Me no go dere; it be bad, Sheriff." His dirty hands were smearing God-knows-what all over his face from the ongoing tears.

"Then tell me, where's your boss, Miss Felders? I'll go see her."

"Her be witz da pigs. I no touch nothin'. I jus' run... ta call ya."

The Mexican was calming down, although his hands were still busy.

The pigs' quarters were quiet, though still occupied. Robert was standing off to the side, waiting on instructions from Ben on what their next step would be. Ben yelled out for Robert to join him.

As they approached the hogs' home, Ben had a foreboding. His rounded gut started to cramp before he could see what it was he was here for; somehow, he knew death was going to be looking up at him.

Silva's body was distorted. Her robe and nightclothes were in shreds. Death was exposed in its grotesque form.

Robert turned away. His stomach was churning. He felt the bile rise, and he ran towards the outhouse the hired hands used. The contents of his stomach quickly emptied.

There was no need for Ben to check for a pulse. Parts of Silva's intestines were on display, eyes bulging from their sockets.

The Mexican, as it turned out, was the one who found Silva's body. The discovery caused the other hired hands to stay their distance.

Johnny failed to tell Ben that Silva would no longer be running her mouth. Ben called out for some of the workers to remove the hogs one by one, but not to cross the gate's entrance, if at all possible.

They complied with his instructions, using long poles, encouraging the pigs to leave their confined area, guiding them to yet another stall. Ben realized potential evidence could be tracked beyond the pen, but there wasn't anything more he could do.

Robert was back from the outhouse. Ben tried to lighten the situation: "I hope everything came out okay!" Robert saw no humor in that statement and said so. Ben grinned with an apology.

Robert stood with his hands on his hips, staring at the naked body of a hideous Silva, when he voiced his belief.

"Phew, what a way to go. Who'd ever think pigs would kill?"

Ben couldn't believe Robert's way of thinking.

"Pigs kill, what the hell is wrong with you? This is no pig killing. Silva was murdered."

Robert thought Ben was crazy.

"Murdered? You can't possibly mean that."

Ben was unrelenting.

"I not only mean it, I'm going to prove it. Have you looked around? Have you noticed anything unusual?"

Robert was blasé with his answer.

"All I see is the body of Silva, naked and dead, lying with a bunch of hogs."

Ben was persistent.

"Have you taken a good look at what she was wearing? No one would venture out into the type of storm we had last night in nightclothes if she was not awakened by someone or something. And where are her boots? She has nothing on her feet.

"Did you take the time to look around and take in the surroundings? Apparently not. Look up at the second floor, Robert. What do you see?"

Robert took his time, and finally he made an announcement.

"Oh, my God, one of her windows is shattered."

Ben was the one this time shaking his head.

"No shit. Don't you notice anything? You're supposed to be observant. This is a crime scene; everything is relevant to solving this case."

"I'm sorry; Ben, but this will be my first murder. I don't know what's expected of me."

Ben apologized, realizing Robert was right. Ben will be his guide.

"This is what I need you to do. Check out the inside of Silva's bedroom. Whatever broke that pane of glass has to be lying about. If we're lucky, the killer left his prints."

Robert continued to stand there, leading Ben to wonder if he was waiting for someone to lead him by the hand.

Ben jumped on his ass.

"Well, get a move on, and don't you dare come back and tell me you found nothing. In the meantime, I'll give a call to the coroner so he can make arrangements to have her body removed."

While Ben waited for the coroner to arrive, Robert was finishing up with Silva's room.

He was shaking his head in Ben's direction when he approached him.

"You can't be serious. You found nothing?"

"Ben, her room was spotless. Not a thing was out of order, unless you count her rumbled bed covering and a few pieces of glass under her window."

"Damn, this doesn't make sense. Something had to have broken that glass."

Robert gave Ben an accounting of the early morning news.

"According to the news this morning, the storm last night had a wind speed of 50 miles per hour. It was reported to be the worst the county has seen in 10 years. Maybe flying debris caused the breakage."

Ben shook his head. The only way he could be convinced was to witness this breakage with his own eyes.

He would put aside his thoughts regarding the object that caused the damage to Silva's window; he and Robert still had work to do. There was only one way to tell Robert of the task before them, and that was just to say it.

"After Silva's body is removed, we have something unpleasant facing us, sifting the mud in the hogs' quarters."

Robert's mouth flew open.

"You can't be serious, Ben. There's nothing in there but pig shit."

Ben expressed his understanding.

"I know it's going to be a nasty job, Robert, but it needs to be done. The killer could have dropped something, anything; it's our job to find it. We need something solid to go on, hard evidence, if we're to find the person responsible for this."

The expression on Robert's face should have brought laughter, but Ben knew better.

"Oh, for cripes' sake, Robert, collecting pig shit is not the hard evidence I'm speaking of. You're just not thinking clearly."

Robert shook his head.

"You are so wrong; there is nothing wrong with my thinking. There is no way I'm getting down on my hands and knees to squash shit. I can't do this, I won't do this. I'll quit this damn job before I lower myself to do that kind of dirty work."

"Then you're out of here. But believe me when I tell you this: you'll never again practice being a law enforcement officer."

Ben's deputy of five years looked shaken with his superior's words. It did not take him long to offer an apology and his acceptance of the disgusting deed.

While waiting for the coroner, Ben made the rounds, questioning the hired help. No one had seen or heard anything. Their boss was sharing the pigs' quarters when the hired hands arrived for work.

Ben was already beat. The heat did not help the situation. This would turn out to be one of the worst days of his life, when he would not be given the go-ahead to start an investigation, although he did not know that yet.

The coroner, Henry White, was a tall gentleman, dressed impeccably and appearing much younger than his fifty-seven years. He was extremely good-looking with a full head of wavy black hair (no dye job here), small mustache and goatee, deep dimples, and fabulous white teeth. Forewarned, he came prepared, as he trudged forward in knee-high boots.

He was not married and was pursued constantly by every single woman and many that were married. He lived in town in a magnificent home that stood empty for days at a time. He was seen in other counties frequenting gay bars.

The townspeople wondered how the men folk telling this tale came to know this as fact unless they, too, were a part of the same crowd. It's no secret all the good ones were taken.

Henry was very patient, waiting for the sheriff after being told Ben was taping off Silva's house. Henry stuffed his hands into his pants pockets. He had all the time in the world to wait. After all, it wasn't as if he had a pile of bodies waiting on him. This was one dead town, no pun intended.

Ben shuffled over to Henry with a grim greeting.

Henry acknowledged him with a nod, anxious to get started processing the remains of Silva. Ben noticed him shaking his head numerous times. Finally, Henry gave his assessment: "Yep, she's dead."

Ben also shook his head, rolling his eyes at such an absurd answer, but that did not stop him from mouthing his opinion.

"She was murdered, wasn't she, Henry?"

"Murdered? My God, Ben, this is clearly an accident. What's wrong with you? Do you have scrambled eggs for brains?"

Ben had no time to think of his brains.

"Silva would not have been in her nightclothes tending to pigs in the dead of night."

Henry acted as if he never heard Ben's last comment. He continued with his say.

"More than likely, the pigs overtook her, which probably caused her to slip and fall. There is no doubt in my mind that the hogs overpowered her and trampled her to death.

"Stranger things than this have happened. Why, just last week, I was called in on a similar case. A deer hunter mistook a horse for a deer and shot the poor animal. The horse, in all likelihood, reared up on the impact, tossing its rider onto the ground. Before the rider could react, the animal toppled over, crushing the guy's head. You talk about a mess. Brain matter was everywhere.

"No, Ben, this is just another one of those unforeseeable accidents."

Ben could not believe Henry's comparison, unless Henry was comparing Silva to a horse. Did Henry really believe he would go along with his theory?

When Henry noticed the look Ben tossed at him, he added more.

"But to satisfy all concerned, I'm going to ask that an autopsy be performed. That way, there will be no doubt as to the cause of death.

"So, if you'll excuse me, I'll go and bag Silva's hands for any possible skin scrapings. I sure wouldn't want to miss any fine details into a possible murder." He gave Ben a somewhat disgusted look.

Ben was pleased with that answer. Henry could give him any kind of look he wanted, as long as he got what was expected. Begging was not his thing, but if it got him any kind of cooperation, he would do it. Hurray for small favors.

Everything was near completion. The only thing remaining was the sifting of the mud and feces in the pigs' quarters.

The ambulance pulled in to bag Silva's body. It would then be taken to the hospital's morgue, located in Pine County. Robert carried out Ben's request, asking around for a donation of hip boots, necessary for the shit job that lay in wait for them.

Ben and Robert spent hours in the mud, many times stopping, the stench that bad. After fruitless hours of searching, Ben called it a day. If a look alone could kill, Ben would have joined Silva.

Robert was boiling. He stomped off, ever mindful of the pig shit still clinging to his body and hip boots.

Ben flew into a rage when the medical examiner agreed with Henry White that Silva's death was an accident. All the arguing would not alter the findings.

Ben had yet another case he felt was murder. He was worn out and fed up with the whole stupid system. When he tried to pursue it further, Ben was told the investigation was over.

Ben could not hold back his temper. He exploded to his superior.

"What investigation? I haven't even begun. This is bullshit!"

Ben's superior could not control his temper.

"And this is the last time I will listen to your bullshit. The case is closed, finished. Find something else to investigate. Just get the hell out of my office."

Ben was ruthless with his words; he was determined to get his point across.

"I'll get out of your damn office when I finish with what I have to say and not before."

The superior's patience expired. He was sick and tired of Ben always wanting to conduct an investigation. He would take no more of Ben's subordination. He showed him to the door with an added comment:

"You want something tedious and time-consuming, work a puzzle."

When the door closed behind him, Ben had no one to talk to but himself.

"What doesn't my superior understand? That's exactly what I'm trying to do."

He began to think he was the one who was crazy and everyone else was sane. Maybe this would be a perfect time to look into another line of work.

Beth's prayer, though drastic, was answered when Silva died. Sloan thought God had taken a vacation from answering prayers, and then realized they could be like everything in life: they are answered in the order received.

The only good thing to come out of Silva's death, other than the fact that the townspeople smiled more often, was when the trustee of her estate read her will, it bequeathed all her holdings to her church. The amount was speculated to be in the millions. Now, that is what you call a mammoth blessing.

One year had passed since the death of Silva Felders. Ben was still the sheriff. He was too tired and too old to make a move. Besides, he was in love with Harriet. But a pall still lingered over the town. Fear of the unknown had once again entered the lives of the townspeople, each realizing how very close they themselves were to being struck down by the Grim Reaper.

Many of the townspeople believed that Silva's attempt to run Harriet out of town and her obsessive contempt of the relationship between the sheriff and Harriet brought about the horror that was slowly creeping over the roads and through their houses.

And when talking of relationships, Marc's obsession for Sloan was bordering on psychotic. Sloan could avoid Marc living a short distance from her home, but school was another matter.

She was a freshman when he was in his last year of high school.

She was always on the lookout, skipping around students to avoid his outbursts of telling everyone in his path of his love for her.

"Sloan might not like me now, but in time, she will grow to love me. Someday she and I will share a home and have many children."

Kids in school would laugh at him or tell him to get lost, although he never did. He would shout in the halls, always demanding an audience.

"Someday Sloan and I will grace the covers of all magazines."

Students thought him unhinged, but marveled at his grades. His I.Q. was near genius.

Because Sloan acquainted herself with various routes to avoid him, he turned his attention to Sunni.

"Sunni, when you see Sloan, tell her how much I love her and I will do everything in my power to have her."

He even had the nerve to grab her arm while she attempted to run. She, like so many, would do anything to rid herself of his presence.

"Let go of me, you creep. Do you honestly think Sloan will ever be seen with you? You'd be the answer to a person's nightmare. What you need to do is take a good look at yourself. You do have a mirror, do you not?"

Sloan had to agree with Sunni. He was hard to look at. Never has she seen a haircut such as his. His barber, if he had one, should have his license revoked. What was the purpose of chopping hair in different lengths?

And his pathetic wardrobe never changed, except for the color of his plaid shirt, worn under faded and well-worn bib overalls. And to complete the look, high-top tennis shoes minus shoestrings, with tongues flapping, trailed after him.

If he thought he would start a trend, he of all people would not be the one. He by far headed the list of the most undesirables.

When she was forced to come in contact with him and no means of escape possible, she stood firm, unyielding to his stare. But a stronger power forced her to look away; fear did that, something she wanted no part of.

Sloan let go of the memories and returned to the present day.

The heat took its toll on her. She found herself speaking out loud.

"So, with all this prime stock, you should go to town? Yes, you should. You never know. That man on the white horse in shining armor just might come trotting into town today. Yeah, and I'm Lady Godiva."

She reached over to check her panties. They were still wet. The sun could bake her, but dry her panties?

She thought about putting on her dress.

"The hell with it. So what if I'm naked? I'm alone." She continued to carry on a single conversation. The sensation from the warmth of the sun tingled her body like a caress, and her eyelids began to flutter.

She knew she must not sleep... but sleep was softly calling to her. Close your eyes... that's it... sleep. And so she did.

Something unspeakable caused her to awaken from her slumber. A feeling of utter terror crept into her body while she was asleep. Something was not right. She again could feel the presence of a danger lurking close, very close.

She knew she had to get dressed quickly. She had to hurry; she had little time to make it to safety. She reached over to gather her panties and dress; she couldn't get into her underwear fast enough.

She then remembered her bra. She kept her eyes focused on the surrounding area while she felt around in the sand. The bra was missing.

She quickly assessed the situation.

"I need a minute to think. When I laid down, I had the bra in my hand. It has to be here somewhere."

She circled the area.

"This is impossible. I haven't moved from this spot." She looked upward; the leaves on the trees were still, nothing seemed to be moving. But maybe, while she was asleep, there was enough of a breeze for it to be carried away. If so, it could be caught onto a bush or a piece of tumbleweed.

She began a search, ever mindful that she had to leave the area. After what seemed like an eternity, she realized it was gone. But how? Where? Surely she was not imagining all that had happened today.

And then it happened. It was if someone whispered in her ear.

'You smell it, don't you, the scent of another? Oh, my God, yes.'

Flinging the dress over her head with the belt and shoes now clutched in her hand, she again made a run for her life.

"Run, that's it, run. Don't stop; don't turn around, for it just might be behind you. Head straight for town; it's just up ahead. Tell someone, anyone. Help is there; just don't look back. You are almost there… "

She stumbled and was completely exhausted as she rounded a bend in the road and ran smack into a nightmare. A scream like nothing ever heard or witnessed pierced the ears of everyone in the cabins.

Sloan slipped away, entering into a state of unconsciousness. She felt the thing hold tight. She fought a good fight; it was now over. She knew, whatever it was, it wanted her, and there would be no escape.

# CHAPTER EIGHT

She could feel the pressure of biting into flesh. She pulled away and took off running, sweat beads beginning to form on her face. But she had to keep forging ahead, least she be caught in a spider's web. The spider with its hideous legs would devour her if she stopped.

But her running path ended with an explosion of fire. The spider's tongue of flames were hungry; she was to be its feast.

She looked to the heavens to be saved, and from its clouds, arms reach down, gathering her close, taking her to a safe house. But instead of finding comfort, she was placed on a bed of thorns. The pain was agonizing. She began to cry, for she knew she was about to endure much worse.

A voice etched in sadness whispered in her ear to look closely at the shadow that would appear before her. Secrets would then be revealed. The shadow appeared briefly, and then faded away.

"Who are you? Wait, don't leave." Sloan was unaware of the gestures she was making, using voice and body language to talk with an unseen entity. She could hear two distinct sounds. She had heard them before, but couldn't remember where.

The shadow reappeared. This time it slowly began to materialize, carrying something wrapped in a small package. The shape and size resembled that of a newborn.

"Please, I must see. Bring it closer. Yes, that's it…" Arms unfolded the blanket. Her arms.

"Oh, my God, no, no, it can't be, take it away. Dear God in Heaven, I don't belong here, please bring me home. Please…Please…" Hysterical crying gradually turned into weeping. She struggled to return, to come back from a visit to the beyond. She tried to focus on the scene before her.

The strength of Marc's arms held her close.

"It's okay, Sloan, I'm here. No one will ever lay a hand on you as long as I have a breath in my body. You will always be safe with me."

She could see Marc, but he seemed to be talking from a far distance. There was something the shadow wanted her to remember, something very important. But Marc kept flapping his lips.

"Why doesn't he just shut up? I need to remember."

Marc could see she was struggling with something; she was somewhere other than with him. She was remembering a night long ago, when her baby brother died, and then it slipped away all because Marc couldn't keep his mouth from moving.

"Sloan, if you're able to see me, nod your head."

As a replacement for nodding, she began shaking her head. "Maybe if I really concentrate, I will be able to recall what the shadow was trying to tell me." Instead, she found herself engulfed in a sea of blue, Marc's eyes.

"Where am I?"

"You're on the edge of town. You passed out. Should I go for the Doc?"

"I'm fine. No doctor, please." She reached out, tugging on his arm for emphasis. It was then she noticed the red welts, a near perfect circle. She somehow knew it was caused by her teeth. Her hand flew to her mouth; a groan escaped.

"Oh, Marc, I did that, didn't I? I am so sorry."

"If you wanted to put your brand on me, all you had to do was ask."

Sloan was mortified, and she showed it.

"Sloan, I'm just joking. I was making an attempt to put a little humor in a complex situation. Will you forgive me?"

"Forgive you? It is I that should ask for forgiveness." All was well. They connected.

Only then did Marc and Sloan notice the people that were gathering, inquiring what the fuss was all about.

There she was, lying on the shoulder of the road, half dressed, barefooted, and dirty. Marc pulled her to a sitting position. She quickly wrapped her arms around her upper body. She was totally embarrassed. She had no idea where the tears came from, but come, they did.

It did not take a genius to see her distress. Marc again came to her rescue.

"The heat has taken its toll. She's been walking over five miles to get medicine for her sick mother. Her father's truck broke down just as he was preparing to leave.

"She offered her help so her father could stay with her mother. I think she ran more than she walked. She worries when it comes to her family."

Signs of relief were heard throughout the crowd. The people assembled were of the older generation and disillusioned with the attitudes of the youngsters that would someday rule our nation. Today, Sloan's unselfish act gave them faith that all was not lost.

A voice sounded out in the crowd.

"Child, is there anything we can do to help?"

Marc took the initiative.

"Would you mind, I see one of her shoes, could you find the other?"

Fifteen to twenty men and women, including children, started rushing about. In a matter of a few minutes, someone shouted out.

"I have it. I found it." A very short, fat, and very old woman with strands of gray hair flying wildly about her face, dressed in a bright orange pantsuit, came huffing and puffing towards them, swinging the shoe above her head. Marc was down on one knee, tending to the woman that would always have his heart.

When the elderly lady approached, Marc stood. She abruptly stopped.

"Glory be, child, this young man would put Goliath to shame."

Sloan took another look at the man that rescued her and she had to agree. Marc was a mountain of a man. The little lady began backing up, never taking her eyes off of Marc. With a fling, she threw Sloan's shoe onto her lap and then took off running. Sloan yelled out a thank-you, but received no response.

Sloan now noticed how Marc had disengaged himself from being the center of attention. He settled his large frame against an oak tree with his arms folded across his chest. And with his legs crossed at the ankles, he boldly focused his eyes on Sloan's partially exposed body. Excitement had died down. Everyone decided the show was over and departed to finish or start what they had set out to do.

Marc was proving to Sloan he had what it takes to make her feel ill at ease.

"Really, Marc, instead of just standing there gawking, you could help me up."

He quickly moved toward her. She tried unsuccessfully to cover the upper part of her legs. The dress refused to move. The top laid like a flap over her arms, providing a poor choice for a cover-up. If anyone possessed a camera, she could be a centerfold for Playboy.

She alone was responsible for this humiliation. The fear that presented itself at the 'hole' did not allow time to close the zipper; her main concern was for her life. Now that her head was on straight, embarrassment set in, causing her to question how such a small thing as a zipper could have held her life together.

"I see we have a problem." With no further thought, he stepped behind her and placed his hands around her waist. She scrambled to stand, her arms still in use for a cover-up. She felt the zipper being fiddled with, and then a tug. Several minutes passed. Was he studying its mechanism? Did he not know how a zipper works?

She couldn't wait another minute.

"I think you need the expertise of a woman's hands. It would be a sad state of affairs if your income depended on the workings of such a dumb thing as a zipper."

She was sorry the second she tossed out the comment, and told him so. It wasn't his fault; maybe the zipper was broken. She did not doubt it; the dress received plenty of abuse.

She could help, but if she did so, it meant full exposure of her breasts. She looked around. Nearly everyone was gone. Those that were in her line of vision were busy doing their own thing. She didn't hesitate; she reached behind, clutching both halves of the dress together, allowing more ease of closure. She told Marc to give it another try.

This time, two hands were not better than one. Four was the number. Once Marc completed the mind-boggling challenge, he came around to face her. She turned away, tucking in her breasts.

He kind of snickered.

"Do we still have a problem?"

She turned back to face him, countering back with a dim-witted answer.

"No, we do not." She then looked at him, really looked at him. This time her eyes were wide open, and eyes an incredible blue stared back. She was caught up in the moment; she wanted him to kiss her. She was no longer seeing the surface, only the soul.

Did he know the effect he was having on her? She prayed not.

She had to pull herself together. Town was waiting, and she changed her mind about her knight in shining armor. He just might show up.

But she needed to break away from the spell that Marc was weaving, his eyes commanding her forward; they were within an inch of making body contact.

She captured his scent, bringing about an excitement she never before experienced. She forced herself to break eye contact, although compelled to stay close. But when he touched her hair, she lost it.

"Just what the hell do you think you're doing?"

Marc threw up his hands and then backed away.

"Sloan, forgive me, I was only trying to remove the fragments of debris that you collected. If this is your idea of hair accessories, who am I to dispute this?"

Sloan was set to defy his response until she thought of the absurdity of his comment. She marveled at his sense of humor. With a childish smile, she tilted her head, hands palm-up, displaying a gesture of not being overly smart. Laughter made everything okay.

Marc returned to the tedious job at hand. This time she did not resist. When finished he turned to face her.

"There. All done, pretty as always."

She could feel moisture begin to form in her eyes, tears to wash her face.

"Oh, Marc, I'm such a mess. Papa gave me twenty dollars to buy… the money... my money is gone. I've lost my money. Oh God, Marc, you have to help me find it."

With a flick of his wrist the now-unfolded twenty-dollar bill was seen between his thumb and index finger.

"I found it lying on the road. I figured it was yours."

She wondered what she would have done had she lost her papa's coveted twenty dollars. Head for the highway came to mind.

"And I suppose you also have my belt?" He dangled the belt in front of her.

"Well, I'm grateful I don't have to retrace my steps. Thank you, Marc. I don't know what I would have done without your help."

Marc's nod was his acceptance. But Sloan wasn't finished with him.

"Could I have the use of your shoulder? I need to put on my shoes."

Now standing secure on the road, dress and shoes in place, she asked for his help one last time.

"Would you mind checking me over to make sure I'm not a refuge can for hauling sticks and weeds?" They were now on the same level, each trying to outdo the other in the humor department. Laughter is a sure-fire way of dealing with stress.

Marc's large hands moved over her back and shoulders, removing all that remained of the trash she collected on her tour of the road. But he didn't stop there. He continued around to the front, then downward onto her breasts.

His face froze; the color of blood came to mind, his embarrassment that obvious. She never said a word, enjoying his reaction. She glued her eyes onto his, while his stared at the hands that lingered on her breast. She had to say something; he appeared to be going into shock.

"My God, Marc, they're only breasts. Even your mother has them. And I know your thoughts are not going in the wrong direction." His face showed relief beyond gratitude.

She ran her hands over her hair and dress, not thinking about the forthcoming comment.

"Well, I can't look any better. What do you think?"

"No, you can't. You're absolutely beautiful."

She got the impression that he thought she was fishing for a compliment. She gave no response to his statement.

Suddenly she felt lightheaded. She needed a place to rest.

"Marc, I need to sit a while. I don't feel well."

Marc placed his arm around her waist, offering support.

"Come with me. There's a bench in front of Cabin 16. I'm sure no one will mind us using it."

Idle talk followed, mostly one-sided, his. The main topic of conversation was Marc's mother, no doubt the great love of his life. He rattled on, though half the time Sloan was not listening; her thoughts were taking her back to the woods and the 'hole'. Was Marc the one that was following her, she wondered?

Marc finally took a breath. She reacted quickly.

"Marc, how did you happen to be here?"

"I guess it was just a coincidence."

"Coincidence, that's crap, you were the one that was following me. You're the one who took my bra, aren't you?"

She stood, ready to again run for her life. He also stood, extending his hand.

She began to back away.

"Don't come near me. Don't you dare touch me! I'll yell for help. Don't think I won't be heard."

"Sloan, whatever you think is going on, believe me, I have no part in it. Please come with me. I want to show you something."

Sloan continued to back away.

"If you're looking for some kind of explanation, you'll come with me."

She looked around. Kids were roughhousing in the playground no more than fifty feet away, supervised by one or both of their parents. Further up the road, the blur of the sheriff or his deputy sat in front of the jailhouse. There was no way Marc could pull her into the woods. Far too many people were within hearing distance.

"I'll go with you so long as you stay your distance, and I'll look at whatever it is that you want to show me. Just don't think I can't get away if I have to."

He stayed his distance as he crossed back over the road. He appeared to be standing in the same area as to where she had collapsed.

He stood, hands on hips, waiting.

"It's over here. You coming?"

She glanced again to the law enforcement. Her approach was with caution.

He hunched down, holding back a mass of twigs, weeds, and overgrown ivy.

"I caught a few squirrels and rabbits – thirteen, to be exact -- but being accused of something I know nothing of, thirteen, as the saying goes, is definitely not my lucky number."

She stared at the blood-coated animals. His gun lay beside his kill. She felt the bile rise in her throat.

"Hunting is something I rarely get a chance to do, with college and work. Nice catch, if I do say so myself. What do you think?" Marc was proud of his catch and it showed. His face was beaming.

She tried to find the words to describe how bad she felt.

"Oh, Marc, I'm so very sorry. This is a terrible thing to do, accuse you of something you apparently have no knowledge of. Will you ever be able to accept my apology?"

"Sloan, you need never apologize to me. You did nothing wrong. What do you say we just put this behind us, and celebrate your safety by letting me buy you a Coke?"

He took her hand in his. She showed no objection.

"Marc, I need to ask you something, but it is rather personal. Do you mind?"

Like her mama said, go directly to the source.

"I think I'm supposed to say it depends on the question."

Sloan's mouth fell open. Before she could think of a reply, he was ready with his answer.

"Ask away. I'll tell you everything you wish to know, if I have the answer."

Sloan has never known anyone like him. Looking past the ugly, how she could have missed his gift of charm and wit?

"Where's your pa?" That's it, Sloan, ask point blank. How dumb.

"I know it's really none of my business. I guess I'm as bad as the others, but why the big secret? Did your pa rob or kill somebody? Is he a jailbird?"

"Sloan, I'll tell you what no one else will ever know, unless you tell them. I never knew my father. I wish I had. All I can do is pray that someday, God willing, our paths will cross.

"I was in my early teens when I gathered enough nerve to ask about him. My mother looked at me with such sadness, I was instantly sorry. Eager to know was one thing, but to upset her was not my intention. If I could have grabbed a hold of those words and shoved them back from where they came, I would have done so.

"What she did tell me amounted to really nothing. They were single and deeply in love. They never doubted that they would marry, but something happened that changed all that, she got pregnant, and they were forced to go their separate ways. She accepted things as they were for my sake. She pleaded with me not to press for further details, that one day I will come to know all I need to know.

"That sums up my life. Not much to tell, really."

Sloan was quick with her questions, for if she thought about it, she just might realize what a jerk she really is for asking about things that were definitely none of her business.

"Except for the fact of money, which your mama seems to have plenty of, and don't tell me it comes from fortune-telling."

"We will never want for anything; my father made a lifetime commitment to provide us with all the necessities of life. He faithfully sends us money each month. This could be construed as a sort of payoff. I pray not, although more for my mother's sake than my own. I guess I'm like her; I trust in the power of love.

"Is there anything else you'd like to know?"

"No, Marc. Like you had said, that about sums up your life." What more could I ask, she thought. I made enough of a fool of myself for one day.

They made their way up the road toward town, keeping their conversations more in line with school.

They were nearing the end of the road when they finally noticed how most of the cabins had cars parked in front. It was apparent the tourist trade had not declined. But it was the car that was parked in front of Cabin 1 that caught her attention, a black Porsche. She was in awe at the sleekness of its design. She couldn't help herself; she went to caress its body.

Marc noticed how she seemed to change. She stood straighter, more poised, more sure of herself.

"Someday you will have a car like that."

"Oh, Marc, I don't think so, although I would give anything to sit in it, maybe go for a ride. Wouldn't that be something?"

"Sloan... I..." Before Marc could finish what he was about to say, Deputy Robert Davis, the one that had his carcass parked in front of the police station, called out to them.

"You two weren't a part of that commotion down the road, were you?" The deputy was sitting in a chair, teetering back and forth on its rear legs in front of the combined office and jail.

"No, sir, Deputy Davis. An opossum decided to show itself during the daylight hours at the picnic site. Caused quite a rumpus with the people staying in the cabins; must be city folks."

"Right so, Marc, right so. My, my, Sloan, you sure are gonna stir up this old town, the way you're lookin.' Lardy, if all the girls looked like you, none of us would ever get anything accomplished. I can see now why your pa keeps you under wraps. And that yellow dress, whew, takes my breath away."

Marc moved closer to Sloan, hoping to give the still-single deputy the impression they were an item. Sloan signed.  It could be worse; she could be working in the fields.

"Why, Deputy Robert, such a sweet compliment, I thank you kindly, sir. I didn't think a big, burly, good-looking man like yourself would even notice such a little thing as a woman's dress."

"Yeah, well, to be truthful, it's not exactly the dress that's a turn-on; it's what's inside the dress that looks yummy."

Realizing his slip of the tongue caused the deputy to lose his balance of control. The chair he was sitting on fell sideways, spilling him onto the porch of the jailhouse.

He scrambled to a standing position, trying to regain his composure from this awkward embarrassment. The deputy turned his head in another direction, making no further eye contact, but finished with a mean remark.

"Don't you kids have anything better to do than to interfere with the police while on duty? You've taken up enough of my time. Get a move on."

His speedy exit was almost like a repeat performance. He tripped over the leg of the chair, slamming his head onto the frame of the doorway. Robert would never again make direct eye contact with Sloan.

Sloan giggled, while Marc appeared agitated.

"Marc, is something wrong? You seem upset. Is it something I did?"

"It was disgusting the way you were flirting with the deputy."

"What, are you crazy? I wasn't flirting. He gave me a compliment. I wanted to be nice back. Is that a crime?"

"Yeah, right, and I guess you didn't notice the way he was gawking at you. The drool was practically running off his face.

"There are only two things I can think of that would cause you not to notice what was on his mind: blindness or stupidity. And since you can see, the only thing left is stupidity."

"Well, since you seem to know all the answers, why don't you tell me what was on his mind?"

Marc was fuming. She noticed his hands were made into fists. She wondered if he was going to hit her.

He took a hold of her arm while making a comment.

"Let's just forget it."

She wasn't about to let him control her life. She voiced her own comment.

"If we're going to argue, I'd just as soon be by myself."

"And if you wait on an apology, you may see it in your next lifetime, and I refuse to argue. I promised you a Coke and I always make good on my promises."

She could not believe how he spoke to her, and she really did not care how he felt. She would have that Coke, but after that she would have nothing more to do with him.

They crossed the road from the sheriff's office in silence. The town was indeed busy. Sloan could never remember her town being so city-like. As far as the eye could see, it looked as if the majority of parking spaces were filled.

The pebble stone walks were overrun with tourists; they were easy to spot by their clothing. Everyone seemed in a hurry. Parents were grabbing their kids from running out in the streets. Horns were constantly being tried out. Many times she rode with her papa to pick up something he had ordered from the hardware store, but never has she seen her town so full of life.

She was caught up in the excitement. She wanted to mingle with the people, eavesdrop on their conversations. She wanted to see, feel, and know what they are feeling. She wanted that kind of life.

Marc calmed down considerably, suggesting they get a Coke at the ice cream parlor. Of the four tables located outside, only one was occupied, by three older women who were arguing over who was to pay the bill.

Marc held the door open, allowing Sloan to enter. As they entered, three girls Sloan had graduated with were seated facing them. Giggles were heard as Marc reached for her hand. That was just what she needed: the most popular girls, and she has to be seen with the pimp.

She refused to act humiliated. She accepted his hand with a smile. For a minute she forgot who and where she was. The glowing smile he returned warmed her heart. She wondered if there was something wrong with her.

Marc ordered their drinks with the intention of sitting outside; therefore, their drinks would be brought out to them. He never once, during this time, released her hand, but as she approached the table, Marc let go, quick to pull out the chair.

She was amazed and stunned by his manners, a perfect gentleman. She wanted to know who he was, this hick with such charisma and manners like no other. She wondered if she was wrong about him; was he always this kind and gentle, serious one minute and then joking the next?

Marc sought her attention.

"Sloan, are you going to sit or stand?"

She was still in a dream state when she answered.

"I'm going to sit while you stand." Their high-pitched laughter caught the attention of the three older ladies. Still arguing over who was to pay the bill, they stopped long enough to giggle along with them.

Now seated, Marc reached out to reclaim her hands. She did not pull away.

"You know, Sloan, I can't remember a day that I didn't love you. I love you so much, my heart hurts. I also know you think I'm a nothing, but I'm trying hard to be someone you will be proud of.

"My dream of being an architect is going to happen. Trust me. Four years of schooling is behind me. Two more and I'm finished. Then, once I get established in a good firm, we can get married.

"The waiting will be hard on both of us, but everything has to be perfect. You deserve no less. And when that day arrives, our wedding day, it will be spectacular, a day no one will ever forget."

Sloan's mouth was hanging open when a young girl of no more than fourteen years of age brought their drinks, along with their bill for

$1.65. As Marc reached into his pocket to pay her, Sloan rose from her chair. Marc also stood, but his was out of respect.

"My God, Marc, I don't even know you and you're talking about marriage. You need to see a doctor, a specialist, one that deals with the mind, for you surely have lost yours."

"Sloan, we've known each other our entire lives. Well, not in the sense you mean, but it's never been a secret how much I love you, have always loved you. If you give me a chance to actually court you, in time you will feel the same about me."

"Marc, I'm sorry, this was a dreadful mistake. I should never have agreed to come here with you. I have to leave. Please don't follow me."

Marc just reaffirmed what Sloan knew all along; his brain hadn't reached its full potential, if there ever was potential. She swung around various people in her quest to get away.

Marc threw the money on the table with a $1.00 tip. He wasn't about to give up.

"Sloan, wait, please wait."

She almost made it to the clothing store when he caught up with her.

"Sloan, please let me explain. I'm sorry for taking you by surprise. I had to; you gave me no choice. You have no idea how long I've waited to get you alone. I thought it would never happen. You of all people must know the depth of my love. I could not let this opportunity pass me by. I may never have gotten another chance. All I ask is for you to consider my plans for our future. Will you please do that for me?"

She would do and say anything to get rid of him.

"Marc, you have to admit you took me by surprise, but you must give me some time to reconsider your proposal; after all, this is something that is meant to last our lifetimes."

"I will give you all the time you need. Thank you.

"I have one more thing to ask: Will you allow me to stay with you to see you safely home?"

She had to think of a way to lose him. She could pretend to try something on in the dressing room of the clothing store, and then, when he wasn't looking, she'd slip out the back door and run like hell for home. She knew this trip would turn out to be a mistake. She knew all along she would not meet that special someone.

Or would she?

# CHAPTER NINE

# YEAR 1958

Jena's weeping was tearing at Charlie's heart. His compassion for this tiny person, whose life was now in shambles with nowhere to go, was eating at him. He was, in all honesty, a kind and thoughtful man.

His full name was Charles Edward Mannigan. He was in his early sixties and of medium height with a full head of gray hair, a fairly decent-looking man. His wife had passed away seven years ago. He had no children and was called by his closest friends "Charlie, my man."

Charles remembered well what transpired a mere week ago, when his boss and best friend, Joe, called him into his office.

Stepping into Joseph Chadsworth's office was like working in the outdoors. Walls of windows surrounded him. The spectacular view was breathtaking. Charlie could live to be one hundred and never would he have what his friend had, but then again he wasn't the owner of this prestigious architectural firm.

Joe was seated in a brown swivel chair facing the walls of windows when Charles spoke out. Joe swung around, first to stretch his arms, and then to place his hands behind his head before he gave a comment.

"What a glorious day. Too bad we have to spend it indoors, but that's life. How's everything going with you, Charlie, my man?"

"I don't have any complaints, Joe, thanks for asking. So what's up?"

Charlie was met with a blank expression. After several minutes of nothingness, Charlie felt as if he should take the initiative.

"I'm here on your request, Joe."

"What's that you say? Oh… that's right; I forgot that I was the one that requested this meeting. Old age is doing a job on me. Too bad I can't do something about it.

"But let's move on to more important matters. I need your help, Charles. It's extremely important and must be kept totally between us. You are my best friend and the only one I can trust."

He has never been called Charles. Something wasn't right. He considered Joe a very close friend. He was one of many architects the Chadsworths' architectural firm employed, but he was always considered to be one of Joe's closest friends, although it was Charlie who chose not to socialize in Joe's circle. Early in his career when he did socialize, he found brown-nosing wasn't his thing. Besides, he enjoyed his wife's company way better.

Something was brewing, and he knew whatever it was, Joe wanted Charles to become involved. How could he refuse? He made enough money as an architect to be more then comfortable. But what was presented to him amounted to more money he could or would ever make in his lifetime.

A $3 million cashier's check was placed into his hand. Joe told him nothing other than he was to be a driver for someone Joe no longer had any need for.

Did he mean what Charlie thought he meant? Joe could see the startled look on his face.

"Oh, God, Charles, you know me better than that, and shame on you for thinking such a thought. All I'm asking is for you to find a home other than New York for one of my employees. It will involve days of travel. I know you will need to rest. Take as much time as you need. I will see you when you return."

Charlie was relieved. Driving, he could do, doing away with someone was another matter. But a gnawing sensation was grinding at him. $3 million to just drive someone out of the state?

Instructions were placed in the same envelope as the check. He was to follow the orders explicitly. He had been sitting in front of Joe's house for well over an hour, lost in thought, when a tap on the partially opened window drew his attention.

Art, Joe's butler, leaned down to face the driver.

"Sir, I have several suitcases belonging to the young lady you are driving for today. Will you please open the trunk?"

"Did you just say a young lady?"

"Yes sir, a Miss Carr will be your passenger."

Charlie was made out to be a fool. Joe knew he would never have agreed to this arrangement if it involved a woman. And then the little guy that sits on his shoulder, called a conscience, had something to say. "Oh, Charlie, come on, you could have asked if the person were male or female, or better still the person's name. Let's face it; you are no better than the rest of the human race. All you could see was the color green. Oh, Charlie, what have you done?"

Although Charlie had been on the road for an hour, he was unable to keep his eyes off the rearview mirror.

Jena, Charlie's little passenger, had her arms wrapped around her knees gathered as close to her chest as possible, rocking back and forth. The weeping showed no sign of stopping.

"'How many tears can someone shed?" Charlie wondered. He needed this to stop; he was hurting, although not as badly as Jena, but enough that his stomach was aching due to her stress. A rest stop was just ahead. He pulled in. The purpose was to try and comfort his prisoner (for that is what he perceived her to be). When he opened the passenger door, the sight before him revealed the sweet innocence of youth.

Jena was the smallest, most pitiful child he'd ever encountered. He prayed he wouldn't frighten her as he positioned himself by her side.

Jena did not move, nor did she shy away from this stranger. She escaped into a world of her own making.

Charlie gently wrapped his arms around her. She showed no reaction. He was in his element; he would know the words to comfort her, for he was a deacon in his church.

"My dear, sweet child, you must dry those tears, for Our Heavenly Father sees and feels your sorrow. The tears you shed, God himself is shedding. The pain you are feeling is God's pain. His pillar of strength makes him your greatest supporter.

"If you need to talk, call on Him. He will listen. And when you feel the need to cry, He'll wipe your tears. If you just need someone to hold you, call on Him. He'll be there."

A calm, reassuring presence unfolded before him. A radiant light appeared upon the young girl's face. Charlie felt the hand of God. Jena was finally at peace with herself.

Charlie told her he would find someplace close for her to live. He emptied his wallet, adding a few hundred dollars to what she had already been given. She tried to refuse, but he wouldn't take no for an answer. She made a solemn promise that he would be paid back.

Charlie decided to take this child under his wing. Joe's instructions would not be followed.

Jena had a suitcase full of clothes, with possibly enough money to sustain her for six months. It would be hard to adjust to a totally different way of life, but never would she allow her son to do so. But as God is her protector, she would make it. She would find a way to get her son back, but she would need a lot of money to do so. But what could she do?

She didn't have to think long. What she thought to be a curse she now realized was God's way of helping her to find her way, and in the process, help others. His gift was going to be put to use.

She was given the power to predict the future and see the past. This ability would hopefully make enough money to hire a private investigator. With determination and the power of prayer, she would find someone to help her, somehow, somewhere. She would find a place to advise and help people. This would be an arduous task, but one she would conquer.

Charlie had been driving for a couple of hours. Jena was stretched out in the passenger seat; she had been sleeping when she suddenly awakened.

"Charlie, you need to turn at the next exit."

"Are you all right?"

"I'm fine. I just found the area I'm going to live and work in."

Charlie was stunned. "Jena, you can't be serious. I wouldn't let a dog live here. This is worse than living in the projects."

"Yes, I know. It's perfect."

Charlie wondered how she knew of such a place.

Jena tapped into his thoughts.

"I just had a vision, Charlie."

Charlie had his doubts about such a vision, but said nothing.

Under her guidance, Charlie would make several left and right turns before she spoke out.

"This is it, Charlie. I've found my home and workplace."

Charlie seriously thought that with all she had gone through, her senses had joined her body, both taking flight.

This was Jena's day to be open to receive Charlie's thoughts, and again she jumped right in.

"Charlie, did you not tell me to have faith? I have to believe in the impossible, if I'm to survive in an unkind world."

There it was, a quaint little shop, listing everything she would need to conduct her business, with a one-room efficiency attached to the back of the shop. The windows were covered with paper that were curled, torn, and brown with age. The streets lacked maintenance and were littered with trash.

Most of the stores were closed, and the few that offered a trade did not seem to be prospering. A mixture of residential and commercial properties were scattered up and down the block, and the homes tucked here and there needed more than a coat of paint. Nothing he said could convince her to keep looking.

"Charlie, all you see is filth. Imagine the street cleaned up, a fresh coat of paint on the storefront. Why, it could be quite impressive to my prospective clients."

Jena was actually smiling. That was all he needed to see.

He boosted her confidence.

"Yes, Jena, I agree, it could be quite an eye-catcher."

Charlie told Jena it was time to call it a day. The shop definitely wasn't going anywhere; they could take care of business after a good night's sleep.

Jena noticed a low-budget motel hidden by numerous trees just before she found the place that would provide a living. Before Charlie could protest, she clamped a hand over his mouth.

"I don't need a down-filled pillow to get a good night's sleep."

Charlie swerved around numerous trees, keeping to the provided path leading to what appeared to be a deserted motel. He prayed it was so. No such luck. A painted Vacancy sign was taped to a dirty window. Charlie shook his head in disbelief. Jena, now a passenger in the front seat, touched Charlie's face.

"It will be all right. Trust me."

Charlie would get two rooms at the appointed motel.

The attendant on duty was bored to death. If somebody didn't show up soon, he was seriously thinking of locking up the motel. He could always find another job. He was sitting on a stool, resting his chin on one of his hands, when he noticed the limousine. "This guy has to be lost. No way will he spend the night in this crummy motel," he thought.

The attendant was as lengthy as he was skinny, a goofy-looking young man with long, greasy hair, wearing cut-off jeans and a knit shirt with a dragon emblem. He could be classified as someone carrying on a love affair with rings and tattoos. His eyebrows, nose, lips, and ears were covered in an assortment of jewelry. Tattoos were sprinkled across every exposed part of his body.

If he thought this would lead to a permanent relationship with either sex, he could possibly wait out his lifetime. And if the young man were anywhere but here, he would be standing in the unemployment line.

The employee who looked to be a biker raised his eyebrows at Charlie and the girl attached to his arm. He winked, before he loudly stated, "I know what's up… ha-ha, get it?"

The gruff-looking man could not control the laughter at his obscene joke. Charlie could have said something, but considered the source and let it go. Jena appeared to have not heard the uncouth remark. Charlie took his lone suitcase from the trunk of the car while Jena selected two of several pieces of luggage.

The next day after breakfast they contacted the realtor. He was shocked that he had a buyer. Charlie felt he was responsible for putting Jena in such a disastrous situation. He had pre-warned her not to seek the position of nanny. Her name had been mentioned in all the society columns as being dishonest and a thief, and the most damaging and degrading, a woman of the night.

Jena would have none of it.

"No, Charlie, I will not allow you to shoulder the blame for the doings of another."

Jena and Charlie became closer than most relatives. She confided in him how she was thrown out of the Chadsworths' estate, a place she called her home for well over five years. She also told him of the trickery they used to kidnap her baby.

Charlie thought of Joe as a fine upstanding man, a man of morals, not the kind Jena was speaking off, but he did not doubt a word of what went on within that house. He never thought he could hate anyone. Joe succeeded.

Jena could now go forth. Charlie gave her that confidence, while reminding her that if she takes one day at a time with God as her companion, nothing will be too hard to bear.

Charlie and Jena continued to stay at the same cheap motel. The low-life that waited on them no longer made with the jokes. He couldn't help but notice how kind and considerate the older gentleman was with the young girl. He somehow knew the little lady was in trouble and this man seemed like he genuinely cared what happens to her.

He wished, at difficult times in his life, which had been many, he had someone to look out for him. Of course, that never happened. When he really thought about life, which was quite often, he always came up with the same conclusion: "Shit happens."

Charlie was on a quest to get Jena established. Once done, he would return to his un-friend.

Joe managed to accomplish his mission. Jena would live in an area that should be condemned. Charlie wished he could turn Joe's cashier's check over to Jena, but it took some doing just to get her to accept a couple hundred dollars;

$3 million would trample her pride.

What he could have told her, but he did not, he would never again work for a man so heartless. He would retire and enjoy the remainder of his life. He would kick back and enjoy what life had to throw at him. The thought of it brought a smile to his face.  What he did not know, his retirement would be short-lived.

Charlie's exterior was totally out of character.

His associates were taken aback at what showed up at their workplace. His clothing was rumbled and appeared slept in, his customary tie did not adorn his neck, and weeks of stubble growth masked his face. Five or six of his associates, two considered good friends, were gathered around the customary water cooler when one of the worst (not a friend), known for trash-talking, acknowledged him with a joke.

"Charlie, my man, is that you? What's with the disguise? By the looks of your condition, I would say someone gave you quite a workout.

"It's about time. Nothing like a good romp in the hay to get your juices flowing.  And if you don't mind sharing, I could use a little action myself."

Charlie ignored his comment, pushing past them. He heard Joe's son Phillip say hello, but did not honor him with acknowledgement. He was about to do a difficult task, but with pleasure. His mind needed to be put to rest.

Charlie blasted through the door to his boss's office. Joe, deep in conversation, comfortable in his massive leather chair facing the windows, turned back towards the door when the eruption sounded. There were no words. Only a camera could capture the horror seen on Joe's face.

This is a man that has it all, a man that never understood the meaning of fear or terror until now. Joe stood, his chair pushed to the side, backing away from the invasion of the approaching creature. He threw the telephone in his direction. Charlie's quick action averted a direct hit.

Evil invaded Joe's private sanctuary. He screamed for security; no one carried out the order. Everyone was sure Joe was playing a joke on them, Charlie as well. Pranks were a part of their pastime. Sometimes they were out of line, but in time, all was forgiven.

Charlie took his time. His steps were slow and deliberate, provoking extreme pressure upon the individual to whom it was directed before the onslaught.

With each step taken, Joe moved further away. The spectacular wall of windows began feeling his weight as his body slid along the glass. And then it happened. The creature grabbed a hold of Joe's necktie, twisting it into a chokehold.

Joe recognized his attacker. He was relieved. He truly thought his life was in danger. Most men of wealth and power have enemies, but Charlie was not one of those men. But if he was not an enemy, then why was Charlie cutting off his air supply? He was being lead like a dog, his tie the leash. And then, like a switch, the gift of oxygen returned.

Charlie commanded him back into his chair.

Joe did as told; it was apparent something unspeakable crossed Charlie's path a few weeks back. But Joe was the boss. He could fix anything, but first he needed to know the problem.

Charlie's relentless obsession could not be shoved aside. He never spoke the word "hate," for he was a man of God, until now. His hatred bordered on madness. To kill Joe would give him much pleasure but for the fact he desired life eternal.

Joe reached out to comfort his friend and began to speak.

"Charlie, my man, my friend, what in God's name happened to you?"

Charlie slapped away his outreached hand. He was quick with a disgusted response.

"How dare you mention God's name in my presence."

Joe was bewildered; Charlie never spoke to him with such utter disrespect. Joe was not about to take much more from him. Charlie would soon be among the unemployed and would never find work when Joe was finished with him.

Before this could be accomplished, he needed to get Charlie out of his office. But Charlie was giving him no space in which to escape. His looming figure and the menacing tone in his voice was that of a man not to be reasoned with.

"You are a disgrace to the human race. What you have done to that young woman, you should be castrated and hung. The despicable torture you are putting Jena through is unforgivable.

"With every breath in my body, I will see that you are exiled from your standing in the community, just as you have banished that sad young woman from her baby.

"The evil deeds you've inflicted upon her will be avenged. The cover-up and lies you have concealed, I will reveal to everyone and anyone of power. You will live to see your life crumble around you.

"And then, when I am done with you, you will return Jena's son to his rightful place, his mother's arms. To think I considered you my closest friend. They say love is blind. Apparently, so is friendship."

He told Joe to open his mouth. Joe obeyed. The $3 million cashier's check was shoved deep into his throat.

"Choke on this, you bastard, for this will be the largest amount of money you will ever see or taste again."

Charlie pushed himself upward from the arms of the chair where he told his boss to sit. When he stood, he couldn't help but admire his handiwork. Joe hadn't moved from his chair, the check forcing drool to run from his mouth onto his chin, continuing onto his $6,000 suit.

Charlie could now continue to do what he set out to do: first destroy, and then enjoy.

The moment Charlie shut the door behind him; Joe gagged, pulling the sodden check from his mouth. His fingers were already dialing when the person on the other end picked up. When that person heard Joe's voice, he knew his debt was being called in. That debt would be paid in full without delay. Never in Joe's life had he been so humiliated by someone of so little importance.

There was only one thing that saved him from further embarrassment. Charles did not raise his voice; what he had to say was meant only for Joe's ears until such time as Charles carried out his promise of exposure.

The office staff was doing their own thing, giving no attention to Charlie's departure. Joe from this day forward would be surrounded by three bodyguards, although he would always be on edge, jerking and twisting like someone with Tourette's disease. Charlie managed to do what no other had done; he put the fear of God in him.

The headline read:

"Tragedy befalls lead architect at Chadsworth & Chadsworth Architectural Firm.

"Charles Edward Mannigan, well- known for his unusual designs throughout New York, died early this morning. Skid marks found at the scene of the accident indicate he was traveling at a high rate of speed when he apparently lost control on a narrow bend at Skinkers Road.

"A witness hitching a ride on the same road watched helplessly as Mr. Mannigan's car flipped several times and exploded. Rescue attempts were impossible. He leaves no family behind. Burial will be private."

In the days following Charlie's death, associates, friends, and family began to question Joe's sanity.

It would take years before Jena learned the fate of her dearest friend.

# CHAPTER TEN

Harriet grabbed the closest thing she could sit on. Clay, her son, was on his way.

She closed her eyes, remembering when her six-month-old son was taken from her. It was the worst time in her life until a special someone by the name of Charlie took control, leading her down a path that would ultimately save her life. Together, they secured a workplace and a home for her to live in.

Her talent as a psychic proved to be a tremendous success. There were those who needed to believe that good does happen to those who are desolate, poor, and with nowhere to turn. Jena gave to them not only a glimpse of their future, but hope and faith within themselves. And if she could help just one person, she would succeed in her trade.

The neighborhood kids, without being asked, began cleaning up the pathways; city sweepers began to maintain the streets. Storefront windows, stripped of their coverings, were now seeing the light of day. Posted signs -- For Sale or Lease --were being replaced with displays of shop wares. Store owners and neighbors pitched in to share the work loads, pooling their talents to blend colors that would complement one another; creating a picturesque view so unique, it would be like nothing ever seen. It not only drew attention from the walkers, but the cars that traveled that route.

The despairing block turned into a masterpiece of art. The streets and curbs soon became overrun with carloads of people; some were running about, snapping pictures from different angles. Several pictures became worthy to cover the fronts of many magazines and newspapers. It would become known as "The Block of Colorful Retreat."

Everyone was indeed not only making money, but friends as well. They were a very tiny community, within a large municipality. The money was adding up, as were the years of not seeing Jena's son. Every dollar earned went from her hand into the hands of three to four investigators working around the clock, firing some and hiring new. She was determined to find where the Chadsworths had hidden her son.

She wasn't naïve; she knew some of the investigators did nothing but take her money, but in the deepest regions of her heart, there had to be that special someone that would do right by her.

That someone was Kennedy Wallace, and no, he did not find her son, but was forthcoming with years of knowledge. And when weeks on the job produced no results, he told her to end her four-year search. Pictures of a newborn up to the age of six months did nothing to help in his search. She did as Kennedy advised; she dismissed the takers.

Kennedy's file on her son would remain open with no further charges, and he would continue his search as time permitted, but he could no longer turn away clients in favor of finding her son. He could not continue taking her money with nothing to show.

Jena made many friends; one in particular she dearly loved was Marnie Allen. She was twenty-five years of age and was considered tall, five-feet-seven inches to Jena's stature of five-feet. Her dark brown hair, parted in the center and cut shoulder length, had a hint of curl, but it was her bluish-green eyes with lashes to envy and a figure only God perfected that drew many men vying for her attention. She could command the cover of Glamour magazine.

But of all these things, most admired is her grace and dignity. She acquired a position that for many women would take years of hard work to attain. But it's like everything in life, if you do not know that certain someone; you will never get your foot in the door. And that someone opened the door that paved the way for her at the tender age of eighteen. She traveled the world as a buyer of women's clothing for many of the elite stores catering to only the affluent.

Marnie had just signed in as a guest at a Hilton hotel when her eyes focused on an editorial in a weekly journal that someone seemed to have left behind at the registration desk. The article talked about various shops that governed a street called "The Block of Colorful Retreat."

She was more than curious when Jena's ad, among the many listed, caught her attention. Marnie was a firm believer in psychics. She would pay a visit to this Jena person.

She quickly changed from her travel suit into something more comfortable. A red tube top tucked under a short-sleeved white blouse was paired with white slacks. She carried a small red, white, and blue shoulder bag; upon her feet, matching sandals.

She called for a cab, and within fifteen minutes she was entering a shop called 'The Truth Beyond.' Beneath that sign in bold, black letters read "PSYCHIC." Marnie let the shop owner know right off she could spot a phony.

Jena and Marnie through the months would become the best of friends. But time was limited. Marnie's position took her to the air, allowing no time to collect a notebook of friends. But whatever time she could spare, she spent with her new-found friend. Her stay this time would be a week. She accepted Jena's warm invitation to stay at her home in the back of her workplace.

Jena's flair for pattern and design reflected the love she had for her home and was a welcome retreat from the lush hotels Marnie frequented.

Marnie no longer wanted to keep her personal life to herself. She took Jena by the hand and together they sat side by side.

"Jena, I have a story I wish to share with you. It is a passionate story of love and loss. I want you to know of this because it's a part of who I am."

Jena nodded; she knew this would be heart-wrenching. She tightened the grip on her friend's hands.

"I found the love of my life when I turned nineteen. After five years of being what I called 'held in total captivity,' my lover and I agreed we wanted that piece of paper. After weeks of preparation, the most talked-about wedding of all times was finally going to happen. No expenses were spared; the invitations themselves were embossed with 10 carat gold.

"My name would have been Mrs. Winston Vaughn, but I called my lover 'Win.' He was a bit older, thirty-four to my nineteen. But as luck would have it, good or bad, depending on how you look at it, if his job hadn't also required extensive travel, we would not have met.

"One week before we were to say our 'I do's' and less than fifteen minutes into the air, the company's private jet that Win had boarded exploded in mid-flight. Following a year of reassembling the plane and examining every minute piece, they could find no explanation as to the cause of the explosion. There was nothing more they could do. They closed the case."

Jena could not hide her feelings. Her tears made quite a presentation.

Marnie wrapped her arms around Jena, offering comfort, when it was she who should have been shown compassion. She wiped Jena's tears away with her fingertips while continuing to tell the tragic ending of her lover 'Win.'

"When I was told my Win was gone, I screamed in agony, pounding my fists on the one responsible for telling such a god-awful tale. I told him he had to have made a mistake. He kept shaking his head. I never felt such pain. No matter which way I turned, more and more representatives of the airline came forth, laying their hands upon me. I wanted the warmth of Win's hands, not theirs.

"I refused their pity and sympathy. I spat at them, accusing them of putting faulty aircraft in the air that could take a person's life and destroy the lives that were left behind.

"But Jena, the worst was knowing I would have to continue to live without him."

It was then Marnie broke down. How could she not? She was reliving her past, something Jena did time after time. But she has more to say.

"I had been on administrative leave for months. I knew I couldn't continue living off the welfare of others. It was time to end my life. It was then it happened, something so incredible it defined meaning.

"Win stood before me. I could smell his fragrance; hear the pleasure in his voice and the sound of his laughter, telling me to remember all the extraordinary things that happened in our time together.

"Then, like a reel of film, our life together began to play out, each scene as we lived it, never forgetting a single detail, including our lovemaking. He was my Prince Charming, and as he would tell me many times, I was his Cinderella. This might seem childish to others, but to me it meant I was someone special."

Marnie was left with unforgettable memories. There would never again be room for tears.

She told Jena a year would not necessarily qualify her as moving on with her life, but it really did not matter. One year or ten years, Win wanted her to move on. She had no regrets; Win took her heart from the beginning and still had it within his grip.

Disclosure was not easy for Jena, but with Charlie it was different. He pulled her to a standing position. Without his help and understanding, she would not be where she was today. Did Marnie deserve less?

She opened up for the second time. She finished with Mr. Chadsworth's promise of $5,000, payable each month, which is now due, but that she had a problem. She was not to live in New York or the money would be forfeited.

Marnie came to the rescue.

"Honey, with me as your friend, there is no problem." Jena listened intently.

"This is what you need to do. Send Mr. Chadsworth a letter telling him your job status requires extensive air travel, and a post office box should be considered your mailing address. And you will accept nothing other then a cashier's check, and should there be a change in the address, he will be notified."

Marnie then told Jena how the plot would succeed.

"I will notify you each month as to where I will be. You will, in essence, mail two envelopes. You will address one to Mr. Chadsworth with your mailing instructions. You will then take his letter and insert it into another envelope that will be addressed to me.

"After I secure a P.O. Box number, I will then forward your letter to Mr. Chadsworth. The postmark of the state will be stamped on the letter as proof of where you are staying at that time. And when I receive his check, I will then forward it on to you. How's that for solving your problem?"

Jena's thank-you could not compare to Marnie's reply.

"You know what I think. I think it's time to put a little excitement in your life. The past is gone and the future is knocking, and I'll be damned if I'm going to let it knock itself out. Tonight, we party."

The nightclub where they planned on spending their evening was a favorite of Marnie's, a club called the Rolls Royce. But first Marnie had to get Jena to agree to a complete makeover. Jena, in the beginning, balked at her suggestion, but eventually Marnie's persuasion paid off, and within an hour Jena was standing in front of Sophia's Salon and Boutique. Jena was given full treatment, not unlike a truck overhaul. She was exhausted. This was a beauty treatment the privileged could keep; Jena would not be back for a repeat performance.

Marnie did have one request, that Jena be blindfolded before viewing herself after the change. When the staff placed Jena in front of the full-length mirror, she was asked, "Are you ready to see the new you?" Jena said she was ready.

She appeared to go into shock. She stared long into the mirror and then approached it cautiously. It could not be. She did not recognize the person looking back at her. She was more than beautiful, she was exquisite. She was embarrassed to be that attractive. In her line of work, she had no use for makeup, and what would be the purpose of owning a cocktail dress when she had no suitor?

But here she was, wearing an exquisite evening dress, revealing breasts that many women had gone under the knife to acquire.

Jena stepped through the draped coverings that concealed the clientele from the public.

Marnie stood, tossing the magazine she was reading onto the side table. She was shocked by the drastic change in Jena's appearance. A miracle was walking towards her. Marnie was made a believer, when a darling young girl entered one door and came out another as a stunning and glamorous woman. Sophia's expertise deserved a standing ovation.

Jena was floating on a cloud, first with her new look, and now with the hand of a man that was leading her onto the dance floor. She couldn't believe her good fortune; the eyes of many women were coveting the man she was now clinging too.

Trevor Hartmann stood six-feet tall while sporting a fantastic tan. Black hair, grey eyes, and deep dimples with a carefully trimmed mustache and goatee suited him perfectly. He was meticulous in his attire; he was definitely a ladies' man. His job title was that of an electrical inspector on high-rise buildings under construction.

He was courteous, respectful, and, Jena guessed, a good lover in bed, for he would hold her close for several minutes afterward, telling her how much he loved her. She hadn't much experience in that area. Phillip was the only one to compare and he was similar in his actions, so she assumed all men were alike in that department. She was totally captivated by his charm. She not only wanted him in her bed, she wanted him in her life.

Marnie beamed with happiness that Jena had found someone. Trevor also seemed enchanted by Jena. They were married by the justice of the peace. Marnie was her maid of honor.

Life moved along happily for three months and then the unexpected happened. Trevor was arrested for assault while committing a robbery. Jena went to his defense. As she stood facing a police officer, she pleaded for his release.

"You have made a dreadful mistake. Mr. Hartmann has an excellent job, his car alone cost thousands, and money has never been an issue."

Jena was shown his rap sheet. You name it, he did it. That expensive car he was driving was stolen. And as bad luck would have it, the first day she met him, he was just released from prison, serving a four-year term for assault.

The time he spent outside the walls of prison could be counted in months. You could say he grew up behind bars, but growing in the wrong direction each time he was released. If he was not behind bars, he was lying his way through life; lies to Jena about being single when he was married. He was now a bigamist, another charge against him.

He drank too much and had a drug problem. She ignored his bad habits. She thought she was in love. This arrest could place him in prison for a very long time, if not for life, for this assault ended in the victim's death.

Jena visited him one last time. She sat down facing him, a screen separating them. Her eyes were swollen from crying. She hated him for destroying her life. The handkerchief in her hand was twisted with wasted tears. The smile that was once captivating now turned her stomach. His orange pantsuit didn't quite fit him as nicely as the clothes taking up the closet space in her home. She kept shaking her head at the man sitting before her, wondering how she could have been so blind and stupid.

She was reeling in anger and could not hold back her fury. She stood and leaned forward.

Using her small fists, she began to beat on the divider, screaming obscenities. A guard was quick to respond. "You will have to take a seat, or I must ask you to leave." She sat, ashamed that the man she thought she loved had brought her to his level.

She had an edge to her voice, but remained calm.

"I allowed you into my home, I gave you my heart, and this is what you give me. I hate you, you bastard. You destroyed my life. The fiery pits of hell are too good for you. I pray God will show you no mercy, for you have shown no mercy to others. You are nothing but a liar, a thief, a bigamist, and now a murderer. I wish you were dead, and if I could, I would kill you myself."

Trevor's welcoming smile vanished, and in its place, evil poured forth. The guards were quick to respond. But not before Trevor gave his greatest performance. He grabbed a hold of the partition that separated him from Jena, screaming a multitude of foul words, many of which Jena had not heard. A shrill scream blasted from his mouth, his nostrils flaring.

"If you abandon me at my worst hour, you will live to regret it. For when I get out of prison, I will find you. And when I do, you will be lying at my feet, dead from the knife I will use to slit your throat."

It took four guards to restrain him, and even then he managed to kick at them and throw a few punches. Security finally managed to get a stranglehold, but as he was being taken away, he put the finishing touches on his threat.

"You'd better watch your back, Jena. I can strike at any time. You hear me, bitch?"

Jena heard every word. She ran from the room, horrified. Where could she go, if somehow he didn't serve time?

Then the worst thing possible happened. She was so caught up in her new life with him that she hadn't paid attention to not having a period. She cried for days. Marnie was in California and would be there for at least two more weeks. She tried to comfort Jena over the telephone.

"Honey, maybe this is a good thing. You will have another baby to cuddle and love. You can give to him all the things you were denied with your son Clay. Maybe this is God's way of lessening the hurt you carry in your heart."

Jena made an appointment to see a doctor, any doctor, she didn't care what his credentials were, and maybe he would tell her she had a tumor. Anything but a baby would be acceptable. She was a very modest person when it came to showing her private parts to someone other than the men she slept with, but this was one time she didn't hesitate in removing her underwear. If she complied with all that was asked, maybe he would tell her she needed to see a head doctor.

"In about five months, you will be welcoming a new life into your world." He was grinning ear to ear. Was it the first time he told a woman she was pregnant? Did he think she would be happy? Now she knows what it feels like to be up shit's creek without a paddle.

There was no doubt she got pregnant the first night she met and slept with Trevor. She knew it could be construed as being a little on the loose side, but it had been years since she had been held by Phillip, the only other man in her life. She wanted to feel the sort of comfort only a man could give. The thought of getting pregnant never entered her mind. She would never again make that mistake.

But if destiny could speak, fate would tell her to never say never.

She did not believe in abortion; she would accept the consequences. There would be a six-year difference in her children's lives.

Jena would be present at Trevor's arraignment and at each hearing until she heard the outcome. By the time the final act was played, her son Adam would be eight months old.

She was hysterical when the verdict was read. He was found guilty of the robbery, but not guilty of the murder, for there were extenuating circumstances. The victim had less than six months; he was dying from pancreatic cancer. Trevor was given a seven-year sentence with the possibility of parole in four years.

Jena had to find another place to live; she would also have a name change. She wanted the kind of safeguarding a person received in a witness protection program. She was not granted that privilege. She refused to worry over something she had no control over. She had four years to make her move.

Adam was growing quickly; he was now two and a half years old. Jena still hadn't decided where she wanted to settle down. She buried herself in leaflets that she requested; the more she received, the more she was unsure. Her choice had to be permanent; her son needed stability and security. Marnie couldn't help; she was all over the place. That was not going to be Jena and her son's way of life.

She was deeply engrossed in yet another brochure when the chime sounded, alerting her of a possible client. She never left the front of her shop unattended to seek her living quarters. Her son was enrolled in a well-recognized day care. She wished she could have him by her side to care for him herself, but she needed to focus all her attention on her customers to give her son the good life.

She was seated at one of two tables. Leaflets representing her services and prices for a range of options were scattered across the tables; costs differed on the length of time involved.

Three very pretty teenage girls did not take another step once inside the now-closed door. The girls were definitely on the wrong side of the tracks; their silver spoons were dangling from their mouths. Jena should know; she had been a part of that lifestyle for many years.

From their expressions, they were in awe of the displays dealing with the supernatural and the hereafter. Vibrant colors were painted about the walls. Jena's artwork was done in good taste, nothing tacky. If the patrons that entered her shop expected to see spirits dancing around or heads poking through sheets, they were in for a huge awakening. Nothing resided here but the living.

She let the girls be. With their hands joined, they cautiously moved about the shop. Several minutes passed before the shortest of the three approached her. She was overweight, but that didn't take away from her beauty. She was extremely nervous when she asked Jena if she could speak to her in private.

When Jena designed the floor plan, uppermost in her mind was the client's right to privacy. She hired a carpenter to enclose a small area, and as extra security, soundproofed the walls.

Jena informed the friends their wait could be several minutes or much longer. She pointed to a stack of folded chairs, should they tire of standing. She guided the teenager into the secured room, encouraging her to take a seat. Two chairs and a table occupied the space, along with a water cooler and disposable cups.

The young girl appeared shy, but Jena's abilities extended further than seeing the past and predicting the future. She had the capability of calming her clients' anxieties.

She took the girl's hands into her own. The touch told Jena she was a runaway, and her father was the underlying factor. But before she could put her talent to work, a powerful sensation swept over her. She knew the child sitting before her.

She closed her eyes, blessed herself, and proceeded to give thanks.

"Dear God in Heaven, thank you for bringing my little girl back to me." The teen was alarmed with the woman's behavior. She stood; ready to head for the exit door, until Jena reached out to stop her.

"Oh, my sweet, sweet Ali, don't you remember me? I was your nanny, honey. You must remember. Please tell me that you do."

Jena's look was one of pleading; Ali's look was one of panic. But Jena refused to give up on her.

"You must think I'm crazy. How can I expect you to remember me? You were just a child when I left." Jena blinked and the tears started.

Ali looked around the small quarters for a means of escape, wondering, "How does this woman know my name and what other nonsense is she talking of?"

And then Ali, like Jena, was caught up in the moment. She, too, began to cry. Memories she buried because of the heartache were now being brought to the surface.

How could she have forgotten the one person who was always there to kiss her boo-boos and scare away the bogeyman?

Ali reached out, tears destroying the carefully applied makeup. Jena pushed her chair and the table to the side. She knelt to gather the long-ago three-year-old close to her heart. They shared tears.

But soon Ali's tears were shoved aside, and in their place came anger. The memory of being told by her parents that Jena had packed her bags and left and that she no longer had a nanny tore a hole in her heart.

She pulled free from Jena's arms.

"I hate you. How could you leave me, and what kind of mother leaves her baby behind?" Ali's tears returned, sobbing at its worst. She began beating her small fists onto Jena's chest.

Jena's struggle with Ali was intense, but in the end Jena was able to still her hands, although the weeping, she could not.

"Oh, my dear poor child, do you honestly believe I left by choice?" Ali refused to look at her. Jena gently cupped her face.

"Ali, you must look at me." Reluctantly, she did as she was told.

"I have never lied to you, and I am not about to start. What I'm about to tell you is the truth in regards to my leaving."

When Jena finished telling the horror of that fateful day, Ali was ashamed for doubting her nanny. Her father could not tell the truth if it meant standing his children before a firing squad.

Maybe Ali could make it up to her.

"Jena, why have you not mentioned little Clay? Is it because it's too painful a subject? Or do you fear that I know something that will cause you more grief?"

But before Jena could respond, Ali spoke.

"Well, I'm here to tell you, Clay couldn't be happier. Phillip adores his son, and if my parents loved me as passionately as they do your little boy, I would still be living at home."

Ali wiped the tears from her nanny's face.

With Jena's mind now at rest, she demanded to know the lie that was told about her disappearance.

"Ali, did not the household help inquire about me? And what about little Clay? Surely, as he grew older, he would have asked about me?"

"Jena, when you left, I longed for someone to talk to. My parents, as you know, were never there for me. I turned to the servants for companionship. They offered comfort, but they, too, were suffering. They loved you as much as I.

"Anyway, they were told by my father that being a mother was not your idea of fun and it was time to move on, and Phillip could have the baby."

"And because all babies have mothers, Father had to come up with a photo, someone little Clay could relate to. Where my father acquired a photograph, I have no idea, but he managed to find a picture that somewhat resembled you and hung it in the grand hallway. He told the household help to never mention to anyone that it was not you, or they would be looking for employment elsewhere.

"But the worst was when he told them if anyone were to inquire as to the whereabouts of the mother of little Clay, they were to say she died in childbirth. I was sickened that my father would say such a thing. But I made a promise to myself that when Clay was old enough to understand, I would tell him the truth.

"But as the years passed, he grew into such a happy little guy that if I told him what I knew, it's possible he would have hated his father and grandparents for lying to him. I'm sorry, Jena, but I could not be the one to break his little heart."

Ali again flooded her already streaked makeup.

Jena hushed and wiped away Ali's tears.

"You must never be sorry for telling me what I longed to hear, that my son is loved and well-cared for, and most of all, that he is a happy child. This is all I have ever wanted for him. Come now, it is time to shelve the tears."

Jena was not yet ready to turn Ali over to her friends. She may never again see her again.

"Ali, could you please stay a while longer? I have means of transportation. I will see that you get home safely."

Ali's nanny returned. How could she refuse? She told her friends they could leave, but with an explanation.

"This woman, whom I haven't seen in years, will see me home."

Ali friends were hesitant, showing their obvious concern.

"Are you sure you will be all right?"

It took some doing, but she finally convinced them she could not be in better hands.

Jena secured the door latch, turning the OPEN sign to CLOSED. They walked hand in hand towards Jena's place in the back of the shop. Ali was impressed with the efficiency apartment. She was excited with the prospect of moving to her own home. A small dining table with matching chairs gave them the seating necessary for a catch-up on how their lives have turned out up to this point.

Ali started first.

"Jena, I ran away. It's been several months since I've been home. I'm in hiding; afraid that my father will find me and force me back to the place I call a chamber of horrors. There is no way

I can go back, especially now. I'm pregnant, Jena, nearly six months; I've been married for as long as I've been pregnant. But that wouldn't stop my father from having my marriage annulled."

Jena should have recognized the obvious.

Ali began to giggle. "Can you believe I got pregnant the first time I had sex?"

Of course, Jena believed. Did she not experience the same fate with Trevor?

Ali was glowing as she continued with her story.

"Jena, he's incredible. I love him so much. I never thought something this wonderful could happen in my life, but it did, and I'm not going to let Father or anyone destroy my relationship with him.

"I ran away from home many times, but always to return. I hated taking advantage of my friends' hospitality and using their money to pay for my expenses. The only thing I take credit for is graduating at the head of my class.

"Who would have thought my father's money, that provided the best in schooling, would lead to walking the streets. I was a drifter with no sense of direction until one of our walks took us inside a diner."

A warm glow gave her face an angelic look.

"The man that would give purpose to my life was seated near the entrance. He looked up, I looked down, and it was love at first glance. My friends still can't believe I'm married and going to have a baby.

"That very day I moved in with him and two other guys. They were sharing an apartment while going to school. I would share his bed, but there would be no body contact until we were wed. That was his idea, as I was eager to experience the unknown. I thank God I didn't have to wait long. Two weeks later we were married.

"Gosh Jena, I never dreamt making love could be so earth-shattering. Explosion after explosion of such unimaginable pleasure ravaged my body to its core. It even caused my toes to curl."

Jena exploded with laughter. Why did not her toes curl? Was there something wrong with her? Or was it a man thing? She will make sure the next time she drops her panties she will feel something before he closes his eyes for the night.

Ali displayed no embarrassment for disclosing such an intimate moment. She continued without taking a breath.

"His finals are this week, and then we're off to Mason's Mill. It's a small farming community that occupies a tiny space in what's called the Land of Lincoln. His father's legacy bequeathed him many areas of land, including a house.

"Oh, Jena, I am so excited. In less than two weeks we will be living in our own home. Although he did have one concern, and that was when I see what he has to offer, I will be greatly disappointed, for there is no glamour in working a farm. And if any of my friends were to visit, they will look upon me as losing my mind for marrying a dirt-poor farmer.

"Those were his words, not mine. I had to think of a way to rid him of his fears. I took his hand and placed it upon my stomach. I asked him if he honestly believes our baby will care where he lives; that that little guy tucked inside will unite us as a family, and I swore to him this is how we will always remain. His lips said it all; I made him a believer."

Jena's heart began racing. Mason's Mill could also be the perfect place to hide from Trevor Hartmann once his release was granted. He would never think to look for her in what could only be described as a little 'hick town,' but would Ali mind? Jena didn't want Ali to begin her new life with her in her pocket, so to speak. She decided the only way to find out was to ask point-blank.

"Ali, would you mind if I looked for a house near you? Could I make my home where your home will be?"

Ali was slow to remove herself from her seated position, ever mindful of her condition. She screamed in delight.

"Oh, Jena, that will be so out of sight. I will have a friend from the very beginning. Just how perfect can that be?

"But Jena, how can you leave New York? This is your son's home."

"Ali, I stayed in New York hoping against hope that someday I would come face to face with the little boy that was taken from me. But it's been years, and staying is only a constant reminder that I'm never going to see him again.

"Besides, something has happened that requires a move, and it involves a little boy that is two and a half years old."

When Jena finished telling the sordid details of her marriage and its ending, Ali was terrified for her nanny's safety and told her so.

Jena calmed her fears.

"Because of you, my son and I will have a home that the devil himself will not be able to find."

It was nearing time for Jena to drive Ali home, and it was also time to tell her what she came to her for. She took Ali's hands into her own.

"Sweetie, you will never again have to look upon the face of your father. He is from your past and that is where he will remain."

Ali's tears this time were a show of happiness. She did not doubt her nanny.

Jena's last words when she dropped Ali off at her apartment were few.

"When I'm finished with my business, I will come to you."

It was nearing the time for Jena to make her move. She had to search her memory to try and remember the name of the town and the state that was to be her home. (Being a psychic has its moments of failures.) She also failed to ask the name of Ali's husband before she left to begin her new life with her new husband in her new town.

It would be quite a while before either of them were to meet again.

# CHAPTER ELEVEN

Clay would never forget the day that brought him to his grandmother's home. His memory refreshed.

His grandmother, Lydia, had summoned him to her bedside. The news would not only change the direction his life would take, but place him into a situation over which he would have no control.

Lydia Diane Chadsworth's nurse, Doleanna, removed Lydia's tray of daily uneaten food, shaking her head in the process. She was grateful when at times Lydia would make an honest effort to eat. Doleanna edged her left arm under Lydia's weightless body, bringing her to her own. Then, with her right hand, fluffed the pillows, allowing Lydia more of a sitting position.

Mrs. Chadsworth was very ill; she was not expected to live more than a few months. This visit with her grandson would be like no other. She had to rid her conscience of a great wrong.

She could not go — hopefully — to her Maker until she righted that wrong.

She loved her grandson more than life itself. Lately she had come to believe it was not the cancer, but the lies that were eating her alive. Today she would bare her soul to her beloved grandson, and this very likely would end the bond she steadily built through the years.

The gentle knock on the door caused her heart to pound. There was no turning back. Tears began to form in her eyes; the time had arrived to break her beloved grandson's heart. Doleanna had been instructed upon Clay's arrival to take her leave. She would be summoned if needed.

As Clay approached his grandmother's bed, he could tell she was in pain. This evil disease was destroying the one person he truly loved. The one who listened, trusted and believed in him, no matter how many mistakes he made, and he made many in his growing years.

He spent more time with her and his grandfather, before his passing, than with his father, Phillip, Lydia's son. He knew the time with his precious grandmother was nearing its end. He felt the tears begin. He quickly brushed them aside. He composed himself for her benefit.

"Grandmother, are you sure you're up to this visit? You look tired. Can't we put this off for another time when you're more rested?"

"If I get any more rest, I may as well be dead. Come sit here on the bed, hold my hand." He hesitated, afraid his weight on the mattress would cause her to scream out in pain, for he had been a witness that whenever the nurse moved her, this was her reaction.

"I know what you're thinking, and you're wrong. I'm in no pain. I was given an extra dose of pain medication before you came. Thank God, this is one medicine that allows me to keep my wit. But if by chance I fall into unconsciousness, or worse, I die before I finish what I need to tell you, I've written everything down. You will find a letter addressed to you in the top drawer of my dressing table."

He took his place beside her, taking her hand into his. He waited for her to speak.

"I have something to tell you, and this is not going to be easy. Truth be told, this is one of the most difficult things I've ever had to do. Lives are going be destroyed. All I ask is that you not interrupt me; you must allow me my say. Promise me." She began to gasp.

Clay was at a loss. Should he promise or should he seek help from her nurse?

When Lydia received no reply, she pushed forward, grabbing onto Clay's arms. Her strength befell her fragility.

"Promise me." He promised.

She relaxed her grip, resuming her present position. Tears were beginning to form in her eyes; the time had arrived to break his trust in her.

"Your mother did not die in childbirth."

Clay's intake of breath was sharp. He could barely say the word. "What?"

From the time he could comprehend, he was told how his mother had tragically suffered a brain aneurysm during his delivery, and died. A picture of his mother graced the grand hall, along with past and present family. He was often caught tracing the outline of her face with his young fingers.

He missed what he did not have but longed for. The picture of his mother, the only one known to exist, was the evidence of no one other than family and the hired help lived in his grandparents' estate. His many questions would soon be answered.

"There are things you need to know about your grandfather, for he had been the force behind what transpired. No one can make excuses for him; Lord knows he doesn't deserve anyone's sympathy or understanding. I know you loved him deeply, but what I'm about to tell you, you will in all likelihood hate the man you so loved. But I must go back to the beginning to give you a better understanding of the man I married."

His grandmother looked away as if going back to her beginning.

"No one could compete with your grandfather for my heart. He was flawless, from his six-feet-four-inch frame to his dark hair and blue-green eyes. His looks were such he could have graced the cover of GQ. His very presence dominated our social circle. He was smart, charming, rich, and a real ladies' man. All my friends were envious, but no one could turn his head in their direction.

"Our courtship was short; we married in less than three months. Every day was like a new day, exciting and full of adventures. Promises were made and kept. I really believed nothing on earth could destroy us, but that was before the governess for your father and your aunt requested a leave of absence, something to do with an illness in her family.

"I had many social obligations and I could not wait for her return. I had to find a replacement immediately."

She sighed as she continued. "The appropriate place to find someone with no ties was St. Mary's Catholic Orphanage. When girls and boys reach a certain age, they are discharged. The transition from living in an orphanage to life on the street can be extremely hard. The Mother Superior relentlessly searches for places of employment months before their discharge. I was given resumes on quite a few of the girls that were due to be released in a year or two.

"The girl I chose was ideal. She had extensive education far beyond the age of sixteen. She was fluent in several languages. My necessary requirements far exceeded what I expected. She was just a wisp of a girl, shy and unassuming. I loved her from the moment I met her. She stepped into our way of life with such ease; no one would have ever suspected that she wasn't a part of our heritage.

"Your grandfather could see the effect she was having, not only on my life, but with everyone she came in contact with. She had a gift, your mother. It was as if she knew what everyone needed and took care of that need.

"I think your grandfather felt threatened. I worked for weeks on her duties and responsibilities in tutoring young Phillip as well as in the care of his little sister, Ali. I created a schedule that suited my needs and worked well with hers. I tried to explain to your grandfather how I had to start the training process all over again. He refused to listen.

"Something happened to him. First I noticed changes in his personality. Then our relationship began a slow downward spiral in nothingness. Our prior life was erased as if it never existed. I was so caught up in my own life, I ignored his. I tried to recover what we shared, but the more I tried to rekindle the flames, the end result was ashes.

"Your grandfather removed himself from our bedroom. My tears had no impact. I was totally alone, not only in our bed, but in my life as well. Conversations took place only when absolutely necessary. I accepted the blame. I allowed myself to become, for want of a better word, his slave. I was his beck and call girl.

"I was taught from an early age that men were superior; I was never to question my husband. I loved and respected him, and yes, I obeyed him.

"Obey,' what a horrible word. Children are taught to obey. I often wonder, if I had been in charge of my own life, been treated as an equal, if things would have been different. But that's something I will never know, will I?

"Slowly, as the years passed, I accepted my way of life. If I hadn't formed a bond with your mother, glowing in her companionship, I think I would have left your grandfather. Your mother had a light about her, always smiling and upbeat.

"I didn't think anything could bring her down, but something did. The change came slowly. The spark in her eyes existed no longer. She was sad, forlorn-looking. I was beginning to think she was no longer happy with our agreed arrangements and she wanted out, but because of our bond, she feared hurting my feelings.

"I voiced my concerns in this matter, but she was quick with a response. She loved our family and could never conceive the thought of leaving us. I pleaded with her to allow me into her thoughts. All she did was hang her head, as if in shame.

"She wasn't a shy sixteen-year-old any longer; in a mere three years, she transformed into a beautiful woman. Our many guests often commented on her looks. Maybe love had a hand in it.

"Anyway, by the time I was aware of what was going on, it was too late. She and your father had been seeing each other in the privacy of her bedroom.

"I should have realized something was amiss when she said she needed to have a weekend off. In her length of employment, she never left the estate, although we offered her nights and weekends off and our chauffeur at her disposal. She would just smile and shake her head, telling me she had everything she needed. If I hadn't taken it upon myself to buy her clothing and personal items, she would have had nothing.

"When she asked if she could have a cab at her disposal for the full weekend, I offered my limo and driver. She thanked me, but refused, saying a cab would suffice. I obliged.

"That was the weekend she found out she was pregnant.

"You are the child she labored for hours into the night, the one she loved from the moment you were placed into her arms.

"I'm sorry. It seems I'm getting way ahead of myself. You must have patience with me."

Clay's response was, "Always, Grandmother, always."

"Anyway, at dinner one evening your father, Phillip, excused himself from the table, stating he had a surprise for us. Your grandfather glanced at me, a rarity. I returned the same, scrunching my shoulders. Phillip couldn't have been but a minute.

"Standing in front of us, your father, boldly holding onto your mother's hand, made an announcement: 'Congratulations are in order; Jena and I are expecting a baby. In about four months, you will carry the title of grandparents. We pray this is as exciting for you as it is for us.'

"They were both 19 years of age and they were going to have a baby. Those poor young souls had fear written all over their faces. Your mother never once took her eyes off your father. His grip on her hand tightened. He stood tall, trying to be the man his father, your grandfather, raised him to be. He was failing miserably.

"Your grandfather stood so quickly, his chair fell backwards. Pure hatred radiated from his eyes. I won't repeat the unspeakable language that spilled from his lips. I tried to calm him; he shoved me aside, lunging at your father.

"I screamed for our butler to call the police. I couldn't get to my beloved Phillip fast enough.

Your grandfather's fist was drawing blood with every punch. Phillip just stood there taking each and every blow.

"I don't remember which punch knocked your father off his feet. He just lay there, taking the beating. Your mother collapsed onto the floor, sobbing for your grandfather to please stop. I shoved myself between them, blocking some of the blows. I tried to protect my first born, my beloved Phillip. My tears mingled with the blood that ran from your father's face.

"It seemed like forever before the police arrived. As your grandfather was being handcuffed, he turned to me. Rage highlighted his eyes; reflected was pure revulsion. He showed no sorrow or forgiveness for what he had just done to his only son, our son, my baby boy."

Lydia's retching sobs at the mention of her son gave Clay reason for concern. He cradled her in his arms, pleading with her to tell him another time. She, of course, refused; given enough time, she was able to control her weeping. But never would she forget the pain and anguish her son endured so very long ago. How the memory of it lingered on and on, and it was a torment she would take to her grave.

The sad tale was not about to end.

"I realized in that moment, that day, that night forever severed our marriage. Your grandfather, of course, never stayed in jail. He was a pillar of the community; name a charity, any charity that his name wasn't attached to. I'm sorry to say, but it's true, money speaks volumes.

"Our butler, Franklin, who served the Chadsworths' dynasty for over thirty years, was fired. He did the unthinkable; he betrayed his employer. It did not matter. It was I who instructed him to call the police. Our faithful butler's name was smeared throughout the city and beyond. I heard he had to leave the country to find employment.

"Your grandfather was very powerful; when he spoke, everyone had better listen. It took months to find a replacement that would agreed to the demands expected of him.

"Art became our butler, the only one you've ever known. Your grandfather at the time would never admit to it, but he was looking for another Franklin."

She took a deep breath and continued.

"I remember when I first laid eyes on Art. It was unbelievable. I felt a rush similar to when I met your grandfather. Art was in his late thirties and single, tall and slim with a body that did not require attention. But what drew me like a magnet, and a few of the servants, were his gorgeous dark eyes and small mustache, similar to that of Clark Gable in 'Gone with the Wind.' My, oh my, he was really something in his heyday.

"I told him numerous times he needed to find a nice woman to settle down with, but he would just shake his head, until one day, after my persistent yakking, he gave his answer: 'You are already taken.'

"He was the only man that ever made me blush. I know a part of me loved him. But those words were never again repeated. He knew his place and stayed there. He has and continues to serve us well. If I told your grandfather what he had said, Art would have joined the ranks of the unemployed, possibly forever. I will never again be a party to destroying a person's life.

"You must think I'm losing it, going on and on about things that really have nothing to do with you."

Clay was ready to give his opinion, but his grandmother put up her frail arm, stopping him.

"Maybe I just feel the need to talk, use up all my words, so to speak, before I lie in green pastures."

Clay just smiled, shaking his head. His grandmother had a talent with word usage. He would surely miss her.

"Anyway, after your grandfather's arrest, he isolated himself from the family. Days turned into weeks, then months. Your father stayed with your mother, while your grandfather stayed hidden within himself.

"Phillip's banging and shouting at my bedroom door in the early morning hour told me the time had arrived, your mother was ready. Soon, very soon, we would welcome a new life into our world. But it was not quick. Your entrance into the world took many hours.

"The unbearable pain etched upon your mother's face, I will never forget. But not once did she scream out in desperation for pain medication, which was offered quite often. Her comment was always the same, to leave her be, she would not harm her baby with drugs.

"Finally, you arrived, and you never cried, even with a swat on your little bottom. You were a perfect baby, and I'm not just saying that because you're my grandson. Your mother is a tiny person. Your birth weakened her considerably, and her stay in the hospital was lengthy. But sooner than expected, she was back to being her old self. She had more strength than anyone thought possible. You gave her that strength. The intensity of your mother's love for you could never be questioned.

"Your grandfather warmed up upon your arrival. How could he not? You were your grandfather; his baby pictures proved that. It was if he were reborn. He became his former self. I thanked God for his return from his evil ways.

"That same day, he called a family meeting. It would take place in his study. Your father, mother, and I, once seated, were taken by surprise when your grandfather removed himself from his desk and got down on his knees in front of your mother. He took her hands into his and profusely apologized, begging for forgiveness.

"Your mother, like I said, was an exceptional woman. She told him no apologies were necessary. Your grandfather cried, as did your father and I. Happy days returned.

"Your grandfather worshipped you. All the minutes he could muster were spent with you. Your mother never refused your grandfather's need. Our home was being washed clean.

"Then the unthinkable happened. Your grandfather called another family meeting. You were then six months of age. At that age, no one could hold you back. The minute your body touched the floor, you were off doing your own thing.

"Your grandfather had this huge smile upon his face. And it wasn't from watching your antics. I will never ever forget that day."

As his grandmother continued, Clay felt as if he were a witness to that day and the obscene injustice inflicted upon his mother.

"Your grandfather was giddy with excitement, but it was not as it seemed. Something sinister was hanging in the air. I felt as if I was invited to a lynching. Your grandfather pointed to the chairs facing his desk as he began to speak: 'Come on in. I have some fantastic news.'

"Papers were laid out in neat rolls; your grandfather was beaming with anticipation: 'Jena, I want to put Clayton in my will, but before I do, I need your signature on a few documents. Two of my close friends will sign as witnesses.'

"And then, out of nowhere, two uniformed police officers stepped into the study.

"There it was, that feeling that someone was about to be hung. My beloved Phillip was the first to speak: 'Father, I am pleased that this family meeting was called, for Jena and I so wanted to speak with you. You presented the perfect timing.

'Clay will never have a need of your money. In less than three years, I will be a full partner in the firm. Until then, Jena and I will manage just fine. In fact, she and I decided it was time for us to find a place of our own; we can't continue to live off your kindness and generosity indefinitely.

'But before we do, we would like to get married. We would like a small ceremony, no fanfare of any kind, and of course, we desire your blessing.'

"Laughter, unlike any ever heard, erupted: 'Married? Are you out of your mind, Phillip? You want to give this slut our name? Never, ever, will she be a part of our lives.'

"Your mother abruptly stood. She turned to Phillip for his support. All he could do was hang his head, tears washing over his face. Jena didn't want tears; she wanted him to stand by her, stand up to his father. She felt defeated, betrayed. She reclaimed her chair to hear her death sentence. She had no recourse.

"You see, Clay, it was a farce. He had this planned all along. He hadn't changed at all. He was a Dr. Jekyll and Mr. Hyde. He was never going to accept her; she was to him a nothing. When he felt the need to speak, he would mumble to himself, and then to me, that she was nothing more than trailer trash.

"I think that saying is shameful, and I told him so. It's as bad as calling someone a nigger. Both are disgusting, and in my opinion, those who say it should be heavily fined or given a lengthy stay in jail.

"Those papers he had lined so perfectly upon his desk were in reality a transfer of sole custody of you to your father. Your mother would never have any say in regards to you. He threatened to take you away from her; she knew he had the power to do so. Although he did have a stipulation, she would have to move out. If she did as he ordered, he promised that she could visit with you anytime, spend hours with you if she so desired. She just could not spend the night.

"He gave her two weeks to make other living arrangements. I thank God for those six precious months she had with you. I knew her heart was breaking. I could hear her weeping long into the night. How could I have allowed this, for you to be taken away from her?"

She took a long breath as if it were her last before she continued.

"I couldn't stand to watch her agony. I approached your grandfather in his friendless study. I didn't bother to knock, something he always demanded. And never did I raise my voice to him, but that day I did not feel like a lady, nor did I behave like one. I left my former self outside the study door.

"A new identity entered his sanctuary. Screaming like a banshee, I told him I refused to be a part of his hypocrisy. He would accept your mother into our family or I would divorce him. I would broadcast to the world, if necessary, what a vile person he had become. I would tear his name to shreds.

"His actions stunned me. His movement came so swiftly, I had no time to react. His fist struck me on the left side of my cheek. I could taste the blood as it pooled into my month.

"I, too, became weak like your father. Your poor father. He loved your mother so much, and yet he just didn't have the backbone that was necessary to stand up to his father."

Clay's grandmother was doing a great job on holding back her tears.

"Your father was young; he was being groomed to be co-partners in your grandfather's firm. Upon your grandfather's retirement, transfer of ownership would then be passed on to him.

"But -- and that was when the 'if' came into play -- if he didn't do as ordered, your grandfather would withdraw all future funds and disown him.

"Phillip was frightened; he had no actual money of his own. His money was in trust. He assumed he could provide a living for your mother as well as himself from his expense account.

"I was wealthy in my own right and offered my funds. He would not accept. Phillip worked hard for a future that was sure to come.

"He now felt betrayed. There was nothing he could say or do that would change his grandfather's way of thinking. Nor could I change Phillip's way of thinking. In his mind, he was a failure not only to himself but his beloved Jena. He could not look in her direction, while she could not take her eyes off of him.

"Lies and more lies became my way of life. I allowed your grandfather to slam our door into your mother's face."

Grandmother's tears could no longer be held back when Jena's name was mentioned.

"Jena confided in me daily on her plans for your future once her custodial rights were returned. I didn't have the heart, really the guts to tell her she would never be given back those rights.

"When she signed those papers, she signed away her life and yours. She trusted us. If she knew she would never again hold you in her arms and cradle you to sleep, I know for a fact she would have lived on the streets, begging for food and shelter, to keep you at her side.

"May God forgive the injustice of all the pain and suffering we have caused your mother and now you. I am not worthy of your love, least of all your understanding."

Lydia's tears seemed to never end, as she begged for Clay's forgiveness for lying and betraying his trust in her. His grandmother did not know him as well as she thought. He loved her now more than ever and told her so. The comfort of his arms while wiping away her tears gave her the strength to continue.

"Another family meeting was called. That day will live in infamy. Only those that were directly involved were in attendance.

"Your grandfather would set up a fund in the amount of $5,000 to be paid monthly until your mother's death, but these funds would not start for four years. She had to go it alone until then.

"An envelope was placed in her hands containing a handful of hundred-dollar bills. He told her this could sustain her for at least six months if she was careful with her spending.

"Your grandfather then announced that day was to be her last; she would never again see, touch, hear, or feel the warmth of your body next to hers.

"I should have known he never intended to keep those prior promises. I never again want to be a witness to what happened to your mother when hearing she would have to live her life without you."

Lydia dropped her head in shame.

"Your mother's wretched screams of unbearable anguish pierced the walls throughout the study. Fury and madness was now a part of her makeup. She tore into the man that ripped out her heart. She pounded on your grandfather's chest. She screamed out for God to destroy all the evil that resided in that house.

"Your grandfather's height didn't deter her, nor did he move away. I actually believe he was enjoying her agony. She couldn't continue with the pounding; she was exhausted, she was shutting down. She collapsed to her knees, holding out her pitiful arms, pleading with your grandfather not to take her baby away.

"Her pathetic screams will never be erased from my memory. She continued to cry and plead, but they were wasted, for they fell on deaf ears.

"The same two officers that were witnesses to the transfer of Clay's custody were again on standby. They were told by your grandfather to remove her; he had heard enough from the harlot.

"Your mother refused to give up. She grabbed a hold of your grandfather's pant leg, weeping uncontrollably, pleading for her baby. The officers had to forcibly tug on her fingers to release her grip, creating a scream not unheard of in the throes of childbirth.

"She lay weeping upon the floor, retaining that position as she was dragged to the waiting limousine. Suitcases had already been packed and placed within the truck of the waiting car. The envelope containing the money that was thrown onto the floor of the study was retrieved and would be tossed onto the floorboard of the limo.

"But your grandfather still wasn't finished. As I told you, we only spoke when necessary; this was one of those times. He demanded that Phillip take his sobbing to another part of the house. He could not stand to look upon a worthless piece of slobbering shit.

"And what did I do for my son? I did nothing. I allowed my one-time friend, husband, and lover to degrade my son in the worst way possible. He demanded I stay. His eyes bore deeply into mine. He needed to inflict additional suffering; I was his third target. But I would bear the burden of his evil. He revealed to me how obliging his associate Charles was to get rid of the whore. His words disgusted me."

Clay couldn't take his grandmother's gasping sobs any longer. They were ripping him apart. He needed an out, a break.

"Grandmother, I need to use the bathroom. I won't be but a minute."

His grandmother's look spoke volumes; she doubted he would return.

"Grandmother, I promise, I'll be right back." She relaxed and closed her swollen eyes, the only thing that looked to contain a semblance of fat. When he took his leave from her bedside with Doleanna back in attendance, the now-closed door to her room felt the pressure of his weight.

He could not hug the door for long. He was anxious to hear the rest of her story, but worried if it will be more heartbreaking than that which was already told. He prayed not, for his grandmother's sake. He wondered how she could have carried such a torment of horror she witnessed on a daily basis, not only with his mother, but her beloved son, his father, Phillip.

In his entire life he longed for a mother. Now, this day, he had one. His mother was alive. He would find her; nothing would stop him. He had a complex journey ahead, but one he knew he could conquer.

He could not keep his grandmother waiting. His soft knock did not fall on deaf ears. She mouthed "Enter," her voice strong, not one belonging to that of a dying woman.

"What's with the knock? If you thought by standing outside my door that I would fall asleep, you were sadly mistaken."

"Grandmother, you are truly one of a kind. Why are you denying sleep? Is it because you fear I will leave? I'll tell you what. If you give it your best effort to eat the food that's sitting on your tray, I'll stay around."

Her answer was curt.

"If I want to sleep, I'll sleep. If I want to eat, I'll eat. I don't mean to sound hateful or rude, but I need for you to understand why I did what I did. If it takes hours, so be it. If you get your wish and I do lapse into sleep, I expect you to be here when I awaken. Today, all will be revealed.

I can't wait. I waited far too long as it is."

"Grandmother, I'll be with you as long as you need me to be."

But his grandmother was not about to close her eyes. Not yet, anyway.

"Phillip holds the key to whatever you need to know about your mother, and that's limited. It's sad that your grandfather was given the privilege of walking this earth an additional twenty years after he threw your mother out. Sounds horrible, doesn't it? But hate does that to a person.

"Like I said, if he had died a year or so later, your father would have searched the world over, looking for her. The only good thing I can say about the tragedy of events, your grandfather did keep one of his promises. Your mother to this day receives the money that was promised and will continue until her death.

"Phillip took over after his father's passing. Your father tried everything he could to gather information, but every attempt ended in failure. Bribes offered also fell to the wayside.

"It seemed no one really knew anything. There was only one person that would have known of her whereabouts other than your grandfather, and that was Charles Mannigan, an architect at your grandfather's firm. He was the driver that took her away, but he died shortly afterward. In all honesty, I believe your grandfather put out a contract on him."

Clay's look of shock did not surprise his grandmother.

"You're wondering how I could say such a thing, to think the unthinkable. The bizarre act alone sends chills down your spine, but you never saw the evil in him. Only in your presence did he show love and kindness, while shutting out his son, Phillip, and Alexandria, who in the beginning was called 'daddy's little girl.' She was only nine years old when he took her out of his heart. If he could have paid someone to give him eternal life to keep you to himself, he would have.

"Yes, may God forgive me; I hated your grandfather with as much passion as a person has for someone she loves.

"Your father has a paper trail on your mother. This information didn't come about until after the death of your grandfather. The years of tolerance and bitter hatred for his father could no longer be contained; he went on a rampage in your grandfather's study. I did not stop him.

"He took an ax, chopping away at everything and anything that got in his way. His father's book collection, first editions worth millions, was destroyed. When his fury was spent and he lay among the ruins, his eye caught a sliver of paper tacked on the underside of a small hidden drawer in the mangled desk.

"It was a list of numbers that could only belong to a safe. He knew of no such safe. He looked in my direction. I shrugged my shoulders.

"He scanned the tangled mess, searching, and there, among the distorted bookshelves tucked inside the wall, was the door to a safe."

Clay was shocked. This was something he could not conceive or believe of his father. He was the most laid-back person you'd ever want to meet, and to perform such an act was beneath him. He was beginning to question his beloved grandmother's sanity. Could this be a concocted story?

"I can see your doubt, but it's true. Your father did do this. It was his way of relieving all the years of pent-up anger.

"He suffered unbearably at the hands of your grandfather. You were never a witness to this. You were away at boarding schools, coming home only on summer breaks, or when your grandfather on a whim took you out of school taking you to parts unknown, sometimes for weeks."

Clay remembered those events. He enjoyed himself immensely. He could leave school at any given time, and no one dared to question his grandfather.

His grandmother regained his attention.

"When you did come home, mostly for the holidays, your father was at his peak of happiness. What parent would confide such an abomination to their only child?"

Clay was ashamed at how he could have doubted his beloved grandmother.

"By the time the knowledge of your mother's whereabouts became available, too many years had passed. Nobody can turn back the hands of time. The safe's contents contained a handbook listing the payments paid through the years, along with the post office boxes the cashier's checks were sent to. There were many. Why the constant moves, I have no idea. Maybe she's trying to run away from herself, maybe she's still running.

"Phillip refuses to discuss anything with me. He's ashamed of what he has become, a very tall man made to feel small, a man incapable of taking charge of his own life.

"I love your father beyond words, but like in all things, I failed to convince him that he had no control over the malicious ways of his father. How could he trust anything I said? I was a participant in this nightmare of nightmares."

Clay tried to hush her. She gently pushed his hand away.

"Clay, I want you to do something for me, really a couple of things."

"I will do all you ask of me."

"Go to your father. I know in my heart, when you ask about your mother, he will reveal his guilt. You are the only one capable of doing this. Maybe his love for you will release him from his private prison.

"But the most difficult task before you will be finding your mother. This longing for her that has been long denied will no longer be. You have the courage and the power within to find her, and when you do, you will find a love that has no end.

"She's out there waiting. It's time to put an end to the suffering you and she have had to bear."

She was trying to reach for something under her pillow. It was agonizing.

"Grandmother, may I be of help?"

"Yes, please. There's a letter I've written to your mother."

He reached beneath her pillow and extracted an envelope. Before he could hand it to her, she closed her hands over his.

"I want you to keep it with you at all times, and when you find her, place it within her hands and tell her I'm sorry."

"I will carry out your wishes, I promise."

"There is one more thing." Her face was now dissolving into a mass of tears. He tried to console her. This time, it wasn't working. She was crumbling into a fetal-like position.

He screamed for Doleanna to call her doctor. His grandmother appeared to be having a stroke. He could not control himself. His tears were no match for hers, but came close.

Doleanna re-appeared in her patient's room and did as Clay instructed. She called the doctor. He would take longer than expected. Because of this, his services would no longer be required.

Minutes passed into a half hour. Lydia's body gradually began to unfold, the spray of tears slowing to a trickle. Clay gently pulled her to himself, rocking her ever so gently. She quickly responded with a soft kiss upon her grandson's cheek. She was back to being herself.

Clay's eyes looked upward, thanking God. His grandmother continued as if she had never lapsed in her conversation.

"I want you to find my baby girl and bring her back to me. I need to see her one more time before I die. Will you please do this for me?"

Clay was confused. What baby was she talking of? He was beginning to think she was hallucinating. "Where's a doctor when you need one?"

Her babbling continued.

"He got rid of her, sent her away."

"Grandmother, I'm sorry, I don't understand. What baby are you talking about?"

"Alexandria."

Clay had not heard her name mentioned for many years. Surely his grandmother's memory of Ali remained just that, a pitiful and tragic memory. What was causing her to bring that up now? For whatever reason, Clay felt she needed to talk about "her baby."      "Grandmother, would you like to talk about Ali? If so, I'm here to listen."

"If only you could see and feel my pain, then you would understand the misery and heartbreak I've had to endure, not having my baby girl beside me. Will you help me, Clay? Will you find my Ali?"

His grandmother had erased from her mind the death of her daughter. Now it was his turn to break his grandmother's heart and take her back into the past. This could possibly put an end to her pitiful and frail existence. He knew he had to be careful with his words. Could he do this? Or better still, should he do this? He could play along with her. Agree to everything she asks of him. He then could start his own list of lies.

No, he could not allow this. All lies end this day.

"Grandmother, what I'm about to tell you, you already know, but deep within your heart you have just forgotten, which is understandable. And you know there isn't anything I wouldn't do for you, but what you are asking is impossible."

She wondered where his conversation was going.

"Many years ago, I think I was about eight or nine years old when Grandfather told me the tragic news. I loved my Ali-Kat. Remember, Grandmother, that was my nickname for her? Remember how Grandfather yelled at me every time I called her that? But that name stuck, didn't it? Ali loved that name. She would tell me that name made her feel special, loved beyond measure.

"When Grandfather told me she died, I also wanted to die. I cried and cried. The pain of losing her was too much. Grandfather grabbed me by my shoulders, telling me men don't cry, that I was behaving like a baby, and that I needed to get a hold of myself. I was acting like a wimp.

"That was the one time in my life I didn't listen to him. I remember telling him I didn't want to be a man then, and as I ran from him, I screamed out my feelings. 'I hate you,

Grandfather. I'll always hate you for telling me not to cry about my Ali-Kat.'

"Grandmother, I was just a little boy, I loved her, how could he talk to me like that?"

His eyes were filling with tears, tears for his Ali, his memory of her made fresh. Only God knew how much he truly loved her.

Angry words exploded from his grandmother's shriveled lips.

"Oh, my God, my dear, sweet grandson. The injustice of everything you have had to endure in your childhood and then on into adulthood is disgusting and degrading."

She gathered him to her chest, soothing away his sobs, and then she gently pushed him away to face her. Taking him by his arms, yes, firmly, she then spoke.

"Now, you listen to me. Your grandfather told you yet another lie. I was told by your grandfather that your father had told you that Ali had run away from home and I was not to talk about it because it upset you greatly.

"I tried to comfort you without bringing up the facts, but you pushed me away. When I would mention Ali's name, you would run from me. I left you to grieve on your own with her departure.

"Had I known the horror of what was told to you, that is one lie I would never have allowed.

"Clay, my darling, sweet boy, your Ali is alive. My Alexandria is out there somewhere. I just have no idea where that might be."

Again, Clay mouthed the word… "What?"

Lydia was now more distressed than ever, but she continued.

"How was she supposed to have died? Did he tell you?"

Clay's whispered response was a weak, "Yes." He repeated what he had been told so many years ago.

"Grandfather told me she had drowned in a boating accident and that her body was never recovered. He told me a memorial would be held, but I was too young to attend; I was to stay in school the day of her service.

"I was so sad. I wanted to do something for her. I picked a bouquet of flowers from our garden to place on her grave. She loved flowers and always had them in her room; I knew this would make her happy.

"When Grandfather saw the flowers, he wanted to know what I planned on doing with them. When I told him they were for my Ali-Kat's grave, he yanked them from my hands, tearing them into shreds. He screamed into my face, 'A watery grave has no need for flowers!' He ordered me to my room.

"As I ran up the stairs, I yelled back, 'I will pick more flowers, and you can't stop me!'

"He ran after me, grabbing the collar on my shirt. He took me over his knee and gave me a whipping and told me never to mention her name. I had to promise."

Clay at this point was sobbing deeply, recalling the memory of his only aunt and special friend.

Lydia felt his pain; she'd lived with it for twenty years.

"Oh, my precious grandson, I wish I had the power to erase the pain you are feeling, but I do not. It was somewhere in that time frame your grandfather demanded Alexandria's pictures destroyed. He wanted no reminder of a daughter that didn't adhere to his rules. He may have removed the material aspect, but never the memory."

She had much more to tell, but her strength and voice were ebbing away. Clay felt her surrender to sleep. He would not leave her. He would stay until she dismissed him. It would be a very long sleep, one that he, too, would yield to.

She awakened, moaning softly, asking for pain medication. Clay awakened to her cries of pain. He didn't think this day could go on. He was perhaps relieved for her sake. She was rapidly deteriorating. He wondered just how long she could hold on.

Could he keep all his promises? Would he be able to find Alexandria soon enough for them to be reunited? He heard his name called out.

"I'm still here, Grandmother." Doleanna rejoined them upon Clay's request.

She quickly attended to her patient's pain needs, rearranging her bedding, trying to make her more comfortable, if that were possible. She again was told to leave. She promptly departed.

Lydia had many nurses; this one was here to stay. This nurse went far beyond her duties. She was a big black woman in her sixties, heavy-set with short, curly red hair. She wore glasses and used no makeup. She was grandmother's best friend. She not only fed, bathed, and dressed her; she spent hours reading all the classics, books his grandmother took pleasure in. Grandmother called her nurse her "jewel."

Clay did not reclaim his original seating upon her bed. He instead drew up a chair to be nearer her face. Her words now appeared strained. He did not want her to repeat anything.

She continued as if she had not earlier succumbed to a three-hour nap.

"Your grandfather was a tyrant not only with your father, but with Alexandria as well. But she was headstrong when it came to her father. She would not give in to his demands. She was a witness to the torture and unspeakable acts performed on her beloved brother and your mother, the nanny she gave her heart to and sometimes called Mommy.

"I suffered terribly when I heard the word that should have been for my ears alone. But this, too, was my fault. When she really needed me, I wasn't there. She began having nightmares, and the only way to avoid her father's actions was to spend days away from home, her whereabouts unknown. When she did re-appear, shouting matches ensued always with her father, prompting more retreats away from home.

"I tried to talk to her in the privacy of her bedroom, reason with her that running away was no solution.

"Alexandria did not hesitate with a response: 'I want a life, Mother. I need a place to live in peace and harmony. This house definitely does not provide those qualities. Open your eyes, Mother. This isn't a home. It's a tower of horrors. I refuse to become another you. I am ashamed of what you have become. You are living in a hell of your own making. You have the means to leave him, but for reasons I could never comprehend, you chose to stay. Why?'

"Everything my lovely Alexandria said could not be disputed. I just sat there upon her bed. This time it was I who hung my head in shame. This house consumed her with hate. I told her I tried to make things right.

"Her comment was, 'No, Mother, you did not try. The last time I looked, the door to this house did not contain a padlock. You could have taken me, Phillip, Jena, and baby Clay out that door. But you choose to imprison us, just as father had. I'm sorry, Mother. I have no sympathy for you. I love you very much, but you also had a big hand in this betrayal, whether or not you try to convince yourself it was not so.'

"I told her I would make changes, put things right, starting that day. Ali just sighed, commenting, 'Yes, Mother, you do that.' She walked away, shaking her head.

"I remember sitting on her bed for hours, crying for all that had been lost. That day, she managed to escape the insanity that penetrated the walls of this so-called home. The day that door closed to her room was the last I saw of my Alexandria. My baby was only seventeen years old."

The first mountain of tissues had been disposed of; a new one would begin.

Clay for at a loss for words. Where could she have gone? So many years have passed. She could be anywhere. His grandmother must have been reading his mind when she interrupted his thoughts.

"Yes, my sweet, many years have passed, and this is one assignment that has no directions from which to start. I believe in you, and trust your father will confide any and all information he possesses.

"Knowing the whereabouts of Alexandria is another matter. Your journey will be long. It will take much patience. You may become weary, you will be tested, but your strength and determination will win out.

"Your life begins anew. It holds much promise. Your time is now, one in which you will thrive. On your journey you will find the love of your life. She is waiting. Your heart will tell you when she is found. Make sure you listen to it. It will never guide you wrong.

"Your grandfather I loved deeply, but a mental illness roamed around inside of his head. But that's neither here nor there.

"You will find another letter in my nightstand drawer. This one was written years ago when I came to the realization my Alexandria was not to return. When you find her, and you will, please give it to her.

"I could not at the time find the words she so desperately needed to hear. I wrote this letter in case I was to die at the hands of your grandfather, for I believed if he was capable of one murder why not another."

Clay at his point did not question the words that spilled from his grandmother's lips.

"May God speed your discovery, my precious Clay. Go now. I will await your return."

His grandmother's eyes closed. She had her say. She appeared calm and relaxed.

Lydia finally found the peace she had been looking for.

# CHAPTER TWELVE

Clay spent a sleepless night. How could he not? This morning he would meet with his father. Nothing would be held back. He was exuberant. When the new dawn appeared, his dawn, his life would take a different course.

He stood in front of the building his father and he co-owned, Chadsworth & Chadsworth, an architectural company his grandfather started. A nameplate bore the company's name. It was attached to the front of the brick building, ground level. He was to approach his father for the first time in matters that did not pertain to company business.

He loved his father; he just never had the same kind of connection as with his grandfather and grandmother. With the data he acquired from his grandmother regarding his grandfather, he refused to allow bitterness to take over his life and to consume him with hatred. His grandmother carried that excruciating weight upon her shoulders far too long. He would remember the good times, even if they were built on lies.

He would find Alexandria. His search would never end until this was so. He would see his grandmother hold her Ali for what he knows will be her last time. His prayer to his Heavenly Father would be fulfilled.

His entrance into the workplace was met with many 'good mornings.' The door to his father's office was open. His concentration on the project before him gave no clue his son was standing at the door's opening. Clay stared at this man, his father, and wondered how he managed to keep so many secrets buried.

He and his father stood eye to eye, sharing a height of six-feet-four-inches. His grandmother's opinion of his father was simple. He was not the looker his grandfather Joe had been. That mark of distinction now belonged to Clay. But no matter, his father had his own qualities. Not to say he wasn't handsome, for he turned many a woman's head. Clay's thoughts were jumbling around in his brain when silence was finally broken.

"My boy, I didn't notice you. Have you been standing there long?"

His father always called him 'boy' even when introduced to a stranger. At first it bothered him, but as time passed he grew to accept it, even took a liking to it. This was something that belonged to him and him alone. It made him feel unique, like Clay calling his Ali, Ali-Kat.

"I've been here less than a minute. You seemed so engrossed in your work; I didn't want to disturb you."

"Never, ever could you disturb me. You will always come first, but you know that. What's up, another contract? You pile them faster then I can keep up with."

He was always comfortable around his father; he always listened intently whenever Clay spoke.

"Father, this has nothing to do with business. The subject matter in question may upset you. I pray not. I spent the day with your mother upon her request."

His father's expression did not change. He continued to wait for the conversation to continue, hoping and praying his mother had not taken a turn for the worse.

"Grandmother called me to her bedside. She needed to tell me things about my life I was not aware of."

His father had been standing, but now he needed to sit. He did not seem upset. The day he dreaded no longer mattered; he was relieved. His eyes never once left his boy's face.

"Grandmother told me everything. I'm not here to criticize. Life is as it is, and we can't change the past. It's the future I'm going to take charge of.

"I need your cooperation and help in regards to my mother and anything you might know about Ali's whereabouts. I also have some questions that have me somewhat confused. I'm hoping you can answer them."

His father did not hesitate with an answer.

"I will tell you whatever you want to know.

"My mother lived for years at the estate. How could no one question where she had gone after her departure? I was only six months of age and yet I would continue to live there. The picture of my mother, gracing the grand hall seems so authentic."

His father removed himself from his chair. His approach to his boy was without hesitation. His arms wrapped around his boy's body, praying he would not be shoved aside. He began choking on his sobs.

"I am so sorry. Can you ever forgive me?"

Clay returned his embrace wholeheartedly.

"Father, there is no need for forgiveness; you did what you had to do."

After several minutes, his father calmed down. Clay would be given all the papers that were rightfully his. Words came rushing out. If there was a word to describe Phillip's feelings, only one word could apply: liberation.

Much of what would be told to Clay would be a replay of his earlier conversation with his grandmother, but not all. A bit more would be added to the disgraceful drama. Clay would show his father the same curiosity as shown his grandmother.

"Because Jena was an intricate part of our staff's lives, your grandfather felt it necessary to inform them your mother was extremely unhappy with her life and that you were too demanding, she needed an out. She said she was sorry, but she had already packed her bags and a taxi was on its way.

"Your grandfather threw in a little drama, performing quite well; he even managed to force a few tears, making everything appear genuine. But your grandfather had to add a bit more drama to the already distraught servants: 'She did not even say good-bye after all that we have done for her.'

"The household help had their own tears to shed, for they not only loved Jena, but grieved for the baby that would be raised without his mother. We had no picture of your biological mother. Your grandfather told his staff he would find a photo that closely resembled your mother because he felt it was important for you, as you grew, to have someone you could claim as your mother. The staff totally understood, and they were told if anyone were to question the photo, they would confirm that it was absolutely your mother.

"He told me in great detail what transpired that day, how he had gone to a specific studio, one that specializes in wanna-be models. The photographer's studio was large, set up extremely well. Pictures lined the walls, plus mountains of photo shoots were laid across tables.

"The photographer was just finishing up with a model when your grandfather presented his request. He requested a photo of a model, but it was to be of his choosing. The photographer asked him what he intended to do with it. He told him it was none of his business.

"The photographer refused. The photos were done with one thing in mind, to find work for struggling models. He told him he was responsible for these young girls' lives. How was he to know if he was going to try and find out where she lived and then use her for unsavory purposes? His models not only depended on him for their livelihood but their safety as well. He would not take the risk of finding out one of his models was missing or killed.

"Your grandfather was never denied anything in his life; he was not going to be refused this request. That picture cost your grandfather $35,000. I would lay odds that photographer had never seen that much money in any one day in his life. Can you imagine what that model would have thought if she had known what her life was worth? You can bet the photographer kept his lips sealed as well as the band that was wrapped around the money.

"Up to the day of his death, the control he had over so many lives sickens me. I made many mistakes in the name of love. What I wouldn't give to live my life over. Sounds like a cliché, doesn't it? But when he ordered your mother out, I also should have made my exit. The threat of being disinherited sealed my future. I wish it hadn't taken so long to realize money is truly the root of all evil."

He continued to rub his eyes, wiping away the stored tears he was unable to show until now.

Clay for the first time felt the strength of his father's love.

"I have everything you need to know about your mother, possibly her whereabouts. By the time I acquired the information on her, far too many years had passed to resume a relationship. She may have stepped out of my life, but she has a claim of ownership on my heart and I will never give it to another.

"Alexandria is another matter; I have no idea where she could have gone. After your grandfather died, I hired private detectives by the handfuls. Soon I began to lose track even of them. In the final analysis, all agreed far too many years had gone by; she could have married or taken on a new identity. When this happens, tracing a person's whereabouts is almost impossible. I'm sorry, my boy, this is something I cannot help you with."

Phillip took a hold of his boy's arm and retreated into a private library, one he designed to suit his own personality, nothing at all like Clay's grandfather. The papers his boy desired were stored safely in a lockbox within his father's safe. It was hidden out of sight behind an oil painting of him and his boy.

While on a business trip/vacation in 1959 to New Orleans, and after Phillip completed a business deal and had taken in most of the sights, he decided his last would be his favorite, the French Quarter.

He was intrigued with the artists scattered along the walk paths and surrounding streets. They depended on the weather and their talent to support them. Two or three chairs, canvases, an easel, and art supplies were their total expense. Samples of their work were on display.

He stopped many times, glancing at the work in progress and then continuing on, until he noticed an exceptionally long line of tourists at one particular stand. He was intrigued as to what was drawing the crowd. The artist was simply called André, no last name, his business cards on display.

Phillip stood back and watched this young, dark-skinned man no taller than a 12-year-old make the canvas before him come alive. There was no doubt in Phillip's mind; this artist, when discovered, would command high dollars for his work. Phillip did not only pay for his plane fare to and from, but provided him with living quarters in his home in the Hamptons.

He would stay until the portrait of him and his boy was completed. Clay had just turned one. Jena had been gone 6 months. André's first commissioned work of art fetched him $25,000. André's portraits in the years to come would fetch much more than Phillip had paid.

The safe now stood opened. Phillip's hand rested upon the metal box. Each month he felt the same sensations: sadness and undeniable loneliness for his Jena, the lost love of his youth. His back was facing his son as he wiped away the start of a lone tear and then turned towards him. Folders containing mounds of documents rested in the hands to whom they rightfully belonged.

Clay's arms embraced the papers like a child would with a parent, for this indeed was his mother. He did not request a leave of absence, for he and his father equally owned the company. There would be no time limit on his return. His father finally released from within the loathing and bitterness in his heart. The demons that controlled most of his life were released back into the hell from which they came. Phillip was a free man.

Clay's findings would bear more skeletons than any closet could hold. He couldn't wait to untangle the mass accumulation of papers contained in the folders. He was at present in his own home -- correction, an apartment worth millions in the heart of Manhattan and within walking distance to his office.

His household staff consisted of three. Chef Sonja, a tall, beautiful blond with an accent, originally from Russia, now an American citizen, was married with two children. The two remaining were housekeepers and unmarried.

Johanna was a brunette with a body any man would love to bed down with. Why she chose a career in housekeeping was a mystery. His take on her, she had a skeleton hidden somewhere.

Mya was another story; she had severe acne, stringy hair, and was extremely unkempt in her appearance. Clay had a hard time dealing with her looks. She would be considered ugly by many. But he was decent and he felt sorry for her. He would let her prove herself. She was by far the best housekeeper he employed, bypassing the servants of his father and grandmother.

If he learned anything from this, it was to keep an open mind; you never know what kind of surprise awaits you. If he had to cut back on staff, 'yeah, right,' Mya would stay; the babe with the bod would go.

Their work schedule was Monday through Friday, 10:00 a.m. to 6:00 p.m., with an hour off for lunch. They loved their hours and he was very generous with salary. A hefty bonus was enjoyed at year's end. He lived the kind of life most of us only dream about. Money begets money, and in his case, he couldn't stop stumbling over his.

When his father placed the folder in his boy's arms, he stated, "I kept every envelope that had an address change. The last check mailed was three weeks ago to Florida. That should be your starting point."

Clay took his advice and placed her last known address in his breast pocket, but first he needed to view the entire contents; after all, this was his mother's life lying in front of him. He wanted to see and touch everything that was a part of her. He pulled out an armchair, settling his weary body into its comfort, while at the same time moving his hand, searching for the switch to the lamp that sat upon his desk.

Night had already taken over, and when through with the paperwork, a new morning would have begun. The long hours of no sleep did not hinder his mind. He would leave immediately for Tampa, Florida, for that was the last known post office address the check was mailed to. Hours before, he called for his private jet to be on standby. He knew the trip could be a waste of his time and money, but time has no value with matters pertaining to the heart.

The cashier's checks were consistently sent on the 1st of each month. Today was the 21st. Had she already picked up the check for this month? Would she move again to yet another state before the first of next month? She moved back and forth, up and down, like a yo-yo with no sense of direction.

Copies of the cashier's checks were grouped in stacks according to the states they were mailed to. A pattern was in play; his mother's stay lasted no more than three to four weeks in any given state. Sometimes she veered off, opting for a week's stay in Chicago, then a week in Texas. Countless times over the years she had a two-month stay in Canada and then in Pennsylvania, avoiding New York, close but not close enough. His mother did as she was told. Was it because of the money or was there something more going on in her life?

Once he landed at Tampa International Airport, a sleek black Mercedes was waiting, his car of choice. He found a decent hotel close to the post office. The waiting would now begin. He did not know fate had stepped in; the check had yet to be picked up. He jotted down the post office schedule for the week. He would park his car precisely at the posted time. A daily newspaper helped pass the time of day, as well as the bathing beauties either roller-skating in their bikinis or strolling along the sandy beaches.

It stretched into two days with no lookers into the post office boxes. He would sometimes sit on a secured bench outside the front of the post office, fanning himself with the daily paper. He was on his fourth long day when security approached him. Big and beefy described the two of them.

"Sir, my friend and I have noticed that you've had your carcass parked here for some time, and we're getting a little concern as to what your intentions are. But first we need to see your driver's license and identification papers belonging to this car."

Clay complied with the requests, while telling security he was waiting to meet with someone he had not seen for quite some time, and the last known post office box address he had was there.

"That's the most ridiculous story we've ever heard. No one in their right mind sits for hours, day in and day out, baking in the sun, looking for... what's that you say, waiting to meet with someone you hadn't seen for a long time."

Clay realized just how stupid that did sound.

"Maybe I could explain a little better." He started to speak out, but was quickly silenced.

"You need to remove yourself from this site or the only person you will not want to meet with will not be a friend. Get our meaning?"

It didn't take a dummy to figure that one out. If this incident were to take place with his grandfather, he would have had their jobs or paid them off, whichever suited him at that time. But he wasn't his grandfather and never intended to be. He would have to find another place, far enough away not to draw their attention, but doing so would prevent him from seeing if anyone were to use their personal mailbox.

He need not have worried. No sooner had he put his car in reverse, a stunning woman entered the post office and immediately went to her designated box, the window large enough to provide a view. Was that his mother? Of course not, she was much taller than five feet.

He continued to back out while the two security guards, with arms folded across their chests, watched his slow departure. He attempted to watch the guards while keeping an eye out for the stunner to re-appear.

They were about to make their move towards him when the door swung open. She stepped into the glaring sunlight, cupping her eyes while retrieving sunglasses perched upon her head. He voiced his comment out loud. "Wow, what a woman." She was wearing a pale green dress that clung like skin on a snake, revealing curves in all the right places. He knew of no one that could make a dress come alive and move in such a way that commanded attention.

Should he follow her? What man wouldn't? But he wasn't there for that. She wasn't his mother, but he felt a compelling sensation to follow her. He wondered where she was going and how he would approach her once she reached her destination.

In a matter of minutes her car pulled into the valet parking lot of the Holiday Inn Express

Hotel. A young uniformed man approached her car, opening the door, allowing her to exit. She had no luggage. Clay assumed she was already a guest in the hotel. His car was barely moving when he felt the urge to speed it up, fearing he would lose sight of her, for he, too, needed the services of the valet. He was about to make his move when another car pulled ahead. All he could mutter was "damn."

As a parking attendant approached him, he leaped from his car, grabbed the ticket from his hand, and stated, "I'll be back as soon as possible; you'll be compensated quite nicely." He couldn't remember the last time his legs moved so swiftly, if ever. Maybe as a boy they had.

The stunner was just about to enter the elevator when Clay shouted out.

"Hold the elevator, please." The stunner reacted quickly; her hand secured the door and then turned around to face the person running toward her.

He was out of breath; he thought if he didn't start working out soon, he might not be around to greet anyone, let alone his mother. He felt as if he were about to pass out. It's called having a sit-down position, or for want of a better word, sitting on your ass. He could barely regain use of his vocal cords to thank her.

She smiled and replied, "You're quite welcome." She watched him struggle in his run for the elevator. She held back her laugh; for she knew it took every breath he could muster to say those two words.

Once he secured his intake of air, he couldn't take his eyes off of her. She had the capacity to put a spell on him if she dared. The elevator door closed. They had no further contact, but he continued to stare. The elevator started moving. She was waiting and watching for some sort of response to floor selection. When none came forth, she asked,

"Do you ride elevators for pleasure or do you have a floor preference?"

She smiled after making that remark. He knew, she knew, he was totally taken in with her beauty. It's called gawking. This had to be commonplace for her. This was a dreadful mistake; he'd never acted so foolishly in his entire life with the exception of the postal security.

So, like the idiot he had become, he blurred out his purpose for being there.

"By any chance, do you know a woman by the name of Jennifer or Jena Carr? I'm her son and I need to find her."

Someone up above must have been smiling down on him when she quickly responded, "Yes, I know Jena. I am her best friend, Marnie, and I know exactly where she lives. Your mother has been waiting a lifetime for you. What took so long?"

Her genuine smile said it all. It's as if the clouds opened and all the angels had fallen to earth, surrounding him with all the warmth, comfort, and love a person would ever need in his lifetime.

She continued her climb to the tenth floor with him beside her. No other words were spoken. She slid her card inside the slot, allowing them to enter her suite. He followed her like an obedient child. He wondered if she were married. He then thought better. He was here about his mother, nothing more.

She threw her handbag down on the entrance table, along with her keycard. She turned towards him and finally spoke.

"Your mother is the most incredible woman I have ever met. I love her like a sister. She and I met after she was forced to live on her own. She suffered terribly after losing you, and it saddened me that there was nothing I could do to help her, but now I can. Do you want to call her or would you like to surprise her in person?"

He wanted to surprise her, but he had to know one thing.

"Has my mother found happiness in her life after all that has been done to her?"

"Clay, I'm assuming she is as happy as she allows herself to be. You were, after all, her heart. I would like to tell you everything that I know, but that would be limited to a very small part of her life.

"It's sad to say, but our time together lasted only four years. It took her months to find what she could conceive as the ideal place to live. After she obtained an address and a future phone number for my use, we said our good-byes.

"Our promises of visits ended up being only promises. We decided, until time permitted, we would communicate by telephone. Time, as it continues, is still not on our side, although I do keep saying, someday."

Clay was relieved his mother had secured her roots and, by Marnie's account, was happy.

Marnie continued with what she felt he needed to know.

"Clay, there is only one way you could have found your mother, and that was through the people that were supposed to love her; instead, they trampled on her heart.

"Something must have happened to bring you to her. What that is, I don't need to know. I'm just grateful for your mother's sake.

"But you need to know something. At a sad moment in her life, she confided in me about an enormous amount of money she could have at her disposal each month if she so wanted, but she was reluctant to take it. She considered it as an exchange for you. She called it a bribe or a payoff, take your pick. She tearfully said she wouldn't use it on herself, but it would give her additional funds to add to her ongoing list of investigators in an effort to find you.

"She said your grandparents owned many estates worldwide. You could have been living in any one of them. She needed money, lots of money to further her search. The guilt she felt was enormous, but I convinced her to take the money.

"She laughed when I told her to hit him where it hurts, not in his crotch but in his pocket, although both would hurt. It would be a monthly reminder that he destroyed a family. I threw in a tidbit, telling her paybacks are a bitch."

Marnie was without doubt 100% lady, but had what you would call balls. It was nearing dinner when they both decided to share what little time they had left over food. She had a prior engagement that could not be cancelled, and because his attire was a polo shirt, khakis, and sandals, they decided on a fast-food restaurant. In the brief time spent together over what some people would call food, his life took on more meaning than he ever thought possible, all because of a woman called Marnie.

When they said their good-byes, their embrace was intense, but strictly as forever friends.

Clay's journey was nearing its end.

# CHAPTER THIRTEEN

Clay's knock on the door was as gentle as a tap. The door opened immediately. Harriet's heart was pounding. The son that was taken from her twenty-eight years ago reached out, gathering her close, taking in her scent, holding her close to his heart. He whispered but one word: "Mother."

Harriet's weeping was uncontrollable.

"Oh, my baby, my precious boy, I can't believe you're here, that I'm actually touching you, holding you."

As her hands caressed his face, she closed her eyes, holding tight to the memories of the first six months of his life. The times he cooed and smiled when she entered his room. Remembering the first time he actually giggled when she played "peek-a-boo." So little time spent to remember.

And then the unexpected happened that forever crushed the fiber of her being when she took him from his crib and he spoke his first word, "Mum," never again to be repeated, for that was day she was removed from the Chadsworths' mansion.

There was no doubt this small woman was his mother, for never had he felt such a connection to anyone or anything. These feelings were the ones reserved for a son and his mother. He turned to close the door, holding onto his mother; never again would they be apart. The sofa would bear their weight for some time.

Jena, alias Harriet, was his mother, and yet she could not convey to her son all she was feeling. All she could do was gaze into the most incredible, beautiful blue eyes she had never forgotten. Their hands clasped together as they sat side by side. Words were unnecessary. The touch of their hands, the eye connection, said it all.

She was more than he expected. An air of nobility floated around her, and yet she took up residency in a town that he considered beneath her. His grandmother described her as beautiful, but God himself would shake his head at such nonsense. She was flawless. She was wearing a loose-fitting grey A-line dress, possibly to cover a little thickness around the middle, but he surmised that could be age-related. (It would be months before he realized she was pregnant at the time.)

He had much to say, but he, too, was in awe of the woman he just called Mother. An hour passed before either of them spoke; she was the one to break the spell.

"I hired so many private investigators; I can't even remember their names. Folders on finding your whereabouts swelled to unbelievable heights. Times when I thought we had a positive lead, it would fall to the wayside. Days ran into weeks, then months, but I refused to give up. You were out there somewhere. You belonged with me, you were my baby, and I was determined to find you.

"The P.I. wanted pictures. What pictures? The ones I possessed were of you as a newborn and mounting albums up to the age of six months. They said it would be impossible to locate someone when they had no idea what that person looked like.

"I gave them your father's name and everything I could think of that could possibly help. If it wasn't one investigator, it was many repeating the same dialogue, how they followed your father around, but never at any time did they see or notice a young child with him. They felt you were being kept from the public eye.

"There was one investigator I really trusted and believed in. His name was Kennedy Wallace. He worked hard, giving it his all. He followed through with weekly reports. He said it was possible they changed your name to protect your identity. On and on the reports continued until he sadly stated it was time to give up the search.

"I still have to this day all his reports. The others were tossed. He said to be patient, that it would take a will of iron, that one day you would find me, it would happen, to trust him. I did, and here you are."

Tears contained for years poured forth. Clay's fingertips gently wiped and felt for the first time the tears of his mother. Jena's baby, snatched from her years ago, finally found the path that led him back to his mother. Never again would anyone deny her the privilege of calling Clay her son. No one would ever again take him from her.

But no one can wave off the hand of fate.

They continued to talk when the subject of Phillip came up.

"Clay, how is Phillip? Has he married?"

"Father is fine. He lives with Grandmother. He refused her request that she live alone after Grandfather's passing. Servants are not family, nor is her faithful, round-the-clock nurse, Doleanna. I spend the weekends with them when possible. Work keeps me busy.

"The answer to your second question is no. Never at any time has father brought a woman into their home, but that's not to say he doesn't date, for he always has a woman on his arm, but only during social functions.

"You see, I was told from an early age that you died in childbirth. The only arms I remember are those of my grandmother. I thought of her as my substitute mother. Grandfather played a larger role in my life than my father, but as Grandmother said, after Father lost you, he buried himself in his work.

"There were many times I would find him staring off into the distance, lost in thought. The look belonged to someone who was living a life of misery. Thinking I could help, I mentioned that he needed someone to take your place. He turned in my direction and, with heartrending words I will forever remember, he said, 'There will never be another. Jena made my heart sing.'

"I'm sad for you both."

Harriet sorrowfully told of her feelings.

"Young love, first love, I believe is the strongest love of all. When that is taken away, you lose a large part of yourself. But memories remain, and you force yourself to move forward. Life is hard enough without living on heartache.

"Now, no more about me, what about you? Are you married? Do you have someone holding your heart?"

He laughed at that phrase.

"I don't have the time. Work consumes my life."

"Make the time. I'm serious, Clay. It can be lonely at the top. Come down and enjoy the life that God so graciously gave you. Living a life with no one to share it is no life. Am I sounding like a mother?"

Again, he laughed.

"Yes, you are, I'm happy to say."

She also laughed.

"Well, okay, then, enough said in that regard. The time has come to tell me what it is that is weighing so heavily on your mind."

She caught him off guard. What did she see in him that conveyed his thoughts? But he had no time to analyze his mother's mind; he was there hopefully not to resurrect feelings that caused such friction between his mother and his grandmother.

"My grandmother is dying…" He hesitated; his voice began to falter from the emotion.

"Please excuse me. I apologize."

His mother moved close, taking her hand to wipe away the start of his tears just as he had earlier done for her. She expressed to him how she totally understood that kind of love. He could feel her sympathy for that special someone he was to lose in a matter of months or a mere few weeks.

He regained his voice, set strong from the strength of his mother's love.

"My grandmother's wish is to see her daughter, Alexandria, one last time, and I'm desperate to do this for her. And then I will truly feel as if I have given something back for all she has done for me.

"She was one never to criticize, but I could depend on her advice. She was exceptionally good at that. One bit of her wisdom has always stayed with me: 'Before you travel the road of uncertainty, think it through carefully, for if chosen wrong, consequences will have to be paid.'

"Only recently have I come to believe this was taken from her experiences. Don't you see how important this is? She needs to know if her baby girl found the happiness she so desperately longed for. Please, Mother, if you know anything, please tell me."

She listened attentively. After Clay had his say, the letter from his grandmother was placed in her hand. She glanced at her name in-scripted upon its facing; she felt its weight tugging at her heart. She has the ability to see the words written within, but would wait to see and touch the actual words.

She had her son. Nothing else mattered.

Clay could not delay. If his mother knew nothing he would have to widen his search. Time was not on his side. His precious grandmother was fading day by day.

When he received no reaction when asked if she had any information on Alexandria, he became dismayed. He was hoping and praying for some kind of input, not the silence she was displaying. But hidden within her eyes, he knew that she knew.

He couldn't hide his desperation.

"Mother, I know I'm asking an awful lot after all that has been done to you, but my grandmother gave me her heart. I can't let her down. With or without your help, I will never give up my search."

Jena glazed loving into his eyes and told him what he longed to hear.

"I cannot lie to you, I have the information you are seeking, but Ali made me promise never to reveal her whereabouts. Until I speak with her, I will honor that trust.

"You mentioned you are staying in one of the cabins in town. If she agrees to see you, I will have Norman, the manager of the cabins; transfer my call to your unit."

But she had more to say.

"Clay, so much has happened over the years. There are things you need to know, but now is not the time. Your grandmother is who we should be concerned with, and I will do all I can to see that her dying wish is granted.

"If you leave now, it's possible I will be able to contact Alexandria, and just maybe when the phone rings, the next voice you hear will be hers."

He was completely overcome with relief and happiness. Everything was coming together; his beginning would now have an ending. From his breast pocket he removed the letter he was instructed to give Ali. Instead, he entrusted the letter to his mother, for something was telling him Ali was close, very close. What he didn't know was that Alexandria was his mother's neighbor.

Clay left immediately for his cabin. It was now 10:45 am. No sooner had he removed his car from her driveway, heading down the road to his cabin, Jena ripped apart the aged envelope.

Four words is all it took for her heart to respond:

"Please forgive me. Lydia"

She clutched the letter to her chest, weeping for what could have been, and yes, she forgave. She found her peace. She all but ran to Ali's, alias Beth's, home, her exhaustion forgotten, replaced with jubilation.

Beth was breastfeeding her one-year-old baby when Harriet blasted through her door.

"Oh, my God, Beth, you won't believe what just happened!"

Harriet was so overtaken with joy, she burst out crying. Beth jumped to her aid. Her nipple freed itself from her baby's mouth, but he was satisfied. Harriet could not stop crying.

Beth placed her hand on Harriet's shoulder while making a comment.

"Let me put DanDan down, he's due for his nap. I'll be right back." Beth assumed something dreadful had happened to her best friend.

Harriet took a seat. A feeling of finality came from many years of waiting, wishing, hoping, and praying for this miracle. These tears provided that.

Beth ran to her side, taking notice her friend's tears had subsided. She pulled up a chair alongside of her friend, taking her hands into her own. The letter addressed to Jena was placed into Beth's hands along with the letter from Lydia to her daughter, Ali/Beth.

Beth was puzzled.

Harriet announced her news.

"He's here, Beth. My baby's here. Clay was just at my house. My son is here. He's staying at one of the cabins in town. He wants to meet with you if you would agree to see him. He called you his Ali-Kat."

No sooner had she heard her nickname, she started crying. Clay forced her to recall the memories of their times together. Their years of separation bore heavily on her heart and now he was here. How could she not see him? He was the only person that made her life bearable when she was forced to live in that house they shared.

The letter addressed to Ali was sealed with a kiss; the imprint revealed aged lip lines. The pale pink shade of lipstick her mother has always worn was unmistakable. Alexandria was inscripted upon the envelope. She caressed the letter as if it were her most cherished belonging. How she could have left her home with so much hate, but if given the chance, she would return with so much love. The word she is looking for is forgiveness.

Harriet spoke, bringing Beth to attention.

"Honey, Clay wrote down the number to the office should you need it. If you decide to do this, you will have to call Norman to transfer your call to his room."

All Beth could do was nod; she was at a loss for words. The slip of paper with the phone number was placed on the table before her. Harriet got up from her chair to hug her used-to-be 'charge' and now her best friend, and simply said, "I'll see you later."

She closed the front door quietly. This time the walk home would be slow, her heart now happy, her steps made light.

Beth looked down at the envelope. She recognized the handwriting. Jena's read letter now rested in her hands, so much heart in such few words. She wept for the years lost, not only for Jena, but her mother as well, their binding love unquestionable. She refolded the letter and tucked it back inside the yellowed envelope. She would return it to its rightful owner by day's end.

One has to wonder what would have been said had they known death was knocking at one of their doors.

Beth's baby had fallen asleep, joining his two other brothers, ages three and two. Beth's daughters were working the fields, minus Sloan, who hopefully was enjoying herself in town.

She pushed her kitchen chair near the window; the sun was shining through, revealing many handprints upon its glass. Washing windows has never been a priority in her home, a job that proved senseless.

She leaned her elbows on the deep windowsill with the sealed envelope held on both ends with her thumbs and index fingers, staring at the imprint of a kiss. Tears fell as she leaned forward, pressing her lips against those of her mother.

It was time to read the letter:

"My beloved baby girl, I pray this letter finds you happy in your life's choosing. Nightly prayers offer some comfort while asking God to watch over you and keep you safe from harm. There are no words to compensate for saying 'I'm sorry.'

"I wonder to this day why God chose me as a parent, for that is an ultimate privilege, and I abused that honor. I could not have been more horrible had I tried harder. Weakness was my downfall; most notably, I was a coward.

"You were always so much wiser than I. If only I had listened. It was if I were the child and you the adult. I would gladly sell my soul to change the past and the horrible events I was made a part of, but not even Satan wants anything to do with me.

"I dread sleep, for that is the makings of the nightmares invading my past, forcing me to relive the pain inflicted upon you, Phillip, and Jena. My arms ache for your touch and the times we did enjoy each other's company. I carried you for nine months close to my heart and there you will remain.

"I cannot end this letter without also letting you know that your father passed away eight years ago. The diagnosis was a heart attack. How fitting, for he broke many a heart when he was alive. Truth be told, I was not unhappy with his death, I was relieved. He is unworthy of tears, so don't you dare waste yours on him. And maybe what I'm about to tell you, you'll waste no tears on me.

"My time on earth is limited, baby girl; I'm dying with that dreadful disease called cancer. I don't want your pity, honey, only your forgiveness. Do you think you can do that? Thank you for being my daughter. My eternal love, Mother"

Tears consumed her; she couldn't accept the fact her mother was dying. She needed her mother; her mother needed her. She would take her advice. No tears for the unworthy. Her father would continue to rot in hell.

Clay was pacing the floor of his cabin. Another thirty minutes had passed since he left his mother's home. Would his Ali call? Was he giving his mother enough time to get in touch with her?

The stress of waiting was beginning to give him a headache. He checked his suitcase, tossing the extra clothing he packed about the room in his search for pain medication. He was a man who never left home without it except for now. He called the office manager, and within minutes a packet of two aspirin was within his grip.

The manager, Norman, stated, "I have to add it to your bill. The cost is $3.00 for two. If you only want one, I don't know what to charge you."

Clay shook his throbbing head at the stupidity of that comment; he, like the sheriff, rolled his eyes, causing more pain. He was in the bathroom struggling with the plastic covering over a glass when the telephone rang. He ran so fast he tripped over the area rug, landing him face down upon the mattress. The phone was on its third ring when his hand made a grab for it. He picked it up in such a hurry it slammed against his mouth, and he could taste blood.

The soft-spoken voice on the other end asked, "Is this Clayton?"

He quickly answered, his blood leaving its mark upon the mouthpiece.

"Yes, it is. Is this my Ali-Kat?"

Beth could barely repeat his name.

"Clay, is this really you? What happened to that wonderful, sweet voice of so long ago?"

Beth could not hold back the tears; a floodgate opened. Clay wanted to be with her, hold her, and tell her he will make everything right, undo what has been done, but how could he? He had no idea where she lived.

"Ali, please tell me where you are, let me come to you, allow me to comfort you like you've always comforted me."

Minutes passed before she spoke.

"I lost a little boy I adored; he was my everything. A little boy who always greeted me with a smile and a kiss. A little boy that depended on my support, and I abandoned him. I ran away, thinking of no one but myself. I never even said good-bye to you. Can you ever forgive me?"

Clay was caught up in her emotions, but was quick with a reply.

"The word "forgive" applies to only those who continuously think they can say or do anything and then ask for forgiveness. That, my sweet Ali, is not you."

It was time to put aside her torment and place the fault to where it rightfully belonged: her father and her mother.

She could hear the sounds of Clay's breathing. She longed to feel those breaths upon her face. She loved him so.

"I called the second after I read Mother's letter."

He was right; his Ali was living close by.

She continued.

"It was wrong of me to run away, leaving Mother to fear the worst about my fate. I very much want to see her and tell her how much I love her and the past is just that, the past.

"I need a minimum of three weeks to prepare, but there is a reason. That is the time span left in weaning my baby off the breast. Once he turns one, his clinging days are over and his source of milk will come from the bottle.

"I pray I didn't embarrass you with that disclosure; country folks are very open about such matters."

There was a lengthy pause before he spoke.

"I'm sorry, I was just trying to get a picture of this in my mind, but it escapes me. Probably because I've never been around young women with babies. But even if I had, I seriously doubt the women in New York would do what you are doing. They would hire in a substitute while spending their time at the spa." Laughter was heard on both sides.

"So what do you think, is three weeks okay?"

"I don't see a problem; the doctor gives her a few more months. She is and will continue to have round-the-clock care. She needs to see you, Ali. The remorse is worse than the pain of cancer. That's what's destroying the little time she has left. She won't let go until her last request is met, and that is to feel the warmth of your body one more time.

"Ali, you must grant her this last thing. I made a solemn promise that I would find and bring you home to her; please help me keep my word."

"I will not disappoint you, Clay. Let me jot down your residence and business phone number and I'll call you when I have booked my fight. You can then pick me up at Kennedy Airport. Do you still live in the Hamptons?"

"No. After Grandfather died and I made partner, I moved into an apartment in Manhattan. I could never live anywhere but in New York. That is my home."

"I never thought I could leave New York, either, until I met my husband. Clay, the day I met him, I knew he was the one. I was only seventeen, but my heart was in a rhythm all its own. I had never felt such a love; it was as if I was thunderstruck. I listened to my heart and it told me right.

"We married within two weeks by a justice of the peace. When I was asked my age, of course I had to lie; thank God the preacher accepted my word. I have never regretted making that decision."

Clay's reply pleased her.

"You sound just like your mother. She said to always listen to your heart, it will never betray you. I guess you are living proof." Laughter was shared.

On a more serious note, she stated, "When I do come, it will have to be no more than two days, three at the most."

This time when he spoke, Ali could tell by the tone of his voice it was one of disappointment.

"Ali, it's been years since I've seen you, and I want you to spend as much time with your mother as possible, but I'm selfish. I would like equal time."

"Clay, if I could, I would spend weeks with you, but that is impossible. I have a family that needs me. Did your mother tell you I have twelve children? Well, eleven now. Our first-born son, Zac, died as an infant. I hated God for taking my baby; it took me years to accept His will, but I am now at peace.

"I wish you could meet my family today, but I, too, have been living a life of lies, and until I make this right with my children, I can't go forward. You will have to be patient. Once I meet with Mother, we can then make arrangements for our families to meet.

"You would have had to live my life to understand why I ran away. I lived in fear with my father's connections that he would find me and physically force me back to my prior life. I held nothing back from my husband and we agreed I would tell everyone I came in contact with that I have no living relatives.

"Once you meet my husband, you will understand why I chose the life I have. My heart is so full of my family that if I were to die tomorrow, I could never have asked for more. My life is complete. If everyone could experience this kind of happiness, there would be no such thing as war."

She waited for a response…silence…and then she heard what sounded like weeping.

"Clay, are you all right? Are you crying? Clay, speak to me."

His voice was quiet but clear, and yes, he had been crying. Tears do not make a man a wimp; it proves he has heart, what many men refuse to show.

"You blew me away. I never expected anything like this. I cannot visualize anyone having twelve kids, but you proved it can be done. I'm overwhelmed with happiness, as will Grandmother be when I tell her about your classroom of kids."

She never quite thought of it as such, but she smiled, realizing how true that could be.

He wished he was sitting beside her when he tells her the upcoming story.

"Ali, I have something to say that is sure to upset you, but it needs to be told. I was barely nine years old when your father told me you died in a boating accident. To describe the years I struggled to accept your death is impossible.

The pain, over time, did lessen, but the love remained.

"If Grandmother had not confided in me, I would not be here today. The list of lies she revealed is phenomenal. How our family functioned, living that kind of life, is beyond comprehension. Thank God everything is now out in the open and we can finally put it to rest.

"But now what you're asking is to turn my back and walk away for an additional three weeks. Do you have any idea just how hard that will be?"

His tears, combined with hers, lasted for minutes.

"Yes, I do, for I am experiencing the same kind of hurt. You managed to do what no one has ever done in our brief years together. You taught me the true meaning of love, and I thank you for that.

"I was not forced out; I left on my own accord. I could not continue to be a witness to the horrors. When I closed the door behind me, I did not say good-bye, for if I had, your tears alone would have forbidden my departure.

"Of everything that was said and done in that house, I never would have thought my father would go to such extremes. He had to have been mentally ill, for no one in their right mind that loved you above all others would inflict such sorrow in a young boy's life.

"But as you will soon see, I am still among the living. Mason's Mill is to me like

New York is to you. It is the place I call home, and this is where I will make my final exit."

Those words will soon come into play.

He now knew what being selfish was all about.

"I'll take whatever time you can spare."

After the arrangements were finalized, he had one last comment.

"I'll be returning home this evening. I prefer to drive at night when the traffic isn't so bad. Grandmother has waited long enough to hear that you are alive and doing well. This will be one part of her suffering I can put an end to, but it needs to be done in person. To see the expression on her face will be my reward."

"Instead of words, I wish it were me you were taking to her bedside. All I can do is pray the three weeks go by quickly."

There was a few seconds' delay before she spoke again. Did some of Harriet's power rub off on her?

"Clay, I know this may sound stupid, but if by chance something were to happen, like I'm run over by a truck or abducted by aliens, please tell Mother there is nothing to forgive, that I've never stopped loving her, and she is always in my thoughts."

Clay would have laughed, had she not spoken so seriously.

"I don't think that will happen, but if it does I'll relay your message."

Good-byes are always hard to say. Theirs was no exception.

The time on Clay's watch read 12:10 pm. He would grab a bite in town and out of curiosity check out some of the shops and perhaps leave earlier than planned.

The shopping center was overrun with cars; few parking spots were left. Was he missing something? This seemed almost ludicrous.

He was standing on the edge of town, his back to the police station, hands on hips, watching the activity. He was trying to figure out what it was that brought so many people to this rather small country town.

And then his heart began to pound, for high up on a balcony an extraordinary beautiful woman who seemed upset with someone or something caught his attention. He was gaining a reputation for a bad display in running, but he was determined this was one woman that would not get away. Marc had the same intention.

Sixteen steps up and you were walking on an eight-foot-wide wooden deck of a two-story clothing store. A four-foot-high redwood rail protected anyone from falling over the side.

Sloan's attempt at freeing herself from Marc was failing, and because of his concentration on not losing sight of her, he slammed into a stranger, knocking him onto the platform. The impact also forced Marc to lose his balance, sailing him backwards onto a rack of miscellaneous items marked for Clearance. An item landed on him that quickly brought chuckles to a few that were exiting the store. The garment, a bra, was lying on him so neatly; you would have thought he was trying it on.

Sloan cupped her mouth in an effort not to be seen or heard giggling along with them. Marc rose, crumbling the bra in his large hand. The look on his face rekindled her old fear. His blue eyes bore deep into her soul. He made her feel as if she had pushed him to make him look like the fool he was.

She stood transfixed. His eyes revealed a great sadness; they seemed to ask why she joined in the laughter. If she had known the hellish nightmare awaiting her, maybe she would have taken the time to reverse the outcome.

His eyes broke away from hers as he threw down the intimate apparel, sideswiping the crowd above and below as they gathered to see what transpired. She followed his departure. He stopped only once to look back and then he was off running in the direction from which they came.

She turned back just as Clay bent over to brush the dust off his pants. She looked onto a mass of dark brown hair. She could feel his eyes moving over her legs, continuing up her body, settling on her breasts.

She held her breath when their eyes connected. She felt her pulse quicken, and her legs began to quiver; for once, Heaven was on her side.

"Please tell that young man, who I assume is your friend, to accept my apology. I wasn't paying attention as to where I was going."

She knew Marc was to blame, but of course he was long gone, leaving it up to her to fumble an apology for which he was totally responsible.

Clay settled the debate as to who was at fault.

"Let's just say it was purely an unavoidable incident and leave it at that, all right?"

She felt weak in his presence. She grabbed a hold of the rail with the intent it would keep her standing. She swayed towards him. He reached out to catch her. An intense heat radiated when their bodies made contact. His arms circled her back, pulling her close. Their eyes spoke what no words could say. Their hearts beat as one.

He whispered in her ear, "Let's get out of here." His hands led her, she cared not where. It happened; her knight arrived.

Before the door closed behind them, she noticed Marc, his head hung low, walking further down the road. She cared not, for that world was left outside. There would be no turning back.

The stranger caught her up in his arms as he carried her to the bed. Gently he lowered her body onto the mattress. His statuesque form loomed over her like a God. Her eyes never leaving his face, yet taking in his every movement as his clothes left his body.

He knelt at the bedside; slowly he began to remove her clothing. Faster, faster, she wanted to shout. She started helping, impatient. For what, she knew not.

A trail of kisses that started on her eyelids, played on her lips, swept over her throat, and danced over her breast could not compare to the magic his hands were performing on her stomach, legs, and inner thighs. Her body moved in a rhythm all its own.

Just for a split second, her mind registered a memory of Papa and Mama in the kitchen, Papa working what she now knew to be his magic on Mama.

She had no idea what was happening. She wanted more and more. She turned wanton for the things the stranger performed; she returned the same pleasures upon him.

She reached a high where she knew her life would never be the same. The pounding of her heart was intense as she was being swept upwards. She gave to this stranger her heart as she surrendered her body.

This day started her beginning, like a newborn babe taking its first breath of life. Her breath of life was now sitting on the side of the bed, head in hands. Her descent from rapture came slowly, only to stare astonished onto her nude form. She couldn't believe she behaved in such a manner. Will she ever be the same? What if she should get pregnant? Oh yes, the teachers pulled no stops when the discussion of sex was brought up. What if her papa finds out what she has done?

All these thoughts were running into each other, juggling around inside her brain. She finally told herself to stop thinking, it's done, there's no turning back, just get dressed and…and what?

She could only mutter a single thought.

"Could I please have my clothes?" She was met with no comment or response.

"Sir, please…"

"Oh, my God, what have I done to you? You are but a child." As he spoke, he did not turn in her direction or remove his hands from his face.

"I beg your pardon, sir, I'm no child. I'm eighteen." She sprang up off the bed to stand directly in front of him, hands on her hips, legs slightly parted.

"Does this look like the body of a child?"

Still seated, the stranger dropped his hands away from his face. His eyes devoured her body. His head rose slowly until their eyes united. A moan escaped his lips. Before either of them knew it, their bodies once again entangled to meet the needs of the flesh.

Time has a way of finding itself, spiraling downward; they found their bodies entwined tightly, the hunger and desire spent. For just how long, they had no idea.

She lay quietly by his side, thinking about nothing but this marvelous creature that she had just bedded down with, a perfect stranger. She could feel the desire rapidly building again. There was nothing, absolutely nothing on God's earth that could compare to this and the spectacular explosions that rippled through her body, erupting time after time after time.

This has to be Heaven. Yes, she thought, that's it, I died and went to Heaven… but… if, by chance, it is a dream, she prayed to never again awaken… but awaken she did.

"I don't even know your name," replied the stranger, all the while caressing her face with his fingertips.

Drained of all energy, she could only whisper.

"Sloan, my name is Sloan."

"An unusual name, but very beautiful."

His gentle hands continued to caress her face as she spoke.

"I am the first born. Papa knew in his heart I was going to be a boy. I was to be named after his pa. He would carry on the tradition; the first boy born from each generation is to be named after their grandpapa.

"The day I was born, when told the sex, Papa had but one comment: 'This is the first time in four generations that the first born is a girl. So be it. She will be called Sloan.'

"So here I am, Papa's girl, with Grand papa's name."

"Lucky for me the chain was broken."

She was waiting for him to tell her his name. When no other comment was forthcoming, she asked, "Well… you do have a name, do you not?"

"Clay, my name is Clay."

No other name could have suited him so well. He untangled his leg that was entwined within hers, raising himself so that they were face to face, body to body, soul to soul.

"Are you hungry?" He asked.

Without hesitation, she answered.

"I'm famished."

He rolled over to the side of the bed, making his way naked to the bathroom, side-stepping the clothes strewn about the floor.

"I'm going to take a quick shower, be back in a flash." He hesitated, and then turned back, retracing his steps. He bent over and pressed his lips gently onto hers and again stated, "I will be right back."

Sloan's lips responded eagerly, raising her body slightly, never wanting to let his lips part from hers. She knew what he was experiencing, for she was feeling the same; he did not want to leave her for one second. She no longer was embarrassed at her nakedness or his. How could she be? His body was a tanned marvel, tall and muscular. She was in awe the way his body moved, the tan lines vivid from swim apparel.

She was given a gift, a package that she unwrapped and was determined to keep. She could hear a trickle of water signaling his shower was over. He emerged, the towel he had wrapped around himself now removed, and began to dress.

"Are you going to get dressed… or do you want me to carry you to the restaurant like I carried you to the bed, only this time undressed?" Their shared laughter united them.

She responded slyly, as she provocatively stretched her body on the mattress. She was becoming shameless in her actions. He had unsurpassed willpower and he refused to let his raging testosterone take control, as much as he again felt like ripping off his clothes. He found himself a tiger, and he knew that from this day forward, she would purr for no one but him. He would see to it.

"Why don't I just pick up something and we'll eat in?"

"Great, that's so much better. I'll hurry and shower and I promise my clothes will be on when you return." He left quickly before he changed his mind about eating.

She made herself useful in his absence by pulling the extra large nightstand over to the side of the bed, making room for one to sit on the mattress and another to sit on the lone chair. She found a flat sheet in the dresser to use as a tablecloth; she hoped the utensils would not be forgotten.

Just as Clay was about to turn the door knob on the cabin, he had an eerie sensation. He felt as if he were being watched.

He looked down the road towards the end of the cabins. On the opposite side were dense woods. He could barely make out a form of something, or were his eyes playing tricks on him? No, he had just seen something move. The movement was swift. Something was moving among the overgrowth of weeds that wrapped themselves around the trees and other vegetation growing there.

He wondered if it was that friend of Sloan's. He felt badly for the young man, but the young man would accept nothing in the way of an apology. He continued to watch the woods. The movement was visible within the brush. He knew without a doubt he was still being watched, but if not by Sloan's friend, then by whom?

Clay's entrance into the cabin was greeted with a sultry comment.

"Welcome, sir. Dinner is about to be served. Please take a bed."

His laughter rang out. There she stood, with a hand towel from the bathroom draped across her arm, naked. She had not done what she had promised; her clothes still lay where he had first thrown them. It was apparent; the dinner she was talking about was her body.

He set the drinks down and threw the bags of food onto the surface that had been set up in preparation for their dinner. He picked her up and placed her upon the bed, their arms twisting together in their urgent need to remove his clothing.

She was on fire. Her arms and legs quickly pulled him close. Her need was no greater than his. They were all over the bed. His lips couldn't get enough of her taste. Her moans could not be controlled. Their hunger would continue for more than an hour until she whimpered, "No more, please, I'm done. I'm completely exhausted. I need to rest a while."

He did not think he could have lasted much longer, but if she still needed him, he would make sure she was fulfilled. He was no quitter. He loved hearing her moans. Her rapid movements made him quicken his thrusts. This was a hungry woman and he would fill her to capacity.

"Do you think we could now indulge in our cold food that at one time was hot?"

He could see she was hungry. She was weak in her movements, and it seemed the only thing capable of moving was her hand, for she was gingerly pulling chicken out of the bag. She could have cared less about a napkin.

She was unlike anyone he had ever known. He had crossed the line when he took her the first time, not knowing her age until after the fact, jailbait being under eighteen years of age. He prayed she was honest with him, although it was a little late for that.

"Come on; get your lovely bones up. We need to get dressed and eat; time is getting away from us."

She instantly jumped from the bed.

"Oh, my God, what time is it?"

"It's a little after six, no big deal."

She started to cry.

"Oh, God, my papa is going to kill me. I was supposed to be home in time for dinner. We always eat at five."

She began running about, gathering up her clothes. She tossed her dress over her head, and then yanked on her panties, not taking notice if either of their placements were correct. While she was crawling around the floor, looking for her shoes, she was still crying. Clay thought she acted as if she were in fear for her life. He quickly changed into a clean pair of slacks and a fresh short-sleeved shirt. He then tried to calm her.

"Sloan, I may be stepping out of line with what I'm about to ask, but I'm doing it out of concern. Does your father strike you, is that what is frightening you so?"

"Oh, no, my papa is loving and affectionate; he has never laid a hand on me. It's the promise I made to him when I left this morning. All he asked of me was to be home in time for dinner. I always keep my word. Oh, God, he'll never trust me again."

She could not stop crying while she continued her hunt for her shoes. Clay also got down on all fours to help in the search. He finally found the shoes; one was in the bathroom, the other behind the headboard of the bed. He would not even attempt to figure that one out.

Once her shoes were on, she made a dash for the door. Clay grabbed her from behind, trying to calm her; he spoke gently as he wrapped his arms around her.

"Babe, the time has expired; there is nothing you can do about it now, and crying won't help either. Come on, I will drive you home. You can save your walking for another time. We'll figure out a story to tell your parents that will be acceptable."

She appeared dumbfounded with his comment.

"Clay, you don't know my papa. He would never expect me to come home with a man. To him, I'm his little girl. I strongly believe he would take a swing at you or maybe even kill you.

"Oh…I don't know what he would do. But I'm not going to take a chance and possibly endanger your life. I'll let you know where you can drop me off. Let's just get going."

He opened the car door for her, the car she had earlier run her hand over. He quickly took his place behind the wheel. He needed to tell her something before he took her home. He turned towards her, taking her hands into his.

"I want you. I need you to be a part of my life. Will you marry me? I would have gotten down on my knees to propose, but you wore them out, crawling around looking for your shoes."

Her worried look vanished, and in its place laughter rang out, making room to give him an answer.

"Yes, yes, I will marry you."

Now was the most difficult part. He had to tell her he was leaving town this evening. He did not want her to think he used the words "marry me" to get out of a bad situation. To tell her he was there strictly for business and needed to return with the results would also have sounded like a lame excuse. But he really had no choice.

After he finished saying what needed to be said, her reply was a simple "Okay." But he still felt awful. Hoping to make her feel better, he told her he would return in two weeks. He received the same response. He knew of no woman so accommodating.

She said she will show him the location where they will meet on the way to her home, but with a requirement.

"We must meet during daylight hours, for you will never find it in the dark."

"Babe, be assured the sun will be shining when we meet again."

He reached behind the driver's side of the seat to retrieve his briefcase. Rummaging through the papers, he confiscated a small calendar. His fingers began running over the days of the weeks. He wanted to be sure about the date so she could mark her calendar at home.

The exact time of their meeting, they both agreed, was impossible to set. Air time, even with his personal aircraft, and driving had to be taken in consideration.

She assured him that on the appointed date she would be there from early morning till dusk.

They reached for one another. The touch of their moist lips began to hurt, their need returned. She was the first to pull away, Papa on her mind.

"Clay, as much as I want to jump out of this car and return to the cabin, I cannot. I really must get home."

His reply was a nod. Unable to speak, the ache in his groin was getting the best of him. He put the car in reverse, backing straight out from the front of his cabin; he then turned his steering wheel to the left and proceeded down the graveled road. The roadside was clear of people and children; he figured it must also be their dinnertime.

As he neared the end of the cabins, Sloan suddenly yelled for him to stop. He braked immediately.

"I need to see if something I had seen earlier in the day is still there, do you mind? It's really important."

"No, of course, I don't mind. Would you like for me to go with you?"

"No, I'll only be a minute. And you need not open my door. I can manage."

She started pushing the brush and weeds aside, trying to locate the spot Marc had laid his catch of wildlife. She kept shoving and pushing at the sticks and trash that gathered along the path on the edge of the road leading into the forest.

Her piercing scream caught Clay off guard, but he was quick to shove the car into park before he rushed to her side. She was on her knees, hands covering her face, crying hysterically.

"My God, babe, what's wrong, did you hurt yourself?"

She removed one hand from her face while the other continued to cover her eyes, pointing downward where she'd made a deep separation of the weeds and trash.

The blood-coated squirrels and rabbits were now twisted and tied with what looked to be a bra. The rifle was gone.

This was a sight no young girl should have to see. Clay pulled her to her feet and guided her back into the car. He worked on calming her down. All she could think of at that moment was if she had not met Clay, this day would have been the worst ever.

He managed to get her trembling under control. She said she had something to tell him about that day. When her story was nearing its end, she told him she was sure that was her missing bra.

"Clay, I over-reacted, I'm sorry. I feel really stupid carrying on the way I did. The reality of that being my bra took me totally by surprise.

"I now know it was Marc who had been following me. He is the one that ran into you at the shopping center. He would never harm me; he loves me too much. I hurt his feeling so badly; he took his anger out on his catch.

"The use of my bra to do what he did was a little extreme, but I think he just wanted to have a little something that belonged to me, something to claim as his own. Now he doesn't even have that."

She hung her head. She was sad for him. She was a nice person and she'd treated him badly.

Clay, too, felt bad for the young man, now more than ever, for he was a witness to the extreme methods a man would go for the love of a woman he considered his and now lost to another.

If this happened to him, he wondered what he would have done. In the deep regions of his brain sat the word "kill." He was shaken with that thought. He wasn't that kind of person, or was he?

He took the car out of park almost as quickly as the evil thought that entered his mind. Sloan told him to turn left at the bend in the road and to follow the path, for that would lead them straight to her home. A couple of minutes passed when she told him to stop again.

"Pull as far over to the right as you can. This is the area where we will meet."

He was not fast enough to open the car door for her. She was already sprinting across the road. He was at her side instantly.

"Gather as many large rocks as you can find. We need to mark this area or you will never find the opening. This used to be the town's swimming hole, but it's been closed for years because of a drowning. This is where I will be waiting."

The opening was apparent only because she struggled with the underbrush and vines that originally kept it hidden from view.

"This in two weeks will again be totally overgrown."

He now understood the reasoning behind the rock display. What now looked to be a monument could not be missed.

Once again they were on their way. When she felt it was safe without anyone seeing her, she told him to stop. She saw a few kids riding their bikes, but they took no notice.

He was reluctant to let her go; she felt the same. But they knew their time would come shortly. They could wait.

No further physical contact was made. They looked at one another for the last time, reveling in the wonders of a one-of-a-kind love. She removed herself again before he could make his exit to open the car door for her. She did not turn around, not once, to glance at his departure.

She would not concede to the fact that he could be a no-show.

This day would end like no other.


Sunni placed a phone call to Sloan's house. When the receiver was picked up, she recognized Beth's voice. She asked to speak to Sloan. Beth told her she had not yet returned from her trip to town.

Sunni looked at her watch. It was 4:00 p.m. She knew the Parkers' schedule and knew they wouldn't allow Sloan to miss dinner with her family. This was a tradition never to be broken.

Something was going on, Sunni was sure of it, but what? She decided to drive into town. She parked and went from store to store. Sloan was nowhere to be found. Sunni returned home after spending an hour in town. She began to pace; she was angry. She would continue to call her house until Sloan makes an appearance.

After the tenth phone call, Sunni was informed Sloan had returned, but Sunni was forbidden to talk with her. She looked at her watch. It was now 7:00 p.m. She decided to bake some pies.

After Sloan removed herself from Clay's car, she ran the remainder of the way home. No sooner had she opened the door to her house, she heard the sound of her papa's shoes pounding the floorboards. She knew she was in for the worst mouth-lashing of her young life. She was prepared; she would allow no one to take away this day or the ones to follow.

Her papa's face was contorted, his anger apparent. He took a hold of her arms; she could feel and taste his spit upon her face. She tried to speak above his outburst.

"Papa, please, I can explain."

He continued the slinging of his words. "How could you do this to us? Your mama and I were worried to death something dreadful had happened to you.

"You are an ungrateful brat. I can't believe you are my daughter, and I don't want to hear your pitiful excuse; no explanation would wash away your deceit.

"You will do without dinner, for we have already eaten, as you are well aware. You will never again leave this house. You are grounded indefinitely. Get out of my sight. You disgust me."

Mama was standing beside Papa; she never disagreed with him in front of their children. She would wait to voice her opinion in the privacy of their bedroom if she disagreed with his measure of discipline, for Sloan would listen at their door whenever one of the kids got scolded and Papa yielded a punishment. She would not be listening at their bedroom door this evening, nor any day thereafter. She remained standing. She made no effort to leave until she felt the strength of his words crushing her heart.

"What the hell are you waiting for?"

She never thought her papa would make her cry. He loved her too much. She removed the shoe that still contained the money she had shoved deep within. She threw his money back at him.

"Here's your stupid money. I didn't use it. I never want anything from you ever again. I hate you, Papa."

She ran crying from the room. Apparently her sisters and little brothers were told to remain at the dinner table, for she caught a glimpse of them staring at her as she passed the opening into the kitchen. She flew up the stairs to take refuge in her bedroom located on the second floor.

She would carry those hateful words her entire life, for something was gaining in force, setting out to destroy. In less than an hour, her mama lay beside her, stroking her daughter's long, dark hair, always amazed at the strong resemblance between her and her papa.

"Your papa loves you so much, all he did was pace the floor, he was that concerned about your welfare. He didn't mean a word of what he said. In the morning he will be remorseful, wait and see.

"Honey, you need to forgive him, for if you carry this with you, it will turn you into a bitter person. Words cannot bring the wrath of God down on your papa and neither should you."

She turned over to face her mama.

"Mama, he was so unfair. Missing dinner one time should not have been the catastrophe he is making it out to be. Something extraordinary happened and he wouldn't let me tell him. He just blew me off."

"You can tell me about this extraordinary thing, I'll listen."

"No. Papa ruined it. I can't tell you without him, I'm sorry."

"It's okay, honey. Like I said, tomorrow your papa will be his old self and then you can tell us together.

"I brought you something to eat. You must be hungry. It's chicken, your favorite."

Sloan would have laughed in any other situation. She politely refused. Beth let her be; she figured Sloan would also be her old self in the morning.

As her mama kissed her good-night and before she left her room for the night, Sloan told her she was going to sleep outside by the barn. She would use the sleeping bag Sunni gave her a couple of years back.

Chrissie, the next in birth order, was also concerned about Sloan. She loved her deeply, and if you want to call it eavesdropping on the conversation between her sister and her mama, she really did not care. Chrissie was happy her mama did not enforce the penalty of being grounded from leaving the house.

Sunni tapped on the door to the Parkers' residence. Chrissie answered the door. They greeted one another kindly. Sunni asked to see Sloan. Chrissie, the younger version of her mama, told her no one can visit with Sloan until papa gives the okay. Sunni respected his right.

As she turned to leave, Chrissie quietly called her back and whispered in her ear.

"She is going to spend the night outside by the barn; she will be using the sleeping bag you gave her."

Sunni gave a nod and thanked her. Chrissie escaped back into the house.

Sunni was back at the Parkers' within a half hour. She made four cream pies for the family.

This time, Chrissie's mama heard the knock. Beth noticed the pies lying side by side in a wagon Sunni had pulled up to their house.

"Mrs. Parker, I know you have a problem, but I'm confident it will go away. I baked these pies hopefully to put a smile on everyone's face, for it's a known fact sugar is the spice of life…kind of corny, huh? But I love you all very much, and when something affects you, it affects me."

Beth gave her a hug and thanked her for being so thoughtful. Together they pulled the wagon into the house. Beth sounded out for everyone to come help her; she had a surprise for them.

The "pack," what Sunni called them, came running. Sure enough, they were giddy with happiness; they loved anything sweet. Sunni said her good-nights. The red wagon was left for a later pick-up.

Sloan made a decision while lying in bed. She would run away with Clay on the appointed day. She would not confide in her folks.

She was by far not stupid; she knew someday she would need proof of who she is. Family birth certificates were kept in a blue folder in her folks' desk. She would bide her time.

Before long her siblings started climbing the stairs; it was time for their eyes to rest. As her sisters passed, they never said a word. They respected her agony.

Before long everyone's eyelids closed. She quietly made her way down the stairs. The desk was located in the hallway just off her folk's bedroom. She cautiously slid the drawer open; the file she was searching was easy to spot by its color.

She quickly thumbed through the papers when she spotted her folks' marriage certificate. Tears could not be contained; she would miss them so.

She did not have time to linger. She urgently searched, and finally she had it within her hand. There was no denying, she truly did exist. She stared at the typewritten words: Sloan J. Parker, date of birth May 22, 1967. She had to get a move on, lest she be found out.

She folded and tucked the certificate into the waistband of her too-tight pajamas and slowly closed the drawer. Lying at her feet was her sleeping bag; she gathered the bag close as she tiptoed out the back door, the sounds of the door scraping on the chipped tile she had no control of. For a brief second that sound reminded her of something. She just couldn't put her finger on it.

She quickly tossed that thought aside as she made her way in the direction of the barn. She would also push aside thoughts of her papa and force herself to dream happy thoughts.

The night would get blacker before the dawn.

The moment Clay stepped into his apartment; he placed a call to his father. It was very late in the evening. The phone rang three times before a pick-up.

"Father, I'm sorry if I've awakened you, but I just got into town and what I have to say could not wait.

"I met her; I met my mother. She is gorgeous and with a wit similar to Grandmother. I can see why you fell in love with her. She is enchanting, and the best part, Ali is her neighbor. There are reasons I never got to see her, which I will explain later, but thanks to Mother and her interaction, Ali did call at the cabin I rented in their hometown.

"We talked for some time, and she promised she will visit in three weeks. I've never had such a feeling of contentment and peace of mind. It's a marvelous feeling.

"And Father, if you are standing, I'd advise you to sit down. Something happened you thought would never happen. I found the woman I intend to spend my life with residing in the same little town as my mother and my aunt.

"Your Cupid days are over. And knowing you as well as I do, you need not hold your breath, for she will be a part of our family in two weeks.

"But Father, please keep what I've told you to yourself. I want to see grandmother's face when

I tell her I found her baby and the woman she said would someday steal my heart."

Phillip would never take away that pleasure. When his boy talked of his mother, he turned back the clock and his beautiful, sweet Jena was still a part of his life. He was dreaming the impossible. He would carry this love till death did him in.

When his boy spoke of finding that special someone to share his life, he remembered his attempt at playing Cupid, setting him up with all the desirables. They were more than willing. Clay shared his arm with many beautiful women, at concerts, plays, and the theater, not to forget the never-ending social functions, always repeating the same tireless reply: "Something is missing."

He decided to give his boy all the space he needed. If it did happen, it would be on Clay's time. Although he would not admit it, he was still on the lookout.

His boy would now have the life that was denied him. His boy managed to do what no one else could accomplish; he not only found Phillip's sister, Ali, but was reunited with his mother.

But Phillip's days of ultimate happiness would come to an end when the core of his soul was ripped apart with more tragedies.

Clay awoke with a smile on his lips. He could not remember a day in his life that brought so much excitement. His beloved grandmother would never again have to endure another day of not knowing if her daughter was alive or dead. He would present her with the gift of life, her Alexandria.

He hurried through his shower and nicked himself while shaving, toilet tissue as always his savior. He placed a call to his chauffer, Gus; his services were primarily used for visits with Clay's grandmother on her estate in the Hamptons. Gus was in reality an errand boy, a sort of pick-up and delivery type guy, but he had no reason to complain, as he was paid extremely well.

As for Clay, he had no use of his driving skills, as he lived within walking distance to his workplace.

Gus was waiting alongside the limo when Clay walked out the main entrance to his apartment. He threw his arms up in the air, similar to the raised hands in church praising our Lord.

"What a glorious day, do you not agree, Gus?"

He agreed with his boss, wondering what was up to make this day grander than the priors. To him, they have all been great.

Gus was a tall black man, clean-shaven and always smiling. He was also born with the gift of gab. He was happily married with one boy. He has been in Clay's employ for over five years. He was more of a friend than an employee, although Clay always treated everyone as he would want to be treated, with respect and kindness. Money does not give anyone the right to thumb his nose at others less fortunate.

No sooner than Gus opened the car door, allowing his boss to enter, he started yakking. Clay noticed Gus's lips moving even after he closed the door. Clay followed his movements as he made his way to the driver's side; he never missed a beat moving his mouth.

Clay had to laugh; he really enjoyed his company. His drive was more than pleasant; Gus never failed to entertain him. God gifted the world with someone special when He made Gus.

The hour passed quickly. Clay did not call ahead; he wanted to surprise his grandmother. Gus pulled up to the entrance. He put the car in the correct gear and then opened his door and ran around to the opposite side, his hand ready to grip the door handle, allowing his boss to emerge. Gus would stay around to drive him back to his apartment.

Art was Clay's grandmother's butler. He had been in her employ close to thirty-years after their faithful and trustworthy butler Franklin was fired due to what the elder Joseph Clayton Chadsworth considered disloyalty. Art welcomed Clay and his huge smile into his grandmother's home. Art knew him well.

Something was up. It was going to be a splendid day.

# CHAPTER FOURTEEN

The night caller from the Doc's office, during Saul's visit, thought the time right. The night hid the stars, the moon its face. Everything was set in motion.

The caller, dressed in black with gloved hands and feet covered in thick socks, was extremely quiet. The plan was well thought out. No mistakes would happen this night while safely waiting until the hand on the clock strikes midnight, the witching hour. The caller was quiet, seeking assurance that everyone would be fast asleep.

Earlier in the day the caller hid an extra large container of gasoline, now in hand, plus a box of matches was ready for use. The first stop was the main floor, stopping long enough to take the family photo from the living room; it was shoved under the caller's shirt.

Proceeding up the stairs to the second floor, the caller entered the large room and finished pouring the remainder of the gasoline. Standing now at the entrance to the room, the caller dropped the lit match and watched as the flames followed the path they were given, searing their way through and beyond.

The running was the easy part. The caller could accomplish any task if it involved the slaying of innocent people.

The top floor was taking off in a blaze. The heavy-socked intruder gained more speed running through the first floor, finishing off the task, and then quickly headed out toward the cornfield. The container of gasoline now empty and clutched tightly would be disposed of deep into the woods. Removing the telltale evidence was a must.

Lying belly down within the field, face resting in hands, elbows pressed onto the hardened soil, the thrill of the caller's life unfolded. Flames were licking at the walls, dancing around the house, bellowing out of the doors.

Two of the older girls appeared at the top floor window. Hair glowing like that of a volcanic eruption; they began pounding on the window glass with objects causing the glass to shatter. This is a definite no-no. The blast of air added more fuel to the already searing flames, causing the blaze to pick up at a faster tempo.

The caller watched as the two flame-coated bodies jumped from the glassless window lighting their way downward. A fire-encrusted wall followed, collapsing on top of them. The caller was satisfied. No one in that household would ever again make decisions that were not theirs to make. It was time to make an exit.

Sirens blasted into the night. Neighbors were awakened to what sounded like an explosion. They began running from their homes towards what they now knew to be the Parkers' blazing home. The wiring that provided telephone service was in heavy use for those unaware, and transportation was provided for those without the use of a vehicle.

As more of the townspeople arrived, arms reached out seeking comfort, when none would come. Screams and cries of anguish matched the sirens. It was beyond belief that the Parker family would never again see another sunset.

This would be the worst tragedy to which this community would ever bare witness. To count those in attendance would have been impossible.

Harriet was in a deep sleep, the kind of sleep she had not had in months. She heard the piercing screams first, and then sirens signaling the arrival of the fire truck. The police on duty were there to lend a helping hand.

She called out for Marc repeatedly, receiving no response. She was in a stupor, not quite awake when she stumbled out into the night. The robe thrown about her shoulders did nothing to cover her short nightgown or conceal her very evident pregnancy.

When she stepped out into the night air, she could smell the smoke. It was everywhere. Men and women, risking their own lives, began helping one another. There was no escaping the bellows of black smoke and the intensity of the heat.

A few that had previously stood no more than sixty feet from the source of the fire were now distancing themselves. If they shoved their friends or knocked their neighbors to the ground, they couldn't have cared less. They were showing their true colors; their thoughts were only of their own safety. They would be remembered by their actions and shunned; they would eventually pack up and leave. Shame is a terrible burden to carry throughout a person's lifetime.

And then there were neighbors that would sacrifice their own lives if they could save the Parkers. They refused to back away when told to do so; they continued to gather numerous buckets of water, doing all they could to help those poor lost souls inside. They would be remembered for their courage. Brains are not functioning at full capacity when the impossible is evident.

The firefighters fought the good fight, but they knew it was useless. They faced a towering inferno upon their arrival. To direct traffic would have been impossible, but they need not have worried; there was nothing they could do.

A few of the neighbors, crying uncontrollably, ran from the horror, something the Parkers were unable to do.

Harriet could not see a thing, the smoke that dense. She could not control her coughing. She thought she noticed some firefighters, but wasn't sure, the smoke was that black. She looked at her hands; they were dusted with soot.

It was then she heard a familiar voice. It was Sunni. She was stumbling towards her, screaming.

"Oh, God, Harriet, I can't believe it, they're gone, every one of them. I tried to get them out, but the flames held me back. What are we ever going to do without them? I cannot continue to live my life without Sloan. I wish to God I had died with them."

She fell to her knees, sobbing. Harriet did not stay around to comfort her. She had no idea what Sunni was blubbering about. Her mind was still in a blur.

Did she mention Sloan? Did she hear correctly? Of course not. She would find out for herself what was happening. She just wished she wasn't so exhausted. The long walk to her friend's house for the second time this day could put her future walking days on hold, but tonight she was determined to seek her out.

Neighbors, friends, and many she was not personally acquainted with were either running or sitting in the road. She wished she could get her bearings. The smoke was blinding her path and the coughing continued. She stopped and turned her head in the direction of her house, thinking, "What if I jeopardize my baby's health with all this smoke?" She made her decision; she would return.

It was then she noticed the Doc. He was walking toward her. He had called ahead for two ambulances, possibly three, if they were available.

The Doc reached out to gather Harriet into his arms.

"My dear, sweet Harriet, I wish I could find the words to ease your pain, to make this disappear, but I cannot. I know the extent of your love for Beth and her family.

"To seek an answer to this ghastly tragedy, you must turn to God. He is your only source to provide the kind of comfort and understanding you will need in the days and weeks ahead." Tears were making streaks down his smoke-covered face.

Harriet looked at the Doc as if he were crazy.

"What kind of nonsense are you talking about? I was just with my Beth a few hours ago. We laughed as we shared fantastic news. You are either out of your mind or you are mistaken. Take your pick."

She tried to push him out of her way. She would return to her best friend's house. She would prove the Doc wrong.

The Doc, in turn, used restraint.

"Let me go. She needs me. My Beth needs me."

Harriet could no longer stand. She collapsed. The ground would be her resting place until the Doc made other arrangements.

She shed no tears.

She began talking to herself.

"I'm coming, Beth. I'll be right there, honey." Harriet had gone into shock.

The Doc yelled for someone to get a blanket and a pillow immediately. Harriet would not return to reality for several weeks.

All the townspeople were either sitting or lying about the ground, bewildered and crying. Many were huddled together in cars and trucks. Some were seen kneeling, praying for a miracle when none would come. Doc was finalizing his ground search after Harriet was taken to the hospital for observation when a piercing scream echoed through the night air; it seemed to have no end.

He started running towards the agonizing sound of unrelenting pain. Lying among the drenched ashes lay Sloan. She was beating the ground with her fists, screaming and crying for her mama and papa.

Her nightclothes were completely embellished with the remains of her home, and soot covered her face and arms. Doc picked her up and drew her close. She gave no resistance.

There was no doubt she would need care in the days ahead, perhaps weeks.  His wife, Miriam, would be more than willing, her home and heart always open to those in need.

The fire chief began asking questions from the folks who stayed around. He wanted to know if they had seen or heard anything that precipitated the fire. Everyone shook their heads. What could they know? All lights were turned out for the night.

When the tragedy circulated throughout the communities, reporters from all the networks bombarded the small town.

The headline shouted its findings:

"Voracious house fire claims the lives of 12 family members, 10 of them children."

"Dr. Malcolm Harrison of Mason's Mill, where the fire erupted, is making a frantic plea for help. He is in desperate need of firefighters that are willing to sacrifice their time sorting through the burned rubble to remove the bodies so they can be sent to the medical examiner for identification."

The dentist, Samuel Otts, has been the town's dentist for well over thirty years. A short, stocky man, married with two adult children, provided his services to the Parkers for free. And yes, like the Doc, a bill was sent each month. Never would they step on someone's dignity. Besides, he enjoyed the Parkers' well-behaved children.

He would have done it for free, with or without digging into Saul's pocket.

He, too, would shed many a tear over their deaths. He would send all the dental records to the medical examiner's office. The Doc as well would provide all the medical files on each member of the family.

Firefighters answered the Doc's plea; they came in droves. The coroner, Henry White, was there to bag each body. Hearses and ambulances were called in to take the bodies to the medical examiner's office. This would be a tedious and painstaking task.

The medical examiner concluded his exam: "The remains of each family member are now correctly identified as to who is who, but it really shouldn't have mattered who lies beneath a specific headstone. Dead is dead."

When those ill-mannered words were spoken, Doc was speechless. This was totally out of character for a medical examiner. He made a grave error. He quickly tried to right his words, but he failed miserably.

"I am deeply sorry. It was a slip of the tongue, although that is no excuse. I have been in this business far too long."

Now he was beginning to sound like the sheriff. Wonders would never cease.

Now that all the bodies were accounted for and identified, the morticians could prepare the remains for burial. Each family member would be provided a casket according to their size. The services could now begin.

The investigation, if that was what you could call it, ended with probable cause electrical, the house being well over 150 years old.

Although the firefighters detected a strong odor of gasoline, they could not tie it in to the full fuel container found locked and stored in a metal cabinet in the Parkers' barn. They searched the property extending into the fields. Nowhere could a gas container be found, and therefore, they deemed it electrical.

The fire chief needed to talk to the lone survivor; he wanted to know how that could be. When he eventually did receive the information about Sloan's whereabouts and why she was where she was, he felt downright ashamed for thinking she had been a part of that catastrophe.

County Valley Hospital, where the critical care patients were taken, were now in capable hands. Doc's personal attention was no longer required, except in the case of Harriet. He called the hospital, making arrangements for Harriet to be admitted into a 24-hour nursing care center located next to the hospital.

A new dawn had begun; the sun bright, the day dark.

Doc's wife, Miriam, was comforting Sloan. She was given some medication to relieve some of her stress. Miriam was about to take her to one of the guest rooms to ready her for bed when Sunni appeared out of nowhere. She stood at the main door to the house, sobbing, distraught and covered in soot.

Miriam had totally forgotten her daughter and the intense trauma she, too, had to be going through. She gently laid Sloan back down upon the sofa, pulling her legs up off the floor, again making her as comfortable as possible. She was in dire need of a bath, one she would not see until the day of her family's burial.

Miriam ran to Sunni, now her main concern. It was at this point Sunni noticed her beloved friend. She pushed her mother aside and took her place beside her friend, cupping her legs beneath her body, her arm draped across Sloan's stomach, her head resting on her breast. Sloan stared into the beyond; no acknowledgment was given.

With the return of Doc in the early morning, he had already decided his new tenant's home would be their home. Sunni would never again be this happy.

Ben had taken several days off work to visit with some of his college friends. Replacements were readily available, whether it be for vacation or sick time. He was not aware what had taken place four days earlier. Doc had many details to take care of before his call to Ben. Ben in his capacity could do no more than what the Doc had already taken care of. This day in Ben's life would be like no other.

The call came in at Motel 6, where Ben planned on staying for the week. Doc requested information on the sheriff's whereabouts at the police station, which was given with no resistance. He also requested time off from his hospital duties. This, too, was met with no resistance. Doc's part-time nurses closed the office until further notice.

It being early in the morning, Ben had not yet taken leave from his room to continue socializing with his friends, for he and his friends had really tied one on earlier in the evening. On the fifth ring, Ben's muffled voice spoke into the receiver.

"What time is it?" No hello was given.

"It's 7:30 a.m. Ben, this is Malcolm. I need for you to return home immediately. Something dreadful has happened, and Harriet needs you. I will be at my office in town. Please make haste."

Doc sounded like an answering machine: get to the point and hang up.

Ben could tell by Doc's voice that he was unable to discuss what was troubling him. Sooner than not, the disaster would unfold, holding him speechless. He couldn't get dressed fast enough. The thoughts swirling around inside his head were making him sick. Doc said Harriet needed him; it wasn't like, "Hurry home,

Harriet died." He felt a little better after analyzing the Doc's words.

He paid his motel bill, left messages with the motel clerk alerting his friends to the call he received, and quickly departed. His prayer beads were hidden somewhere in his car, although they were never used. He was determined to find them. Fifteen minutes later they were put to good use on his hour journey back home.

Sad but true, the majority of us are guilty of the offense of calling on the 'Guy' upstairs only in the time of need.

Ben crossed over the bridge into his town and noticed how it appeared ghost-like. He pressed his foot to the gas pedal, braking quickly in front of the Doc's office, the closed sign hanging lopsided. You wouldn't think, with his size and weight and always seen sitting in a chair, he could move as swiftly as he did.

Doc was seated in his waiting room, head cupped into his hands, sobbing for all the young lives that held such promise, but now will never be. Ben's heart started pounding, his gut speaking out.

He flew through the door. Doc turned his face upward. His tear-coated face shook Ben. He did not want to hear or see anything the Doc had to say.

He started crying without any warning of what was to come. They usually shook hands;

this time they embraced. They continued sitting, each waiting for the other to speak; one to ask questions, the other to give answers.

Doc was the first one to find the courage to speak out. When he finished with the nightmare and how Sloan had survived and was now staying at his home, Ben felt a slight measure of relief, for his beloved Harriet adored her. Ben totally understood why his sweetheart had been placed in a nursing home, but Ben had questions of his own.

"Doc, does the fire marshal have any idea as to what caused the fire? Is there going to be an investigation?"

"Ben, the fire marshal said everything pointed to electrical. Frayed wires were exposed throughout the house. The Parkers' house, sad to say, was a fire trap. I'm sorry, Ben, but the investigators that were called in concurred with the fire marshal. End of story."

Ben was beside himself.

"Something is going on in our town and no one seems to give a shit. Malcolm, we need to stick together on this. You have to back me up. We must demand another investigation. With you in my corner, we just might get what we ask for. Are you with me?"

What could Doc say? He was tired.

"All right. If that's what you want, I'll go along with your request. But if they don't comply, we let it go, okay? I mean it, Ben."

"Yes, yes, of course, but I know they won't turn both of us down."

Doc knew Ben would want another investigation. Let's face it, all of us at one time or another get plain tired of just sitting on our asses. Ben was no exception.

In the end, Ben would have to settle for electrical. His superior would not reopen the investigation. Most men would roll with the punches; Ben was not such a man. He would spend his career chasing his rainbow. An investigation, any investigation would do.

Doc had not yet finished with what he had to tell Ben about Harriet.

"Have you talked to Harriet since you left on vacation?"

Ben shook his head. Harriet knew his whereabouts, but she would never interfere with the little leisure time he managed to grab for himself.

The Doc picked up from where he left off.

"Well…she came to see me. I would not ordinarily divulge any information on my patients because of the privacy issue. But in this case, I feel you need to know, only because it involves you personally and because of her present state.

"Harriet is pregnant with your child, Ben. Your baby is due in about five months."

Ben's gasp sounded much louder than it really was. He started crying and would not stop until his tears were spent. He was to be a daddy. He was past the point of being happy; he was elated. There was no doubt his sweetheart would now marry him.

Doc also alerted Ben to the possible complications because of her condition.

"Harriet is in shock, and I have no idea how long it will take for her to come out of it. Sometimes it takes a few days, other times weeks or months. The baby could come early.

"I'm telling you this so that you will be prepared. I will monitor her and the baby every day. The mind has to have time to heal. It's no different than the body. She will return to the living when she's ready."

Ben understood, but he couldn't sit still any longer. He removed himself from his chair. What he really needed now was to see his sweetheart, if only for a few minutes.

He apologized to the Doc for his abrupt departure. Doc was relieved Ben was happy with the news about being a daddy. You just never know what someone's reaction will be to that kind of news.

Ben wept for his sweetheart when he saw her. Nothing he would say or do brought forth an acknowledgement. He left her with four words: "I love you, sweetheart."

Sheriff Ben and the Doc would work side by side making the funeral arrangements. The tombstones would be inscribed with the Parkers' full names, their birth dates and death.

In time, something extraordinary would take place, and because of this, the Parkers' grave site would be as much of an attraction as the fishing.

Mercy Church the Parkers attended did not believe in cremation, despite the fact their bodies were near that point. The Baxter Mortuary was within walking distance to Pleasant View Nursing Home where Harriet was admitted. They were contracted to take care of the Parkers' remains.

The caskets, headstones, and burial grounds, plus the services rendered by the funeral home, were donated with the funds left to the church following the death of Silva. If it wasn't so horribly sad, the townspeople would have snickered, their thoughts on Silva.

"I'll bet she's rumbling around in her grave over this."

The funeral services would be conducted outdoors due to the attendance and the many caskets that would have overcrowded the funeral home. Pastor Riley of Mercy Church, along with the funeral director, decided to hold a service in the Parkers' memory in the park overlooking the lake, the same lake the many tourists fished. There would be neither tourists nor fishing that day in the park.

To show respect to each victim, twelve hearses, many of which had to be bought from various funeral homes throughout Pine County, were escorted by two limousines that proceeded down the highway towards Mason's Mill.

Cars, trucks, minivans and motorcycles traveling the road pulled to the shoulder when they realized an out-of-the-ordinary tragedy had to have occurred for so many hearses. Many were wiping their eyes with tissues; some just placed their heads on their hands secured on the steering wheel, praying they would never again see such a sight. Others stared straight ahead, ignoring the convoy; they did not need for this to be a memory.

When the procession of hearses pulled into the shopping center in Mason's Mill, the tourists stood rooted to the sidewalk. Many began to cry, and some cupped their hands over their mouths, stunned. Many were making the sign of the cross, while others fell to their knees in prayer.

The motorcade of hearses followed the exact path the tourists took to the lake.

The pastor, the Doc, and the sheriff, waiting at the lakeside, guided the limousines to the designated areas the caskets were to be placed. It is now six days since the fire.

Sloan had refused to allow anyone to touch her; she retained the clothes she was found in, pajamas. Miriam gave her the space she needed, but enough was enough, she needed to bathe.

She pulled her off the bed she'd occupied since she had been forced to live with them. Sloan tried to push her away; Miriam pulled harder. "Sloan, the harsh reality of your family's deaths can no longer be denied. Their memorial service is today and you need to shower. Honey, you smell."

Sloan pulled away, calling Miriam a bitch, but she agreed to the shower. As she made her way to the bathroom, she began removing her pajamas. When she closed the door behind her, she was naked. The top and the bottom lay on the hardwood floor of the hallway. She stood for several minutes in front of the vanity mirror, staring at someone she didn't recognize.

As her eyes traveled over her body, she noticed something that was clinging to her waist. She peeled it away from her body; it had seen better days, but was readable. Her hand trembled as the memory of that dreadful night replayed. The one thing she felt she needed so badly now seemed useless.

She placed the document on the vanity, keeping an eye on it as she quickly showered and washed her hair, all the while thoughts roaming around in her head. She reached toward the rack that contained the bath towels. That piece of paper, her birth certificate, did have a purpose; it would provide a new life for her. Everyone needs to show proof that you are who you claim to be.

She ran to her room, towel flapping against her.

Sunni had picked up some things in town, dresses, shoes and personal items she felt Sloan would need in the coming days. Among the items was a small black purse with a long strap. Inside was a small zippered compartment; this section would conceal the document. The small handbag would never leave Sloan's side; it would be her bed companion. She was dressed from head to toe in black; she was now ready to attend services for her family.

This July day was beautiful. A soft breeze whispered through the trees. There would be no sweat on this day, only tears. Twelve caskets, side by side, lined the lakefront. Three of the caskets, toddler size, contained what was left of the bodies of Steven, aged three; Tony, aged two; and DanDan, aged one. A male guitarist played 'Amazing Grace' throughout the service.

Pastor Riley stood on the pulpit that was removed from his church by several parishioners; its use today will be for the Parkers.

The pastor started the sermon with a verse taken from the Book of Joshua 1:9.

"Have not I commanded thee? Be strong and of good courage; be not afraid, neither be thou dismayed: the Lord thy God is with thee whithersoever thou goest."

Out of respect for Sloan, the service was not lengthy; a few more words from the pastor would end the sermon.

"God now has in His presence the Parker clan, a family who prayed together, stayed together, and now joins their Heavenly Father together. How fitting is that, for they entered this life as a single entity. Praise be to the Lord. Let us pray."

Everyone bowed their heads in prayer.

At the beginning of the service, everyone was given a dozen white roses. One rose from each will grace each casket, purity in its sweetest form. Hundreds of those roses will end up as cloaks for each of the caskets.

Sloan was led by her pastor to each casket to say her final good-byes. Her papa's casket was the first in the long line, his rightful place being the head of his family.

She remained a robot throughout the service until the pastor took her arm. She fell across her papa's casket, weeping and screaming.

"Papa, Papa, I'm so sorry for what I said. Please forgive me. I don't hate you, I love you, Papa…I love you. Please, Papa…please come back…I need to hear you say you forgive me."

She was out of control. Pastor Riley thought it best to take her away and again place her into Miriam's care. As Sloan was forcibly being drug away, she began biting and scratching anyone who tried to make contact with her. She screamed out for her mama.

"Mama, Mama, I need you. Please, Mama, come and help me…Mama, why won't you help me?"

Cries of anguish could be heard for days. Then silence came calling in the form of reality, for did she not have a date to keep?

A flash of her hours spent before that dreadful night could never be erased from her mind, nor should it. She felt as if she'd waited for that special someone her entire life. She would not take a chance on losing him as she had her family.

She would have someone to love and take care of her, just as her papa had done for her mama. She would not reveal to anyone her newfound love, not even her best friend.

Sunni was overjoyed with her friend's return from possible insanity. She spoke out for the first time since Sloan's loss.

"Sloan, you need to get to the bank immediately and see if they can check out your papa's title to his property and the insurance policy your folks surely would have carried on the house and its contents. You are their only living heir and you are entitled to everything they owned.

"The sooner you get all your affairs in order, the quicker you can get the house rebuilt and sold. This is money in your pocket. It belongs to you, honey."

Sloan did not hesitate. She took her advice. She would waste no more time, for time was not on her side. She would go that day. Sunni offered to drive her to the bank, she declined. She needed to take her papa's truck; she wanted to feel the steering wheel where his hands had been. The slow walk to her house brought forth memories no one should have to remember under these shocking circumstances.

She stared at what used to be her home, now charred and blackened, and soon to be totally discarded as if her home had never been a haven of laughter and happiness.

Her papa's smoke-encased truck needed to be wiped clean. The barn located in the back contained boxes of rags. This, too, in all probability would be cleared away, which was appropriate. The barn belonged with the house; you could not remove one without the other.

The moment she sat where her papa had sat, caressed the steering wheel his hands had touched, her tears returned. She prayed her papa would hear her.

"I miss you so God-awful much, Papa. Please tell Mama I love her. I hurt so badly, the pain is unbearable. It never goes away. I do not know if I can live my life without my family…but I know I have to try. I will never forget you and Mama. I will love you until I breathe no longer. My heart will store all the memories. And I will take all of you on every journey I make."

The key was where it should be, for it never left the ignition. The truck started on the first try; did her papa have a hand in it? She was in a hurry. She would soon have a new life. It was waiting.

She strolled into the bank. If the employees looked in her direction, it was with indifference. The bank was there to service the needs of the people, not to dwell on someone's tragedy.

She approached the first desk she came to, announced her name, and then asked to speak with the bank president. The young woman named Mary sitting at the main desk had dark blond hair that was held back with barrettes, securing straight hair that reached her waistline; she could not have weighed more than ninety pounds.

Her large brown eyes, with no visible iris, were her best asset. Her nose was perfect as well as her pink-coated lips that matched her blouse, skirt, and barrettes. She was like a dainty flower, but would not win a beauty contest.

Mary dialed a number on the phone, spoke a few words, replaced the receiver, and then scooted her chair back from the desk. She stood before speaking.

"Mr. Hewlett will see you, Miss Parker. Please follow me."

The man, who had sworn off women, noticed Miss Parker approaching his glass-enclosed office. He'd known her since she was just a baby. Only now, he really noticed her. He watched her body move like in slow motion, the sway of her hips, the nipples erect against the sheerness of her blouse. This baby was now a voluptuous woman.

He quickly composed himself. He was beginning to get aroused. He swore under his breath, "Damn all women." He rose from his black leather swivel chair, swung around his desk, and managed to open the door just as she was to enter.

He extended his hand toward a seat at the front of his desk; he did not trust himself to shake her hand without feeling the need to touch and caress her body. He returned to his chair. It was women like her that were his downfall.

Well, not exactly like her. No one he ever bedded down would come close to measuring up to this magnificent creature that was now seated before him. This man, William Hewlett, "Willie Boy, the skirt chaser" was not a man to mince words.

"I assume you're here about your father's debt."

"Yes, I am. I know my papa was still indebted to your bank, and I plan on paying back what he owed, but I need to know the exact amount because I plan on selling the property. I was wondering what you think the house would be worth once it's rebuilt, and of course, the land would be included.

"I was informed by my friend that that's why people have insurance. If anything were to happen to someone's property, whether through vandalism, fire, or flood, the insurance pays to replace what has been lost.

"When the house is rebuilt, I plan on putting it on the market, and once it has a buyer, I plan to move away. I can't continue to live here with everything that has happened. Hopefully, I'll have enough money left over from the sale to make a new start."

Mr. Hewlett would have laughed if it weren't so absurd.

"You must be crazy to think you have anything coming. When your father purchased that new tractor and all the necessary attachments to maintain his farm, your house, land, and personal contents were required to secure that loan.

"Your father's loan was five months in arrears. We notified him we were foreclosing well over three weeks ago. He was to be served an eviction notice two days after his death.

"The fire marshal said the fire was definitely of a suspicious nature, but he lacked the evidence to prove it, leaving the only alternative, electrical. I think Sheriff Ben is going to request an investigation.

"I believe your father was embarrassed and ashamed of the many mistakes he made in his lifetime. He was facing a life without a cent in his pocket and nowhere to take his family. He had one out and that was to end his life and the lives of his wife and children. I have no doubt that your father started the fire."

Sloan rose so quickly from her chair; it toppled on its side. She refused to show this lower-than-life creature the tears waiting to escape her eyes.

"I beg your pardon. My papa loved his family, and for you to suggest such a thing is unforgivable. And because he had pride, he doesn't deserve to be tagged as inadequate to care for his family.

"And if anyone should be ashamed, it should be you. In the length of time I've been here, you have yet to express your sympathy over the loss of my family. Twelve people died horribly, three of them just babies."

His comment was swift and curt.

"I'm sorry for you, Miss Parker."

"Sorry for me. You feel sorry for me. How dare you. You are pathetic. These children could have been yours. You have shown no compassion for a family dearly loved in your own community, neighbors of yours, so to speak.

"I didn't come for a handout. I wasn't aware of my folks' circumstances. I now know my papa and mama probably went to their fiery deaths thinking how they could pay their loan before you threw us out onto the dirt road.

"Sir, I will tell you this. You'll receive every penny my papa owed, plus interest, if it takes me my lifetime. This is one promise I intend to keep. Good day to you, sir."

She turned to leave.

The red-faced president thought about what he had to say. He was sure the information would help him make amends.

"Miss Parker, I believe the debt will be paid. We plan on putting the land on the auction block next month. I'm sure we will get what is owed."

Sloan was standing with her back to him, her hand on the door knob, ready to exit. She turned around to face him.

"I don't care what you do with the land; you can stick it where the sun will never set."

The bank president did not hear the door open or close. His eyes misted over; tears dripped from his chin. He could not remember the last time he cried. Oh yes, he does; when his child support payments go out each month. Now, those were tears.

Sloan did not show her true feelings as she walked out of the bank. Once out, she jumped in her papa's truck, knowing full well she was not licensed to drive, but she drove the truck many times when it did start to fetch her papa when her mama needed him.

Rambling over the road back towards Sunni's, she pulled off to the side of the road, for she was blinded by tears. Tears wretch agony deep within. She would cry for a very long time until Sunni drove up in her Jaguar.

Sunni was worried about her friend. It seemed like it was taking way too long for Sloan to get her affairs in order. When she noticed the truck from afar, she slammed on her brakes, jumped out, and flew to her friend. No sooner than Sunni opened the door to the truck, Sloan collapsed into her arms, sobbing hysterically.

"Oh, Sunni, what am I do? The bank owns the land and everything that had been on it. I own nothing and have nothing. Even the clothes on my back belong to you.

"Oh, God, Sunni, why did God take them? I loved them. But all I did was complain about how poor we were. I know this upset them, and yet I never stopped talking about what a waste my life was. Why was I always so cruel to them? They tried so hard to please me.

"Why didn't I return all the hugs my sisters gave me? They were always telling me how much they loved me, yet I can't remember telling them the same. My baby brothers always wanted to give me their slobbery kisses, throwing a storybook on my lap for me to read to them. The words that came out of my mouth were not from a book, but to tell them to get lost,

I had better things to do than read or play with them.

"There has to be something wrong with me. They were just babies. But Sunni, I truly loved them all, I really did."

"Of course, you did. And they knew it. You need to try really hard to put this behind you. You can't continue torturing yourself over something you had no control over. Your papa and mama loved you so much. They would not want you to spend your life grieving over them."

"But Sunni, you have no idea what I'm going through. My stomach is twisted in knots; I can't stand living with this pain. It hurts too much. I just want to die.

"You have always taken care of me, been there for me when I needed your help. I need your help now. I want you to end my life. That is the only way to put an end to this misery. If you truly love me as much as you say you do, you will do this; if you don't, I will find a way myself."

Sunni's hand viciously slapped her across her face. Sloan never in her life had been hit, and to be struck with such a brutal slap by her so-called best friend astounded her. But it accomplished what it was intended to do. She snapped back to reality, her tears ended. She stared at her friend, not believing what she'd done. She could still feel the harsh sting upon her face and the individual finger welts that would surely be there.

"Honey, I'm sorry. You left me no choice. You were out of control.

"Now, you listen to me and you listen well. You will come and live with me. You will never, ever be alone. I love you and I will always take care of you. I will help you get over this pain, and someday your grief will subside. And when it does, you will find happiness where you least expect it."

Sloan indeed knew where she would find her happiness, but it would not be with Sunni.

Both of them were seated upon the running board of her papa's truck, when Sunni gently began rubbing her hand back and forth across Sloan's back, trying to comfort her the only way she knew how. Sloan's hands lay in her lap. She needed what Sunni had to offer, and she would always need it.

They continued to stay parked off the main road. A few trucks passed, noticed the girls, and honked their horns.

Sunni then took notice of a pyramid of rocks across the road from them.

"Sloan, look at that. I've never noticed that before. Who would have done that? It looks as if someone really took their time stacking those rocks. It's huge. That's strange. What would be the purpose?"

Sloan was quick with a reply.

"It was probably just some kids playing around; you know kids and their rocks."

"Sloan, look at the size of those rocks. Many are bigger than a basketball. There is no way kids could pick them up. This had to have been built by adults. I think…"

"Sunni, please, I'm not feeling well, I feel sick at my stomach. I really need to go home…ah…your home."

Sunni stood, pulling Sloan up from her seated position.

"My home is your home, honey, please remember that. Would you like for me to drive you home in my car? I can come back with a neighbor to pick up your truck."

"No, I will not leave my papa's truck stranded. I'll be all right. I just need to lie down. You can follow me. If I have any problems, I'll stop, okay?" Sunni nodded.

Sloan had only a few days left to keep her appointment.

# CHAPTER FIFTEEN

"Where "Where is Marc Anderson?" That was the question on all the townspeople's lips. No one had seen or heard from him in thirteen days. Suspicions in regard to the fire were beginning to focus on him.

Everyone knew his relationship with his mother. He would never leave her alone for one day, let alone two weeks. The sheriff posted a note on the church's bulletin board for a town meeting to be held on Thursday, July 18th.

Today was that day. The townspeople took to their seats as was custom when they attended church services. When the pews were filled, the remainder stood along the perimeter.

Pastor Riley Bucannan shook his head, bewildered his parishioners could attend a meeting, but the majority could not make time for their Creator. He wasn't kidding himself; he already knew the answer; gossip, the key ingredient that was sure to ensue following any meeting. The Pastor relieved himself of his appointed podium, turning it over to the sheriff.

Ben spoke frankly.

"I want to welcome everyone who took time out of their busy lives to attend this crucial meeting. I think many of you probably know what this is all about.

"The tragedy this town has had to endure is beyond words. We all wonder how this could have happened. No one seems to know. All we know is our community has twelve less people gracing us with their presence.

"We have had far too many mishaps occurring in our hometown. Is it just a coincidence or do we have an evil among us, threatening our very existence?

"Well, I'm here to tell you, I will no longer sit by and watch whatever it is destroy us. I will find the predator reigning his disease and put an end to it. So help me God."

Everyone in the pews rose from their seats. The applause was deafening.

This day there were smiles; there would be no more tears. Ben would do his job. Finding Marc was high on his list. Getting out of the church was another matter; everyone had an idea where he could be, roughly shoving to be the first heard. If he took the time to listen to the stories thrown at him, he would see tomorrow's sunrise.

He had neither the time nor the energy. He spoke his thoughts.

"Please, everyone put your comments on paper. I have an enormous undertaking before me. I would appreciate your patience. When I'm able, I will look at each one. But for now, I just don't have the time. Thank you."

This time there was a parting of the ways.

# CHAPTER SIXTEEN

Marc was reeling in anger with Sloan and her reaction to his tumble. If she had any compassion, she would have known how humiliated he was, and yet she laughed along with the others.

And who was the stranger he collided with? He surely didn't live in this area, and his manner of dress didn't qualify him as a great fisherman. No, he was here for something else, but what?

His ability to see into the past and predict the future, a gift from his mother, was growing at a snail's pace. He ran away to escape the embarrassment he was left to endure. He sought out a wooded area after he reclaimed his rifle, taking no notice of his kill. He would not be responsible for the death of some child if they happened across the gun. His catch was no longer of interest.

He was well-hidden from the view of passersby, settling himself in the woods across from the cabins midway down from the sheriff's jail house. He would wait patiently for Sloan's return; he would still see her safely home.

He dropped to the ground, his rifle safely beside him and the road barely visible as he pressed his back onto the truck of a tree, his knees drawn up to his chest. Hours passed; he refused to take his eyes off the road.

When the stranger appeared again, he was seen coming out of Cabin 1. The car Sloan caressed had to belong to him. He was as tall as Marc, that being the only comparison. He watched as he closed the cabin door and then the screen. He thought he might be leaving, but instead he turned left into town. Marc continued to wait.

The stranger returned, carrying two bags. He stood to get a better look, tearing at the brush in front of him. The stranger stopped just before entering his cabin, his back facing towards Marc. Slowly he turned. Marc quickly pushed the tangled mess back into place. Did the stranger see him? No, of course not. Marc was secure in his choice of coverage.

The stranger started to turn away, thought better, and turned again to peer into the woods. He was aware of something, but saw nothing. He shook his head and entered the cabin.

Marc glanced at his watch. The bags the stranger had in his grip could contain food, for in his calculations, it was nearing dinnertime. But still Sloan made no appearance.

She must have returned home, he thought, remembering their earlier conversation. Dinner with her family was a must. He was heartsick with missing her. He turned to make his way towards home. If he had waited a little longer, would the outcome have been different?

No, for destiny was fast approaching.

Marc continued to make his way deeper into the woods. He took no notice that he was wandering off his familiar track, his thoughts never off Sloan. He walked and walked, mumbling to himself all the while. "I love you, Sloan, and if you think that by laughing at me, I will give you up, I've got news for you. I will have you, and by God, you will accept me as your husband. This is my solemn oath."

Finally something shook him out of his dreamlike state. He was bewildered. When had night shown its face? But that wasn't all that was baffling him. He was lost. He would have to wait until the sun warmed his face. He crouched down against a tree, thinking he would wait the night out, but sleep hunkered down with him.

He knew not the time when awakened by an ungodly amount of smoke invading his lungs. His coughing could not be heard among the screams and cries of the night.

He grabbed his rifle, running back to where he'd previously come from. Fresh air was what he was seeking. When it was found, he huddled back down. Only until he was fully conscious did he wonder where the smoke was coming from.

He continued to sit, his rifle now his constant companion; then a bulb turned on. He started running again, this time towards the smoke. He pulled a handkerchief from his pocket to cover his mouth as the hacking cough began. He was blinded by the smoke, but recognized the townspeople, yet they took no notice of him. They appeared dazed and disoriented.

He apparently was among the first of several to arrive; to what, he had no idea. His mind contained one thought: "What the hell is going on?" He had to find the source from where the smoke was coming.

A very small child, whose age he was unsure of, was seated on an old log close to the ground, where it appeared as if there wasn't much smoke. Marc thought, "Smart kid." A scarf was tied around his face; his eyes the only things peering out. It must have been helping; he wasn't coughing like the adults.

Marc approached him and crouched down by the little boy's side.

"Are you all right, my little man?"

"I'm okay. I'm just sleepy. Mama yanked me from my bed and started running to her car. She said a house was on fire and she wanted to see if she could help. She put me here and told me to stay put. I just want to go home and go to bed.

Will you take me home?"

"I can't take you away without your mama knowing. She would be sad if you were missing. Can you tell me your name?"

"My name is David J. Mitchell, but everybody calls me DJ."

"I think I'm going to stay with you, D.J., until your mama comes and gets you, okay? We don't want your mama to get lost."

"No, she gets lost a lot! I'm glad you're staying with me. I saw the fire and it's really big. I'm afraid of fires. Are you afraid of fires?"

"You bet I am. But your mama picked out a safe place, so you'll be okay. Do you happen to know whose house caught on fire?"

"Yeah. Mama started crying when she saw it was the Parkers' house."

Marc gasped. The tears would not be from the smoke. This little man could be mistaken, couldn't he? Of course he could. But he'd made D.J. a promise to stay with him. Promises are not made to be broken.

"I'll be right back. Don't you move from this spot, you hear me? You have to promise me." D.J. promised.

Marc took off running toward Sloan's house, running down anyone that got in his way, the rifle, with its safety on, slapping against his leg. The smoke was getting much worse. He was hacking so badly, it felt as if his lungs were about to explode. But he would stop at nothing until he faced his nightmare, a sweltering fireball.

He screamed out, "God in Heaven, no, please don't let it be." He ran towards the flames. A firefighter managed to grab a hold of his shirt, forcing him away from the bellowing flames.

Marc screamed at him.

"Get the hell out of my way! My girlfriend is in there. She needs my help. Please let me go to her."

"I'm awfully sorry, fellow, but there is no way anyone could survive such a horrific fire." Again, the firefighter gave his condolences.

Marc fell to his knees, sobbing for a life he now knows will never be, wishing he'd died along with his love. He would not stay around to see the remains. He turned back towards his home; he needed to get far away. But before he could try to outrun this hideous nightmare, he couldn't forget his little man. But when he got there, he had already gone. He prayed his mama had come for him.

He managed to make it home. His mother's car was parked next to his truck. Their home was in total darkness. It was apparent his mother wasn't aware of what was going on. He thanked God for that blessing. His mother was safe; he could leave -- or escape, for want of a better word.

He was in shock, not realizing as he went

about doing things he normally did under such dire circumstances. Ben took over the role of a father figure when Marc was a youngster, teaching him how to hunt, and the most important aspect of hunting was to always return the rifle to the locked storage unit located in back of his house; there were no exceptions to the rule.

That task now completed, he all but ran to his truck, gunning the tires as he sped out of the driveway, taking off to parts unknown. He cared not where his truck took him so long as it was nowhere near Mason's Mill. He took nothing with him but the clothes on his back. His checkbook was like his car keys; he never left home without them.

On his first night out, he stopped at a Wal-Mart. He loaded up on shirts, jeans, socks, underwear, deodorant, shampoo, toothpaste and toothbrush, comb, hair brush, and disposable razors.

He would travel hundreds of miles, taking no notice of where he was going or where he had been. He slept when it was forced upon him. He would not remember the many motels he stayed in. He ate only when he felt a headache announcing its arrival, no doubt coming from the lack of food.

No matter how hard the firefighters struggled in their attempt to get the fire under control, it was useless. It was if the fire hoses contained gasoline instead of water. It was if the gate of hell opened, consuming everything in its path.

The town hadn't seen a drop of water for weeks. Everything was parched; even the creeks running helter-skelter throughout the town were beginning to dry up. The fire continued to light its way among the trees and bushes as the smoke made its deposit into the lungs of the townspeople. Oxygen being administered was never-ending. The firefighters would continue long into the night until they were convinced not a spark could be seen. The night was at its end when the firefighters started gathering up their equipment, readying themselves to take their leave. It had an ending that many would carry to their graves.

# CHAPTER SEVENTEEN

Marc had been gone long enough, thirteen days; it was time to return home. It was early morning when his truck pulled into town. The townspeople who owned and operated these shops along with the hired help were a part of the Parkers' community, and yet the activity was as if nothing had happened. Life definitely does go on.

It took all thirteen days to realize the suffering his mother must be going through. She needed him now more than ever. He was ashamed for thinking only of himself. Together they would work through the grieving process.

He pulled into the driveway, her car still parked as when he left. She was safe. He knew, once he entered their home, it could be hours or possibly days before he could leave her.

He needed to see what maybe he didn't see, for his eyes had been badly blinded by smoke. He could have gotten disoriented, mistaking her house for another. Sloan and her family lived a minimum of six blocks; a slight hill blocked his direct view. The house set back a ways from the main road; trees covered most of the front.

He stopped his truck; there was no mistaking the now-blackened and charred trees. He grabbed the steering wheel and buried his face into his knuckles and wept for what he prayed would not have been. His tears blinded him more so than the smoke had.

"Dear God, why? I loved her deeply. I was raised to believe in 'Thy will be done,' but I cannot cope with this. I cannot let her go.

When You took her, You took my heart, for she had a stranglehold from the moment I saw her. You have to tell me, what am I to do now that she is gone?"

His visible tears will not end that day. He turned his truck to return home. He would never again pass this way; the road which led to his heart had vanished.

He pulled alongside of his mother's car. No sooner had he turned the key in the ignition and stepped outside, Ben's patrol car pulled up behind him.

Ben was ready with the handcuffs.

"I'm sorry I have to do this, Marc. I love you like a son, but if I don't arrest you, someone just might take a potshot at you. You'll be much safer in jail. If anything were to happen to you, it will destroy your mother and I as well."

He chose to cuff him in the front. "Marc, I'm sorry, but I need to read you your rights. You have the right to remain silent. Anything you say can be used against you in a court of law. You have the right to have an attorney present during questioning. If you cannot afford an attorney, one will be appointed for you.

"Do you understand these rights as told to you?"

Marc responded with a "yes." It wasn't as if he had a choice. This had been the most insufferable thirteen days of his life, and now this.

"Ben, I don't know what this is all about, but I need to see my mother before you take me off to jail. I haven't seen her for two weeks. I know how much she loved the Parkers and I know she's devastated with their loss."

Ben refused his request. Marc was puzzled when Ben reached for a handkerchief in the back pocket of his uniform. He turned away, pretending to blow his nose, when it was evident he was wiping away tears. Marc screamed out of fear for his mother.

"Oh, my God, there is something wrong with my mother, isn't there? Is she hurt? Is she sick? Oh, my God, she's dead, isn't she?"

"No, no, Marc. She's okay."

"Then what in God's name is happening here? You arrest me for God only knows what, and then you refuse to let me see my mother. No way am I not going to see my mother."

He took off in a run. He was three steps up and just about to kick in the door of his house when Ben shouted.

"Marc, wait! She's not inside."

Mark turned back towards Ben.

"She's been placed in a nursing facility. She went into shock after learning about the Parkers' deaths."

Marc lowered himself onto the top step. This was much more than he could handle. He just glared at Ben.

"You inform me of this after you arrest me. What was I supposed to have done, murdered somebody?"

The look Ben gave him left no room for doubt. Ben then told him he was being charged with arson and murder of the Parker family.

"This is obscene. No one will conceive I could do something so horrendous.

"What is wrong with you, Ben? You know me. I may as well take a gun and blow out my mother's brains. She couldn't live with the knowledge I destroyed the one person she loved more than life itself.

"Ben, do whatever you want with me. Jail me, hang me, shoot me, just let me see my mother first…please, I beg of you."

Marc's tears were now for his mother. Ben would not have been at Marc's house to check it out if he had not begun to get numerous phone calls at the police station. It seemed as if all of the townspeople had their nose stuck out their window on the lookout for this hardened criminal.

Ben knew in his gut, and no, it was not hurting, that his son, as he would be proud to call him, could not have committed such a heinous crime, or any crime, for that matter.

He grabbed a hold of Marc and removed the handcuffs, telling him to get in the back and lay on the floorboard. Ben would take him to see his mother, come hell or high water. He deserved that much.

Their driveway sloped downward. Six cars could easily park. The only thing visible from the road would have been the woods, part of her house, and the roof. It was hidden quite well from prying neighbors. Neighbors could only notice the sheriff's patrol car when it backed onto the roadway.

He drove cautiously, keeping an eye out for any of the townspeople walking about. He had to drive through town. That meant someone could wave him over either to chat or ask questions. His solution:, turn on the siren and speed it up. They would move out of his way thinking he was in hot pursuit of Marc. To the townspeople, that was the reason for the flashing lights. You'd have to live in a small town to understand how these people think. Some of them shouted as he flew past.

"Go get him, sheriff, get that baby killer."

Horns blared as he passed. The nursing home was a ten- minute drive. Once he was on the highway, he turned off the siren and the flashing lights. He pulled over to let Marc sit in the front as a passenger. He began talking about his mother.

"Marc, I've been visiting with your mother every day since she was admitted. I'm sorry to say she is not responding to anyone or anything. They are feeding her intravenously.

"For the time being, she is in her own little world. They do get her up to prevent bed sores. Her nurse takes her outside in a wheelchair to allow her some fresh air. She said she seems to prefer the outdoors.

"I think she just says that to make me feel better. Your mother would have to give some kind of reaction if this were so, and trust me, she is not. I spend as much time with her as I can. I love her more than I have loved anyone in my entire life. She's my little sweetheart."

He again removed his handkerchief to wipe his eyes while making the statement, "I've never grown out of my childhood allergies."

"I know what you mean, I have the same problem."

They looked at each other with understanding.

"Before I go to see her, I light a candle in church. I pray to God he will bring her back to us. Maybe you are the one she needs to see and hear. If she doesn't respond, don't get discouraged. The doctors say she will eventually come around. We just need to have patience."

Marc understood.

Ben pulled up in front of the nursing home. He parked in the designated area for police. The design of this "home" was brilliant. The landscaping, with a multitude of trees, evergreens, and flowers of every imaginable color, graced the entrance. In front of the home was a circular drive that drew attention to an enormous seven-tier fountain surrounded by a colorful array of begonias. The waterfall was an invitation to God's feathered friends as well as the wildlife that roamed the fields and forests.

Immense columns stood firm under a canopy offering shade to all those who entered. Marc's mother would appreciate the architectural beauty of the place that would be her home for some time.

Ben and Marc approached a well-appointed desk, behind which sat the full-time receptionist, Alayna. She was a light brunette with wide-set hazel eyes and a rather large nose. Her lips were well-defined, painted with scarlet red lipstick. Her chosen outfit, a pantsuit, matched the color of her lips.

As was customary, they both had to sign their names and time of arrival. Upon leaving, this was repeated with time of departure.

The nurses called out with a "hello." Ben was a daily visitor since Harriet's admittance and was well-liked.

The corridor had recessed lighting throughout. The walls, painted a soft melon, were complemented with tan overtones; the wainscoting that covered the lower part of the wall was the color of wheat. The wood flooring was made of a high-polished smooth bamboo with a runner the color of cinnamon.

Each patient had their own room. Harriet's room, with its massive opened bay window, gave an outside view of a grand garden; flowering trees and mounds of planted flowers gave off a delightful scent captured within the room. The outside tables and chairs were arranged in such a manner the patients could have their own privacy with or without guests.

Upon each table sat an impressive bouquet of fresh-cut flowers. This nursing home did not need to advertise. Once seen, the healthy could not wait to make this their permanent residency.

Harriet was seated in a wheelchair facing the window. If only she could appreciate the beauty that was displayed before her. In time, hopefully.

Ben allowed Marc his privacy with his mother, although he was still considered under arrest. He entered her room silently. He loved this woman, his mother, more than anything in his life; he could not bear the thought of ever losing her.

He stood behind her, taking his hand to stroke her beautiful hair. This tiny person, no more than five foot tall, had the heart of a giant, the soul of a saint, and a mind full of wisdom. Her life evolved into helping others. Her motto had always been do to others as you would have them do to you.

He moved around her wheelchair to face her. He was astounded. She appeared to have gained weight, a lot of weight. She stared straight ahead, taking notice of no one or anything.

He got down on his knees and took her hands into his. He stared into her brown eyes, eyes that would allow no one to enter. Marc's eyes began to form a mist.

"Mother, what have I done to you? When you really needed me, I left you to suffer alone. This act of mine is unforgivable. I was a coward. All I could think of was to run, run as far as I could, knowing full well I would have to eventually face the horror of that unforgettable night.

"I am terribly, terribly sorry, I know the extent of your love for the Parkers, and nothing I say or do will ever mend your broken heart. But if we work hard, maybe, just maybe, we can put our lives back on track.

"Please, Mother, come back. I need to feel your strength. I will never again desert you."

His mother was in there somewhere. Today was not that day, but maybe tomorrow. Yes, tomorrow could be that day. He left without saying good-bye. Good-bye means forever.

It was now Ben's time to say hello. Marc would take a seat in the waiting area, near the front entrance. He promised Ben he would not run. Run where? Everything that meant anything to him was contained within that room.

Ben placed himself on bended knee in front of his sweetheart. He caressed her face and then took her hands into his.

"Sweetheart, I'm here again, waiting for you to join me. I have so many plans for us and our baby.

"Yes, the Doc told me. The only thing I can call it is a blessing. Just think, sweetheart, me a daddy. Can you envision that?

"I haven't told Marc. We'll do that together. Can you imagine the look on his face when we tell him we're expecting? You know he will be thrilled to have a little brother or sister, the way he loves kids.

"Sweetheart, you have to try really hard to get well. I need for you to rejoin the living, the sooner the better."

He needed to give his knees a break; the status of being a senior was already here, his bones feeling the effect. He rubbed the area that bore the weight of his body. It was time to say so long for now.

He took her face into his large hands and gently kissed her mouth, still receiving no reaction. He felt as if he were giving a repeat performance, the words always the same with each visit. He was looking forward to the day it would be a two-way conversation. It would happen. God would not forsake him in his time of need.

Marc was still seated; he stood when Ben approached, hands held out.

Ben shook his head with a reply.

"Enough of your foolishness, it's time we get back." Ben was praying for a miracle for Marc's release. What do you think Marc was doing? His mind was building the church for the prayer to be heard.

Ben wanted no fanfare when he placed him in a cell. He told Marc to assume his position on the floorboard in the back; he would alert him when no one was looking. He would then make a run for it. Where? Why, into the jail cell. Can you imagine the anticipation of running to your own cell?

Ben was hiding a so-called criminal on the floorboard with no handcuffs and the prisoner would then lock himself in his own cell. This was getting ludicrous and downright shameful. He felt like hanging it up. He needed to turn in his gun and badge and run like hell for a little sanity in his life.

The antique shop in their hometown stood empty for five years when, lo and behold, a SOLD sign found its way to the store window. That was three years ago.

A not-so-tall young man named Simon Sonderson, with a fantastic personality in his thirties, took ownership. He had long blond hair tied with a headband across his forehead. He had blue eyes and tattoos of a cross on both sides of his neck. His only distraction was the wide spaces between his teeth.

He was single, with no intention of marrying. Many of his friends were divorced, and the ones that were married wished they weren't. You're damned if you do, and damned if you don't.

He loved antiques and kept the shop as such, but added a printing machine. He was then and now in the newspaper business. His paper was called "The Happenings." It contained information on the comings and goings of the townspeople. And we cannot forget the tourists; they, too, have much to say.

If truth be told, and not always, the newspaper was run by a gossip columnist. Yeah, that guy with the…ah…personality. The paper's cost was $2. Sounds high? Who's kidding who?

This paper would reveal more information about you than you knew about yourself. Who doesn't like to look behind someone else's curtains?

The tourists really were the worst. They could reveal all they knew about their friends, even their families, and who would know. This was a small town; it would never get back to them. If anyone came up with something really spicy or scandalous that Simon thought was headline news, they could also get their picture printed for the world…ah…the town to see.

So far, no pictures had been taken. Everyone chose to remain anonymous. Really?

Marc was big-time news. When it became known, and Ben knew it would, that Marc was behind bars, everybody would bombard the police station to take a peek at the prisoner. Ben shook his head at the stupidity of Marc's schoolmates; they were acting as if they had forgotten what their neighbor/criminal looked like.

Ben had to stop wondering if there was any other job out there for him; he just needed to get up off his ass and look. No need to take a vote on the #1 procrastinator.

Simon was a huge part of the circus. Ben remained behind his desk and let everyone do their own thing. Eventually they would have to leave; all he had to do was bide his time.

Simon's camera was clicking away, taking many angles of Marc, some kneeling, others standing. A side shot was impossible, but try, he did. It was Marc's turn to put on a show, flashing a smile for the photographer. Simon was thrilled; a jailbird behind bars with a smile. That would make front cover; he couldn't wait to develop the film.

The paper with the news of his capture would be available within three hours. He was already counting his money. Once the papers hit the newsstand anchored into the stone walkway, they were snatched up.

Simon could hardly keep up with the demand. He was basking in glory. He thought maybe he could be a news reporter. Yeah, and a monkey was going to jump out of his…well, you know.

People were stomping their feet when their friends refused to move out of their way. They needed that paper. It was as if someone were hoping to win the lottery; the prize, Marc.

"The Happenings," Simon's paper, lay across the dinner table at the Mitchells' home. Mrs. Mitchell was about to step out the side door of her home to hang some clothes while Mr. Mitchell worked on his sixth cup of coffee. Their daughters finished clearing away the last remains of the family's dinner twenty minutes earlier and were chit-chatting about the day's activities.

David Mitchell Sr. had dark hair, dark eyes, white teeth, clean-shaven, and was a man who stood tall in the eyes of the townspeople with his unending offer of free help to those unable to pay for a handyman, as were many. His heart was bigger than his height of five-feet-three.

His daughters knew, without being told, they were to pick up "The Happenings" on their way home from work. He never believed half the trash printed, but he had to admit Simon was gifted; he had a way with words that never failed to bring forth laughter. He always finished his dinner with Simon's paper. That was his dessert; he enjoyed a good laugh.

The headlines took him by surprise. He yelled out to Carrie, his wife, or anyone within hearing.

"Carrie, you have to see what's written about the Anderson boy." This was no laughing matter. Carrie backtracked with her laundry basket to take a look. The Mitchells' two daughters, Sissie and Sassie [no twins here] favored their mama and were also her height, five-feet-five-inches. They worked at the local post office after graduating from high school.

They removed themselves from the table, crowding behind their mother to also take a look. They knew Marc from high school.

Carrie voiced her opinion.

"How sad Harriet must be to have her son accused of murder. You know as well as I, that boy could not have done what they are saying. I think it's shameful that Simon printed that picture of Marc smiling behind bars. But Marc, being the kind and thoughtful person he is, accomplished what he intended, to put on a show strictly for Simon."

Her husband agreed, as did their daughters. After the story was read aloud by

Mr. Mitchell, everyone took their leave. Carrie reclaimed her dropped basket. The girls scooped up their own wash-load, following their mama out the door.

Mr. Mitchell scooted his chair back, stretched his arms and yawned as he, too, made his way out the side door. His job was to work on the brakes in his truck. The paper, no longer of any interest, remained where it had been read, upon the kitchen table. Everyone was now aware of Marc's arrest, everyone except D.J., the youngest in the household.

The headline of Marc's arrest blasted the front page:

"Sheriff Ben Davidson single-handedly apprehended Marc Anderson of Mason's Mill as he attempted to run from his home. He is the main suspect in the murder and arson deaths of twelve people."

Leave it to Simon to beef it up with a little added drama.

D.J. came tearing into the house, a red tablecloth wrapped around his shoulders; he was pretending to be Superman. He stopped suddenly when he saw Marc's face looking up at him. He screamed for his mama.

Carrie could be a contestant in a beauty pageant, with a figure to die for. She was never without a ribbon tied to secure her very long, curly brown hair, highlighted with natural streaks of blond. Her eyes were a light brown, her lashes long, and no one in their township could match her smile. She was blessed; she needed no makeup. She was and would always be a natural beauty.

D.J. resembled his papa. His dark hair had many curls and his eyes sparkled with mischief. He may have been pint-sized, but he, like his father, shared the same kind of heart, that of a giant.

Carrie came rushing into the house, blessing herself in the process. Her reclaimed basket, once again disposed of, fell to the floor. She knelt in front of her baby, her hands gently stroking his arms.

"Sweetie, it's all right, Mama's here. Did you hurt yourself?"

D.J. pressed his index finger against the picture of Marc.

"That's the guy I was telling you about; remember… the one who stayed with me because I was scared of the fire. He was really nice. He talked to me a long time. He thought you were lost, remember?

"Anyway, I wanted him to take me home because I was sleepy, but he said he had to talk to you first. Don't you remember, Mama?

"Anyway, he asked me where the smoke was coming from, and when I told him the Parkers' house burned up, he starting crying and told me not to move, he would come back to me... and then he took off running.

"Don't you remember, Mama? He was sad. I feel sorry for him. He could have been my buddy, huh, Mama?"

When D.J. started talking, you may as well pull up a chair. He would babble on and on until he finished what he had to say. That was his calling card. Carrie gathered the baby of the family into her arms.

"Yes, D.J., I do remember, and you know what? He can still be your buddy. Come on, Superman, we need to rescue your buddy. Okay?"

"You bet, Mama. Let's go get my buddy."

The ones that managed to squeeze their way into the police station finally had enough; they got what they came for, a look at their long- time neighbor. If Ben wasn't careful, he would shake his head into a migraine. He was finally able to close the door and turn up the air conditioner.

Marc had his hands tucked behind his head, lying on his back. The jail's cot smelled new; bodies were hard to come by. Ben had taken a similar position, his hands also tucked behind his head, only he was seated.

They both took notice of each other and started to laugh. Sometimes you just need to lighten up; this was one of those moments. Suddenly the door burst opened. Ben stood, as did Marc.

"Sheriff, Superman has something to tell you."

Carrie had her arm draped around her son. D.J. was definitely not shy. When Superman finished, everyone was hugging one another. There were tears and there was laughter.

Marc was exactly like his mother, always thoughtful and considerate. This time it paid off for him. He got down on one knee as he reached out to give his little man a hug. Finding the right words were easy.

"You just saved my life, Superman. You are my hero and my lifetime buddy."

D.J. glowed with happiness when Marc called him his hero and buddy. D.J. raised his tiny fist high in the air and shouted out, "Superman saved the good guy!"

No one could contain their laughter at this little man who was smarter than a whip, standing just 3½ feet tall. He would grow no taller than his papa.

Ben slapped Marc on the back.

"You just got a reprieve. What does it feel like?"

"I thank God for using D.J. as His instrument in giving me back my life. My mother's philosophy on life is simple: When God ends one chapter in your life, He starts another."

Marc then asked Ben if he would accompany him to the cemetery. He was ashamed for not being there when the services for the Parkers' were conducted. This would continue to bother him for months, more so when he found out Sloan survived, and then went missing.

Ben offered to drive his patrol car, for Marc's truck was still parked at his home. Marc did not realize the woman that would remain locked inside his heart had returned to the living and he had just missed seeing her.

The time of his release was 4:00 p.m. They headed out immediately for the cemetery. The time Sloan looked at her watch upon arrival at Sunni's house was precisely the same time Marc and Ben were entering the grave sites, 4:10 p.m.

They removed themselves from the sheriff's patrol car. This was going to be one of the worst and happiest moments in Marc's life.

Marc fell to his knees when he viewed all the newly dug graves. Hundreds of flowers were gracing the Parkers' headstones, their fragrance filtering through the breeze. Tombstones are generally not in place until the fresh dirt has settled. But the Doc and the sheriff could not bear for anyone to look at thirteen mounds of dirt; they would add dirt as needed.

The lonely casket containing the remains of baby Zac was dug up, and now rested between his papa and mama. He was finally reunited with his family.

Marc stood up, his eyes glancing from the beginning of graves to the very end. He did not take the time to read the inscriptions. He spoke for the first time since leaving the police station. He was not ashamed to show tears.

"Ben, this is so totally unbelievable, I can't stand to look at them, it hurts too much. What are we ever going to do without them? I not only loved Sloan, I loved her family as well.

"Saul was difficult, but I understood him. He loved Sloan dearly; he didn't want anyone to hurt her. I don't think he could stand the fact that one day she would have left him. It looks as if he got what he wanted. She will now be with him for all eternity." His sobbing was at its worst.

Ben, who was standing a ways from him, rearranging some of the flowers on Zac's grave, was flabbergasted.

"Marc, my dear boy, do you not know that Sloan is alive and well?"

Marc just stood there, speechless. He had difficulty comprehending what he had been told. He was a witness to that fire; he remembered well the firefighter's comment: "No one could survive that fire." Now he was being told she was alive.

He ran to Ben, grabbing a hold of his arms. He repeated what the firefighter told him.

"Marc, she wasn't in the house. She took her sleeping bag that night to sleep outside. She was nowhere near her home. God spared her, Marc. She could well be the new chapter in your life."

Marc blessed himself with the sign of the cross.

# CHAPTER EIGHTEEN

Sloan had to say good-bye to her family today, for she would not have time tomorrow. Tomorrow could not come fast enough.

Sunni happened to see her slip out the door of her house. She yelled out, "Sloan, wait up." Sunni ran, catching up with her. Sloan did not appear happy.

"What's up, honey? Running away?"

She thought that would bring forth a laugh; instead, Sloan has a curt reply.

"Can't I do a damn thing without you always trailing me? God, Sunni, I can't make a move without you asking. Why are you moving?"

Sunni dropped her head.

"There, you did it again, always dropping your head when I get upset with you. I need some breathing room. Is that too much to ask?"

"No, I guess not. Do what you have to do." Sunni turned and walked back into the house.

Sloan jumped into her papa's truck, the handbag tugging on her neck; it started again on the first try. She stuck her head out the driver's door window and looked up into the heavens.

"Thanks, Papa. You know I'm coming to see you, don't you?"

Yes, she did feel sorry for Sunni, but it was time for their friendship to end. She would not be seeing her after tonight anyway. It would be easier for Sunni to stay pissed; this way, Sunni would not say anything if she happened to see her leave early in the morning.

She traveled slowly, briefly taking her eyes off the road when she came to the remains of her home. She shed no tears. She continued down the road, swerving in and out of the newly formed ruts.

The roads were a disgrace; Silva's money had always taken care of their community problems. When the state was notified and was made aware of the road conditions, their response was always the same, to look away. After the state filled their pockets with the taxpayers' dollars, there was never enough left to take care of the needs of the little communities.

The damage done to her papa's tires from the roads really should not have mattered; the tires were already threadbare. But care, she did.

The cemetery was in the opposite direction of the town's shopping center. She tried to avoid the rocks and other debris that gathered on the road. The road the tourists traveled, from the shopping hub to the lake, was quite nice. At last she came to the path that would lead her to the cemetery. She could see the lake, but it wasn't accessible from the road she traveled.

A boundary was in place. An eight-foot elaborate black steel fence enclosed the acres surrounding the lake and beyond. The lawns were well-manicured, with many trees, some hundreds of years old, giving off plenty of shade. Picnic tables were in abundance, as were gazebos.

Recreational sites for children provided swing sets, see-saws, sliding boards, jungle gyms, and sandboxes, as well as an eight-foot tall grey and white dolphin fountain with a twenty-foot rubber base for safety. The filtration system allowed no more than an inch of water to accumulate within its base.

The playground with the waterfall is a child's paradise. This, besides the fishing, is the town's drawing card. Admission into the park was paid at the cabins office: $8.00 per day for adults, $3.00 for children to the age of 12. The town's belief in the honor system never wavered. Their motto was "Let the patrons' conscience be their guide."

Sloan pulled her papa's truck to the entrance of the cemetery. The fencing used for the enclosure of the lake also complemented the graveyard. An arch reaching a height of twelve-foot by twelve-foot was attached to the fencing and was inscribed with scrolled letters,

"HEAVEN'S GATE." She stood, tearing at the wording.

"Is it, Papa? Is it really Heaven's Gate?"

She proceeded forward; she did not need to search them out. Their headstones were placed in a straight line facing the entrance. It had been ten days since her family's funeral and memorial, yet hundreds of fresh flowers were placed in front of their tombstones.

She first went to her papa's grave. She stood looking at his name inscribed upon the headstone until her legs could no longer support her weight and she fell to the earth. Tears streamed from her eyes as she yelled out.

"Why, Papa, why? Why did you allow Mr. Hewlett, of all people, to humiliate me? Why didn't you have enough faith and trust in me to tell me the trouble you were in?

"I considered us a team; together, we could have found a solution. What were you planning on doing with your family once the eviction notice was served? Did you even have a plan?

"I was always proud of your stance on life and that stubborn pride of yours that so few possess. And Papa, I so wanted to be like you. You were my rock, did you know that? You could do no wrong.

"Well, Papa, your pride ended up being your downfall. You should have done what every other man would have done when his back was up against a wall: beg, borrow, or steal to keep what was rightfully yours. Maybe you would have done just that. But I will never know, will I?"

She knelt down and kissed his gravestone, tracing her fingers along his name. Of course, she still loved him; she would not stop loving him because he fell off his pedestal.

She would not leave until she had finished kissing and tracing each name. She was beyond happy to see ReRe had joined his family. She held onto his stone as if she wanted to take it with her. She loved him the most, maybe because she knew her papa adored him.

She took a few steps back to take one final look. Never again would she return to a place that caused her to endure a tragedy no one in their lifetime should have to bear.

As she turned to exit, she glanced upward.

"Please, God, wrap your arms around them and love them hard, like I should have when they were alive. May they rest in peace."

She could feel the liquid that contained tears within her eyes, but she refused to let them fall. She vowed she would cry no more. She backed out her papa's truck, turned the wheel sharply to the left, put it in drive, and sped down the road, her papa's threadbare tires peeling off what was left of the rubber.

She arrived at Sunni's home at 4:10 p.m. Her time for departure would have to be very early, before anyone in the household awakened.

Sunni heard the truck as it pulled into the driveway. She needed to talk to her best friend, but did she dare?

Sloan was copping a bad attitude towards her since her parents died. You would think she would be falling all over Sunni, for now she could have everything she ever desired, Sunni would see to it.

She met Sloan as she opened the front door and entered into the house.

"Sloan, honey, I really need to talk to you. I hate it when you're mad at me. I just don't know what I've been doing to upset you so much. You need to tell me. If you need your space, you've got it. If you just need to be alone, you've got that, too. I'm only trying to make your life easier, not harder."

Sloan listened to what her friend had to say. How could she not? Sloan did love her. She did not want to hurt her best friend.

She was caught in a web. If she revealed she had a lover and was leaving with him the next day, she just might try and stop her. How could Sunni accomplish this, she didn't know. That is why she could not take any chances.

Sunni sometimes pushed their friendship a little too far, though in all honesty, she herself was guilty of doing the same. Sunni could show a bad side when it came to Sloan, she was that protective, but then again, so was Sloan when it came to Sunni.

Sloan decided to adopt a philosophy: be discreet.

"Sunni, I don't want to hurt you anymore. I have been downright rude to you and my behavior cannot be justified. Please forgive me. I sometimes just want to be by myself. I need to sort things out in my own time frame. Please allow this until I say otherwise. Okay?"

Sunni felt some relief. "Of course, honey, whatever you say. From this day forward, I will not question your comings and goings."

She held out her arms, praying Sloan would walk into them. She did. They would take their dinner together.

Sunni's parents, if the Doc found the time, always ate at the restaurant in town. To prepare a meal and the Doc not be there was absurd, for Sunni and Sloan always ate something light, body weight always on their minds. Doc and Miriam did as expected; dinner would be enjoyed in town.

Sloan really put on a show, talking and laughing all evening, when all she really wanted to do was get the hell away from her boring friend.

Dinner was over, and Sunni felt it was time for horseplay; she made a grab for the strap on Sloan's purse. She instantly released her grip when Sloan angrily told her to back off.

Sloan never realized how annoying Sunni had become, or had she always been this way? Had she been walking around with blinders this whole time?

It no longer mattered; she had clear sailing from this night on. She would leave at whatever time she chose, feeling comfortable with the knowledge she would not be followed. A peace like nothing ever felt settled over her as the sleep that had been denied for two weeks was reclaimed.

She awakened; the pounding in her heart was intense. Today was the day her life would begin anew.

The time on the bedroom clock read 7:22 a.m. She had overslept. She wanted to be up and ready to go by 6:00 a.m.

She all but ran to the bathroom, the shoulder bag slapping against her side. She removed the purse, care taken when she placed it on top of the toilet tank, proof of life hidden within.

She turned the shower on full blast while her head pounded with the thoughts to hurry, hurry, hurry. She threw her nightgown onto the black-and-white tiled floor as she grabbed up a washcloth and towel.

The water was still cold to the body; her nipples felt hard, like marbles. The shampoo was also cold. She could not believe in this July heat the water could be this cold, but of course, Sunni's folks had air-conditioning, a luxury she had never known. She would not be in the shower long. Her teeth began to chatter.

She plugged in the hair dryer while the towel around her body removed the chill. She touched her lips with gloss and added a bit of blush from Sunni's coveted cosmetic bag. She chose the dress she had worn when she first met Clay. She loved that dress, and for a split second her thoughts turned to her best friend, remembering when she was given such a marvelous gift.

Sunni would never do to her what she herself was about to do. She refused to go there, rehashing their long-time friendship.

She wanted to leave; she needed to leave. Clay was giving her the means to escape, and she would be damned if she would allow anyone to take this away from her.

She would take nothing but the dress on her back, shoes on her feet, and the handbag that found itself a home. She wore no bra, but felt it necessary to wear panties. Purchased by Sunni, they were the bikini type. Lifetime panties would never again be part of her wardrobe. She was about to begin a new life, and that also did not include hand-me-downs. She was through with that kind of life.

She peeked into Sunni's room; she was snoring. Miriam was a late sleeper. In the two weeks she had been living with the Harrisons, the nights that failed to bring sleep, she would notice the Doc's car missing, the daylight not yet visible.

She moved quickly, but silently, through the house. Her hands held onto the door as she stepped onto the porch. She turned, allowing the door to quietly close. Upon her arrival the day before, she backed the truck in, parking it as close to the end of the driveway as feasible. Her intention was to make as little noise as possible when she pulled away.

The key, as always, still maintained its present position. She hesitated before turning the key; she felt a foreboding. She tried to push it aside, but was failing badly.

"Papa, you are there, aren't you? Please don't leave me in my time of need."

She turned the key…nothing. Again, she tried…nothing. She shouted out, beating her fists upon the steering wheel.

"Don't do this to me, Papa! I can't bear to live here another day. This town is not going to take my life as it did with you, Mama, and my sisters and brothers. Please, Papa, I need to be set free."

She released her vow, tears freeing themselves from their confinement. She wept as one hand covered her eyes while the other searched blindly for the key.

She then heard a loud knock. Blurred eyes turned toward the sound. A young teenage girl with grimy blond pigtails and badly discolored buck teeth in a stained blouse, torn jeans, and bare feet stood at the driver's door, asking if she was all right.

She did not want this to happen; she did not want anyone seeing her leave. She said a silent prayer. 'Please God, do not allow this person to remember this day.' Instead of acknowledging the young girl, Sloan, without thought, turned the key. With her foot still positioned against the gas pedal, the truck was brought back to life. The tires squealed their way out onto the road. Papa spared her life. But she had not instituted a plan to rid herself of her papa's truck.

Her papa's truck was now her enemy.

Look for the exciting drama *"Rest in Peace"* to continue in *Book Two: Changes* and *Book Three: Starting* Over

# Author / Evelyn Sciarratta

Mrs. Sciarratta resides in St. Charles, Missouri. She is a widow with five children, 17 grandchildren and eight great-grandchildren.

*Rest In Peace* is her first full-length novel.

The *Rest In Peace* trilogy is as follows:

> *Rest In Peace Book One: The Beginning*
> *Rest In Peace Book Two: Changes*
> *Rest In Peace Book Three: Starting Over*

The novel initially appeared as a synopsized serial newspaper feature in 1988. She's excited with the prospect that the new novels will bring as much enjoyment to readers as they brought to her as she was penning them.